The Perilous Journey of the much-too- Spontaneous Girl

LEIGH STATHAM

Month9Books

THE PERILOUS JOURNEY OF THE MUCH-TOO-SPONTANEOUS GIRL
by Leigh Statham
All rights reserved. Published in the United States of America by Month9Books, LLC.

ISBN: 978-1-944816-57-5

Published by Month9Books, Raleigh, NC 27609

Month9Books

For Evan & Georgie,
little boys with big dreams.
Fly hard and fast,
and keep your mouths closed
or you'll get bugs in your teeth.

The Perilous Journey of the much-too-Spontaneous Girl

Chapter One

L ady Marguerite Vadnay strapped herself into the tiny
compartment and slipped her goggles over her eyes. A glass
hood lowered over her upper body while she sat snug in the
cockpit of the single-man aership. The wind blew enough to rock
the small cabin back and forth as her envelope filled beside her,
eventually leaving the ground completely, its seams tight with
helium.

Her hair was pulled into a neat bun, and her flight suit was
no longer a man's hand-me-down. It was custom made from the
finest industrial cloth she could get her hands on in Montreal,
complete with lots of pockets. Lady Vadnay loved pockets. Little
brass buttons stamped with her monogram ran from her chin
all the way to her trousers. She had fully embraced her life as a
woman of New France and soon-to-be aership pilot.

Plenty of men flew the tiny contraptions. It was the aercraft of choice in New France, perfect for charting high-mountain passes and performing night raids on neighboring New England. France was far ahead of any country in the world when it came to avionics—unless, of course, you counted the pirate nations of the seas, which Marguerite did not. All of their technology was stolen, mostly from France.

It had been a long road getting to this point. Only six months earlier she was being abused by her high-priced governess, Pomphart, back in mainland France. Her father was a wealthy Lord, determined on marrying her off to anything that crawled around with a decent title and bank account, and her friends were either boring or deserting her for adulthood.

Marguerite quickly took matters into her own hands. She'd volunteered to be a Daughter of the King and sailed away without her father's knowledge. All she wanted was to start a new life with her childhood friend Claude and have some adventures; unfortunately, the adventures were more than she'd bargained for. Friends were lost, and new ones made. She was lucky to be alive and studying at His Royal Majesty's Flight Academy for Resilient Young Women after the harrowing trip.

"Tighten the lift lever, pull in on the altinometer. We're going to remove the anchors now!" Her professor yelled at her over the sound of the roaring single-motor engine. It sputtered and spit steam. The solar panels had been fully charged the day before and the fuel tanks filled with fresh water that morning. There was nothing left to do but fly.

"Ready?" the professor called to Marguerite. The ground crew, consisting mostly of her classmates from the flight academy, scurried to finish their assignments. Marguerite nodded, and the assembly went to work loosening ropes, moving sandbags, and generally getting out of the way.

Marguerite adjusted her goggles out of sheer nervousness. Claude had made her a new pair, with even better dark vision and a scoping feature on the right eye. They fit her face perfectly, but she didn't even need them today. She had a glass dome to protect her from the elements. Still, she loved having them on, and she couldn't help but think that they brought her good luck. Her first pair had saved her life not too long ago.

This was her inaugural solo flight for His Majesty, Louis XIV. If all went well, she'd spend the rest of her life an independent woman doing what she loved—flying. If not, she was going to have to do a lot of backpedaling with a lot of people, Jacques Laviolette, being person of interest number one. She spotted him walking up to the edge of the group of onlookers. She'd hoped he would come today. She'd mentioned the event offhandedly the night before while they shared dinner with her automaton, Outil, but she wasn't sure he'd understood how important this day was or if he could get away from his own duties at the school.

Jacques—handsome, brave, and annoying Jacques. He was an entirely different issue. But there was no time to think about that now.

The professor gave the signal. She tore her goggle-tinted gaze away from Laviolette's tall, dark-haired frame. Lifting one hand, she gave the sign for all go, pushed the buttons and pulled the lever. The launching mechanism shot her little ship into the air like a Chinese rocket. She had never traveled this fast before in her life. It felt like invisible arms were shoving her back into the seat with tremendous force, until she reached her cruising altitude, and the balloon took over as the thrust let off.

Marguerite glanced up from her controls and caught her breath. Her new home city of Montreal lay beneath her in all its splendor. The river wound like a loose ribbon through the brick and wood dwellings. She could see her school almost immediately, its roof littered with experimental equipment for weather and aviation. The chapel caught her eye next, its soaring crucifix and brightly colored windows winking in the perfect morning sun.

Her heart filled like a mini aership envelope, happiness threatening to burst it open. Marguerite sighed audibly, realizing that she'd held her breath during the entire launch. She eased her controls to the right, and the thrusters kicked in, propelling her forward and to the right.

This was amazing.

"Yes!" she cried out to the endless blue sky in front of her.

The controls felt so right in her hands. She began to execute more maneuvers. The tiny ship felt like an extension of her own body. She dove to the left, steered it back up, turned tight to the right, centripetally swinging her own compartment in the opposite direction.

She laughed. What a thrill! Months of study and hard work, tiny rooms, and terrible food—this was completely worth it.

A flock of birds flew past her, swirling around, welcoming her. They dove and skimmed the surface of the St. Lawrence River, then swooped back up along the edge of a brick building.

"That looks like fun," she said to herself.

Laying on the controls, she took the little ship in a steep dive toward the aerstrip. Her heart floated in her chest, her breath caught in her throat, and she giggled with delight as the ship responded to her demand and swooped back up. It leveled off like the birds, just in time for the envelope to catch on a breeze and drag Marguerite, ship and all, into the windsock tower.

The birds continued on without her, the sudden lurch throwing her forward and forcing her to close her eyes. When she opened them again, it was just in time to see the metal trusses of the tower approaching at top speed.

Before she could call for help, Marguerite was whipped around the tower, her envelope caught in the trusses. She banged into one pylon and then another; the glass around her shattering and tearing at her exposed cheeks and nose. She cried out and braced herself for impact with the ground, her giggles from the moment before turned to cries for help.

This could be it, she thought. *How appropriate that I work so hard and then die in my first solo flight. Poetic even.*

She braced herself for death, but a final jerk left her shaken yet alive. Unfortunately, she dangled several feet above the ground from her own rigging, tangled beneath the windsock. She opened her eyes, realized her precarious situation, and groaned. She could still fall and be hurt, but her broken pride was worse than death at this point.

"Marguerite!" Jacques was the first on the scene. "Are you alright, my dear? Quick! Someone get a ladder. Call the medic! Move!" He barked orders like the Air Captain he was born to be. Marguerite cursed herself and pounded her fist on the altinometer.

The little dial spun around and fell off its clasp, landing in the bottom of the circular compartment, completely useless.

"Yes, I'm fine," she called back. Then more quietly to herself, "Just feeling like a complete idiot."

"Lady Vadnay," her professor called up, "I'm sorry, but I'm afraid you failed your first flight test. Very glad you survived, however. Very glad!"

"Wonderful." She laid her head back against the seat. "Just wonderful."

Chapter Two

After much finagling, and procurement of a very tall ladder, Marguerite was freed from the trap of her own making.

"Are you sure you're not hurt?" Jacques asked as he examined the scratches on her face, his hands on either side of her head.

"Yes. Yes. I'm fine." She swatted his hands away. "My body is in perfect working order. My spirit, however, is crushed beyond repair."

Jacques eyes twinkled. "I'm sure the ship feels the same way. He looked up at the envelope and battered cockpit still dangling from the windsock tower and covered his mouth with the back of his hand, failing to stop his laughter.

"I'm sure you find this hysterical, but I just set myself back by at least six months or more," Marguerite said.

"They will give you another test flight before then. Everyone crashes—eventually." He laughed again. "I'm going to climb up there and try to help them cut the poor beast down. Wait for me?"

Marguerite didn't answer. She'd had enough of the field and his chuckling. As soon as he mounted the grey metal ladder, she gathered what was left of her pride and walked back to her dormitory.

The next day she sat at attention on the edge of her wooden chair, furiously scribbling notes as her teacher lectured on the mechanics of the next generation of aership thruster systems. Something sharp pricked her ear. Annoyed, she reached up to rub it, without breaking her concentration on the lecture.

"With improved aerodynamics and lighter construction materials, we should be able to see improvements in speed and process efficiency." The professor, old and balding with a long white beard and a moth-eaten uniform, poked at a diagram on a chalkboard as he walked through the final information the young women needed to know for their exams the following week.

Another prick, this time to her neck.

Marguerite rubbed it again and heard giggles behind her. Annoyed, she glared behind her at the pack of simpering girls having a laugh at her expense. She looked at the ground. Two pieces of paper lay folded in the shape of stars with sharply creased corners jutting from each edge.

"Here." The girl next to her bent over, scooped them up, and handed them to her. "You dropped these." She barely hid a chortle as she turned back to the other girls, then pretended to listen to the lecture.

"Fortunately for us, France has a leading edge on mechanics

and steam engineering. Our solar harnessing powers are unmatched, and our Royal Corps of Engineers is unparalleled in the world. The best that other countries can do is hope to steal our technology, then pick it apart, trying to reproduce it." He chuckled at his own joke. "Why, we even have engineers from other countries denouncing their birth homes and swearing allegiance to the King just for the chance to go to our schools— schools such as this, ladies." He flashed a wide, squinty smile around the room then turned back to the chalkboard. "Where was I?"

Marguerite knew she shouldn't, but she couldn't help it. She slowly unfolded the first paper and read the tiny script inside:

Why are you acting like you need to learn this material?
Everyone knows your lover will make sure you pass the exams …
Unless you keep crashing.

Marguerite crumpled the scrap in her hand and forced her thoughts back to the lecture. She endured this kind of torment regularly. Jacques Laviolette was an instructor at the school, but not *her* instructor. And he was most certainly not her lover. He'd captained the ship that brought her to New France. They spent time together; they enjoyed each other's company; and they frequently debated engineering and the latest science out of Paris. He'd made it clear more than once that he intended to marry her, but she had made it clear that she was not going to get married until she was good and ready, and that probably wouldn't be until she was done seeing the world.

The most ridiculous thing about the whole situation was that she kept hoping the notes and comments from the other girls might be friendly at some point. But no, they just got uglier and more cruel.

She wadded the second note without reading it and tried to memorize what the professor said about thermodynamic possibilities. If it weren't for the amazing subjects she was free to learn in this school, she would have left long ago. She certainly wasn't here for the female companionship or the housing. But small, grey, and dingy as it was, at least she was able to secure a room to herself.

The teacher wrapped up his lecture and dismissed his class. Marguerite tucked her papers neatly into a satchel as several girls bumped into her shoulder while filing past.

She sighed and rose as soon as they were gone. Outil peeked around the corner of her classroom, and Marguerite smiled.

"Hello, how was the oiling?" Marguerite asked.

"Lovely, m'lady." Outil nodded and took her bag of textbooks from her. "There is a new machinist who is most cautious with all of my gears. He was admiring Master Claude's handiwork."

"It sounds like you have a little bit of a fancy for this new boy. Was he human?" Marguerite grinned wickedly.

Outil stopped walking. "This theory is illogical in the extreme, m'lady. I was not designed to exhibit feelings other than loyalty, in any form, much less for a human I do not know. And I can't imagine developing a *fancy*," she repeated the word carefully, "as you call it, on another bot that is also not designed to return feelings."

Marguerite laughed. "I was only teasing. Relax. Where is Jacques? Have you seen him? I never know how to find him now that his teaching duties are completed for the term."

"I believe he is in the chapel, m'lady." Outil moved easily away from the strange conversation of human emotions.

Girl and robot made their way to the school's chapel, the oldest building in the neighborhood, possibly the oldest building in Montreal. Its soaring stone walls were already turning black with age. Inside the mammoth wooden doors, stained glass windows shed rainbow colors on all the pews. A man in a uniform sat with his head down, while an automaton meandered from one candelabrum to another, trimming wicks and mopping up spent wax.

Outil waited at the back of the massive, echoing room while Marguerite moved silently up the aisle. She slipped into the pew next to the man and sat quietly for a few moments until he lifted his head and smiled at her.

"Hello, Lady Vadnay," he whispered.

"Hello, Jacques. What are we praying for?" She was half-sarcastic, half-concerned.

"Nothing really … I just received some news, trying to digest it and figure out the next steps." He sat back and stared ahead at the pulpit.

"Anything you'd care to include me in?" She slid her hand across the bench toward him.

He swept it up and kissed her knuckles without taking his eyes off the front of the church. He kept her hand at his mouth for a moment longer than was appropriate, and then exhaled and kissed it again. "I have a commission. The ship leaves next week." He smiled, but happiness did not fill his eyes.

"Oh! Where are you going?" Marguerite's heart leapt at the prospect of going with him to finally use all the knowledge and skills she learned.

"To the Atlantic. The corsairs are moving farther and farther from the Barbary Coast. King Louis himself has decreed that we must stop them from attacking our trade routes and drive them back to the Mediterranean. They are also afraid that the British may be aiding them in attacks on our merchants," he spoke quickly. "We will have the finest warships France has ever built, and I will captain one."

"That's wonderful! When will they have our tests sorted out?" Marguerite didn't miss the fact that fulfilling her dream of serving on an aership rested on her ability to pass this test.

"Next week. They should have the students cleared before the ship departs—but, Marguerite, my love, you cannot go." The corners of his mouth turned down, matching his eyes at last.

"What are you talking about? Of course, I can go. I have but to volunteer. We will work together. It will be wonderful!"

He let go of her hand and folded his arms. "Marguerite, you failed the flying exam, and there won't be another opportunity to retake it until after I have departed." She began to protest, but he stopped her. "Do not argue. There is no way around this. Besides, this is not the type of voyage I think you should be on for your first assignment. You've already survived one pirate attack. There is no reason to see the world from a battleship."

He reached up to stroke her cheek, but she pulled away.

"This is ridiculous, Jacques. You said it yourself; I've already proven myself in battle. I'm a crack shot, and I think quickly under pressure. Outil and I are a marvelous team. School is merely a formality so I can get into a cockpit," she whispered fiercely, trying not to disturb the quiet of the chapel. "And why must you leave so soon?"

"Because the supply routes are being attacked daily. His Majesty's aeronauts have to constantly devise new routes and carry more armory than is usually necessary, which leaves less room for supplies. In short, it's costing the king a pretty penny, and that doesn't count the bounty he's losing when the pirates win skirmishes."

"I suppose the ship will be outfitted with modern weaponry?" she asked.

"Yes, in fact, your friend Claude just finished a commission to create a defense system to thwart their blasted air cannons." She shuddered at the thought of the giant bursts of wind that rocked the ship and tore it to pieces. "We won't be going in to save anything. We are going to search and destroy. This is going to be a dangerous mission, Marguerite. Trust me, you are not ready. In fact, I doubt they will have any female crew on the battleship."

"I'm not planning on being in hand-to-hand combat. I'll be on the bridge with you. It won't be like the last time where we were attacked from out of nowhere, and I had no idea how to help or what I was doing. I'm ready now. I can help you lead the attack."

Marguerite couldn't believe this conversation. All these

months she thought they had the same goals. She thought he knew that she wanted to work on an aership and eventually command her own in the Royal Fleet.

Jacques laughed. "Darling, you won't be on the bridge."

"What do you mean?" She folded her arms and stared at him.

"Even if you passed all of your exams and were granted a post on this mission, first-year cadets don't serve on the bridge. You would be below in the engine room or on the galley ship."

"The galley, as in where food is prepared?"

"Yes, I'm afraid so. It's the order of things."

Marguerite sat back and put her hands in her lap, methodically smoothing her skirt as she choked back disappointment. "I want to fly."

"And you will!" Jacques reached for her hand again. "In a year or two you'll be on the bridge, and we will be married. Besides, you will be able to pilot a small ship privately before that." He took her hand again and kissed it more softly this time. "Your accident yesterday … I'm sorry I laughed. I know that was uncalled for, but it frightened me. I don't want to see you in danger ever again, especially if I can prevent it."

She couldn't argue with his logic, but it bothered her that a man was still deciding her future. Even if he was a handsome, kind, thoughtful, and funny man, who knew exactly how to make her insides melt at just the wrong times. Even if his plan aligned with her dreams perfectly, she still felt squirmy about it.

And she didn't like him assuming she would go along with all of this. She wiggled her hand free. "I don't think so, M. Laviolette." He smiled at her.

She glared back, heat rising to her face.

"You always laugh at me, but I am not making a joke. You act like this is all just a hobby for me. I don't think you take me seriously when I tell you I want to fly, and I *will* fly. I also don't need your permission or your timeline in order to accomplish my goals." She stood. "And I *do not* need your proposals any longer."

Even though her hands were shaking, and she felt as if she would explode, right there in the middle of a church before the altar and God and everyone, she regretted the harsh words as soon as she said them.

"I know you are upset, but that is no reason to take it out on me." His tone was serious.

"If you love me so much, why are you running off to battle pirates without me? You expect me to wait here and be a good girl. This is Claude all over again!" She threw her hands up in the air and turned to leave the pew, then thought better and twisted back to point a finger in his face. "Except this time I'm not a stupid girl. I've done things. I've seen things. I know what I want and it has nothing to do with you."

Jacques' jaw hardened as he spoke. "Your pride is the only thing standing in the way of your dreams. No man. No society. Just *you*. Certainly not me. Maybe if you'd been paying attention during your flight test and hadn't started showing off you might have passed," he shot back at her. Then added, "And I am no Claude. If you would just pay attention to men a little more carefully, you would have seen that he never loved you that way, but I always have."

"Love, love, love. It's easy to say sweet things and buy presents, but when it comes right down to it, you march away without a backwards glance. That is not love, Jacques." Marguerite forced herself not to consider his words. They were pricking at a very soft place in her heart, tempting her to cry, but she would not let herself give in.

"That is my job, my dear." He stood and made a move to take her hand. She pulled away. "I'm an aeronautic officer. I have to leave when I am called." Then more quietly, "There are very few exceptions."

A million retorts filled her head; everything from accusing him of being a very poor officer—letting his first ship get blown up—to begging him to resign. It was all ridiculous. She didn't need him. She didn't need *any* man.

"Fine then. Go chase your pirates. Enjoy your battle. Kill a few hundred people and try not to get blown up this time." She started to walk away, then turned back to finish. "No, go ahead and get blown up. I have the perfect flight suit to wear to your funeral."

"Marguerite! You don't mean that!" He called after her.

"Yes, I do." She marched resolutely to the wood doors of the chapel and pushed them open. "Come on, Outil. I'm famished."

The bot followed dutifully. "Yes, m'lady."

"I could use a decent meal myself," Jacques ran to catch up to them just outside the chapel.

After a course of soup, mutton with roasted vegetables, and fresh bread from the nunnery down the street, Marguerite felt much less cantankerous. She still fumed about Jacques's news, though, and resolved herself to finding a way around his stubborn attitude and the rules.

A young boy approached their table, his voice loud. "Lady Marguerite Vadnay?"

A chorus of chortles erupted at the other end of the hall—the other school girls enjoying the boy's announcement that a *lady* was serving alongside them in a government-run institution. The rumor was that her father had disowned her for having an affair with Jacques. Marguerite and Jacques both ignored the idol gossip, and Marguerite made sure she was at church each week and on good terms with the priest. The last thing she needed was a guilty conscience on top of the stress of living in a new world with all of these commoners.

"I have a missive for you from Paris. Came in just an hour ago." He puffed his chest and handed her a slip of paper, obviously proud of himself for finding her and delivering the important message.

Normally she would have tipped him handsomely, but the last six months she'd been living on the money Claude set aside for her from his family jewels, and she didn't want to waste one franc. Instead, she smiled prettily at him, handed him the last coins from her pocket, and said, "Excellent work. Thank you." The boy smiled back and made a tight military turn before leaving the dining hall.

"Who is it from?" Jacques leaned over the table, trying to

catch a glimpse of the formal lettering on the page. Marguerite read the lines quickly, her face pinching slightly. Then she had a thought. She sat forward and looked him in the eyes using her most serious voice.

"Help me get a commission on your ship, and I'll tell you what it says."

Jacques leaned forward and answered in his most serious voice, "Marry me, and I will."

Marguerite rolled her eyes and sat back to reread her message.

"What? Most women around here think I'm a fine catch." He leaned back and smiled at a group of girls at the next table, nodding his head slightly. They actually tittered and turned away. "See?" Jacques whispered.

Marguerite gave up her game of blackmail and handed him the page. "It's from my father," She said, "He's coming to see me."

Chapter Three

"Well, that's wonderful news!" Jacques cried.

"Not necessarily," Marguerite said as she poked at the leftover carrots on her plate.

"How could it not be good news? You have been wondering about him all these months, and how he felt about your wild wanderings. This is wonderful. If he were going to disown you, he wouldn't do it in person. That's much too messy for the aristocracy."

"You don't know the Vadnay aristocracy, Jacques. He could very well be coming here to spank me with his own hand."

Jacques laughed, and Outil approached the table from the corner where she waited as chaperone. "M'lady, I doubt that your father will come all this way to administer corporal punishment. You are much too old for that, and it goes against the dictates of refined society," Outil said with concern.

"I was exaggerating, Outil. He is unpredictable at best. Who knows what Pomphart told him about me when she got back to France." Marguerite's mind flashed to her horrid governess who'd followed her across the Atlantic only to be thrown in jail for threatening to kidnap Marguerite, or worse.

"You really think he visited her in prison?" Jacques asked.

"I don't know," she answered.

"Well, cheer up. He can't possibly get here for another few weeks. You've got exams to worry about, and I'm sure he'll be most impressed when you pass with top marks." Then he quickly added, "And learn to land correctly." Jacques was always trying to put a positive spin on situations she was sure would be positively dreadful.

"Oh no, this note was not from Paris. It was sent by ship-to-shore wireless telegraph. He will arrive in three days."

"That is not much time, m'lady," Outil said. "And that is right in the middle of your first written tests."

"Exactly, Outil. I'm going to have to figure this out." Marguerite folded it carefully and put the paper in her pocket.

"I would offer to help you, or meet him at the docks, but I'm afraid I may not be available next week," Jacques said.

"Why not?"

"My ship leaves next week." He smiled but did not look happy.

"So soon?" Marguerite felt her anger bubble up again, but she didn't want another scene, especially not in front of her ridiculous classmates.

"The sooner I leave, the sooner I will return to you." He

stood from his seat and made a low bow, sweeping up her hand and kissing it.

"That's *very* reassuring." She was trying to be mature and more level-headed these days, but sarcasm came so easily. Jacques liked a bit of her coquettish, spoiled rich girl side, but he could only take so much. Then again, she wondered why she was even concerned with what he did and didn't like.

"And now I must bid you lovely ladies farewell. You need to study, and I need sleep. It's going to be a long week for us all." Jacques crossed to her side and placed a kiss on her cheek before leaving. The other girls in the room fanned themselves and whispered giggles into each other's ears.

He *was* rather dashing. Marguerite couldn't deny that.

She spent most of that evening and all of the next day in her dingy room with Outil, going back and forth over the facts of the semester.

"What is the fastest possible speed of an aerschooner?" Outil asked.

"Cargo, passenger, or warship?" Marguerite asked.

"Each, m'lady."

"It obviously depends on weight and design. The schooner is the fastest of the aerships because of its combination of sails, motors, and envelope, but a heavy load will slow even the sleekest of vessels. Whether that be passengers, goods, or guns."

Marguerite stared out the window at the golden spring weather. Other girls were congregated on the lawn with their books and papers. The scene pulled at her heart a bit. Outil, poring over the facts and figures, reminded her not to get bogged down in the details, but to give concise and complete answers. Marguerite, however, was preoccupied with memories of sitting in the grass with her friends, Claude and Vivienne, back in France.

It had been several months, but the rot of guilt still ate at her gut when she thought about how her childhood friend Vivienne had died crossing the ocean with them.

"You are tired and distracted." Outil's voice cut through the moment.

"Yes, I am," Marguerite replied.

"Would you care to tell me what bothers you?"

"I was just thinking of Vivienne." Marguerite continued to stare out the window. "It's strange. I don't feel as bad about her death as I do about the way I treated her when she was alive.

"I mean, I wish she were still here, of course. She would love the thought of a husband, a little farm, and babies crawling all over her. I can't help but think that if I'd actually paid attention to her back at home, that she might not have suffered so much. She might still be alive." Marguerite's voice trailed off.

"M'lady, at that time you did not yet understand many of the aspects of true friendship that you understand now. You were never required to sacrifice or to give much of yourself. Please forgive me for speaking more openly than is appropriate, but I do so to prevent you from punishing yourself for a situation that was beyond your control."

"That's just the problem, Outil. I did have control. I could have paid more attention and been kinder, and then I might have seen what she was going through. I might have helped her sooner." Marguerite stood from the end of her bed and shook out her hair. It hung loosely in long dark waves down her back. "Never mind. It's done now. If I ever get the opportunity to make a friend again, I will just have to do a better job. Even if she is the most obnoxious girl on the planet, I will be a good friend." She folded her arms and held her head high as her resolve sunk into her chest like a pebble to the bottom of a lake.

"Now, would you fetch me some supper? I'm starved, and I don't feel like dealing with those imbeciles in the dining hall." She nodded toward the girls outside gathering their materials for dinner.

Outil sighed an automaton sigh, shifted uncomfortably but answered dutifully, "Of course, m'lady," and left the room.

Chapter Four

Sunday was long and tedious. Marguerite's brain kept jumping between test questions, and what her father was going to say when he arrived. She was starting to formulate a plan for getting her way with Jacques, but she had no idea what to expect from her father or the exam. The fact that she crashed and nearly died on her first solo flight test meant she had to do that much better on her other tests, so she barricaded herself in her room and studied until she couldn't keep her eyes open any longer.

The next morning Marguerite was up before the dawn, poring through her books one last time. She wasn't due in the main lecture hall until late morning, but she felt there were still a few subjects she could brush up on; propulsion was a big one, and so was maritime aerial law. Plus, she'd never taken an examination before in her life. Her father always provided her with the very latest publications and occasionally a competent tutor. She wanted to get it right and get her failure behind her.

Outil came to life with the morning sun as usual.

"M'lady, would you care for some breakfast?"

"No, I couldn't eat a thing." Marguerite didn't look up from her text.

"It is a fact that you will perform at a higher level if you have a healthy morning meal and a full stomach," Outil pressed.

"Fine." Marguerite looked up and remembered herself. "Yes, that would be lovely, please fetch me an egg and some bread."

"Very good." Outil left the room quickly, happy to have something to do with herself. Marguerite took a moment to stretch, stare out the window, and get dressed. Today was definitely flight suit time. She didn't think she could stand one second in a corset and still think clearly. Plus, it was an aviation examination. That called for an aviator's attire.

She pulled the pants up and buttoned the pretty brass buttons on top. Then she fastened the belt and picked up her bottle of perfume; the original bottle she'd brought from France hadn't survived the trip. Jacques had purchased her a new one as soon as he'd found out her favorite type from Outil. He was very thoughtful. She had to give him that.

She put on a squirt and set the bottle down, looking out the window absent-mindedly. The door opened behind her. She didn't turn around. "Thank you, Outil. You can set the meal on the nightstand." A booming male voice shook her core and scared her to death. She spun around at once.

"I am no automaton, and I'm certainly not serving you breakfast. What in the world are you wearing?"

"Oh! Father!" Marguerite's first reaction was to run into the old man's stout arms and hold him tightly. She stopped herself midway, however, suddenly leery of his response to her new life, remembering she was no longer a little girl.

"Come here, then. I won't bite you." He beckoned and stepped closer to her.

Relief flooded her heart. He didn't hate her.

She leapt for him, nearly knocking him over. He returned her affections with a tight squeeze and a rough peck on her cheek. "My dear, dear daughter," he said reverently.

"I was so afraid you would never want to see me again." Big salty tears ran freely down her cheeks, soaking his shoulder.

"I'll admit I spent quite a bit of time ready to disown you— or kill you—for the grief you caused me. But of course, I wanted to see you again. I'd have to see you to knock sense into you." He laughed at his exaggeration and held her at arm's length. "What in the world are you doing here?" He gestured to her tiny room and indicated the low status of her life with only the raise of his eyebrows. "Your letters were so vague. I only knew you were alive and nothing more."

"I know. I'm sorry, Father. I didn't want to trouble you, but I'm so happy here, and I didn't know how to explain by letter. I feel like I'm finally using my brain and my talents. People respect me because I'm working hard and doing well, not because I'm your daughter or because I have money."

She knew this wasn't all true, but it fell off her tongue so quickly and easily, and it just sounded right. She was happy. And wasn't this what a father would want to hear? Not that his daughter was laughed at and tormented because of who she was and where she came from?

"Well, money is something we must discuss." His tone turned dark. He looked her up and down. "Please explain this clothing. I arrived last night, and I haven't seen one other lady wearing anything of this sort. However, I have seen several young men in similar." His glance was accusatory and suspicious.

"When our ship went down, I lost everything I brought." She hesitated before explaining further. It was still hard to think back on that day. "My gown was soaked in seawater and blood. All they had for us to change into on the rescue ship was a flight suit. It was so warm and comfortable, and such a relief to get the soil of the wreck off, I couldn't resist. I suppose it's become a symbol of my new life."

"Darling, it's been several months," he said with eyebrows raised again. "You must know that there are rumors ... er ... more than just about you leaving home. Now that I see you face to face, I'm beginning to worry these rumors are not without substance."

Outil appeared in the doorway, carrying a tray and followed by Jacques. Suddenly the tiny space felt close to bursting.

"I see the automaton survived. Curious," her father said.

"Lord Vadnay," Outil dipped low, balancing the tray perfectly.

"At least you aren't without a servant." He did not acknowledge her piety. "And you. Explain yourself." He looked at Jacques, who seemed just as stunned as Marguerite to see her father this early in the morning, two days ahead of schedule.

"Sir," Jacques stood tall and offered a small bow in greeting.

"I am an instructor in this school and an acquaintance of your daughter, as you will remember from the ball at your home several months ago."

Marguerite noticed that he left off the part about being the captain of the ship that was bested by pirates, or the fact that he blew it up and was investigated by a formal inquiry.

Her father's face grew dark nonetheless. "Oh, yes. I know who you are." He turned back to his daughter. "Marguerite, I'd like you to move into my quarters for my duration in New France. I can send a man for your ... things." He looked around the room with disdain once again, his eyes rested on the humble meal Outil was carrying. "And we will get you some proper food."

Marguerite's stomach jerked in upon itself as she fought to get the words out she knew she had to speak. Defying her father in the middle of the night with no one watching was a far cry from openly disobeying him to his face.

"Father, I ... " she began.

Jacques stepped forward. "Lady Vadnay actually has a very important examination that will keep her engaged for the rest of the day. She is required to report to the lecture hall within the hour and will complete the exercises sometime in the afternoon."

Within the hour ... the words made her stomach even more upset. It was almost time. She was almost finished. She just had to get past her father first.

"Marguerite?" Her father looked at her, his hands on his hips and his chest puffed out. "What is he talking about?"

"It's a school, father. I've been learning aeronautics and steam engineering. Today is my final examination before I am assigned my own ship to pilot." She took a deep breath and suddenly felt five years old again, begging for a mechanical pony. "I'm going to be a pilot, father. I'm going to fly!"

He looked at the ceiling. He looked at the floor. He took a deep breath.

"Sir, she has attained the top place in her class—academically," Outil added without mentioning the test flight disaster. "She is the brightest student in the history of the school."

"Outil is correct … " Jacques tried to add.

"Enough." He cut them off and then looked at Marguerite. She thought she saw tears welling in his eyes, but he spoke with the authority of a king. "My man will collect your belongings from this closet. You will report to my home immediately." His voice was even and deadly serious. Marguerite set down her book, picked up her cape, and stepped past him into the hall by Jacques and Outil.

"Father, I will meet you for supper this evening at any location you choose. Outil will take down the address and escort me. If you wish for me to live in your rooms, I accept, gladly. I have many things I wish to discuss with you as well, but only after my examination. I've worked very hard to learn this material. I've paid my own money for this experience. I will see it through to the end." She dipped low in a curtsy, made ridiculous by her flight suit, and turned to walk down the hall.

"You are just like your mother! Stubborn and hard headed!" He hollered after her. Marguerite did not look back.

Chapter Five

Her hands twitched and trembled as she tried to hold the pen steady and scrape it on the edge of the ink well. She blotted it carefully and began to write. The more she lost herself in the technical details of the questions, the more she felt the drama of the morning melt away.

Her thoughts began to flow more easily, and the knowledge she'd pored over for the past few months all came together. There was even a portion of the test that she knew she bested simply because of her time on Jacques's ship, *The Triumph*.

They had a small break for lunch. Marguerite was a bit saddened that Outil and Jacques were not waiting for her in the dining room, but she ate quickly and sped back to the lecture hall, giving herself time to stretch and think and breathe deeply before the second half began.

Much to her relief, Outil was waiting for her at the end of the day. If the automaton had been anything softer than brass gears and panels, Marguerite may have fallen into her arms and wept for joy. She was exhausted, but also confident that she'd passed without a flaw. This was her passion. This was her talent. It was just a shame, for her father's sake, that she hadn't been born a boy.

"M'lady, congratulations!" Outil used the most excited version of her mechanical voice for this exclamation. "There is an autocart waiting to take us to your father's home. He has already removed your belongings from the school."

"Thank you, Outil. How does he seem?"

"He is not in good spirits."

"That's not surprising."

Outil adjusted a button on Marguerite's shirt that was about to come undone. "I believe that although he did not wish to, he may have enjoyed the tour of the city Master Laviolette and I took him on today."

"You took him on a tour? With Jacques?" Marguerite was incredulous. "That's a small miracle, Outil. I was sure he would have you sent out for scrap and me chopped up for chum after this morning."

"Excuse me for saying so, but I believe he loves you much more than that." Outil motioned down a path to their left. "This way."

"What is it they say? Out of the gearbox, into the oil," Marguerite mumbled.

The cab was the latest model from Paris, of course. Marguerite had seen a precious few on the streets of Montreal up to this point. She wondered if her father secured it as a rental. or if he'd brought it with him on the ship.

The rear seat was plush and comfortable and made from the softest velvet. Marguerite caught herself running her hand across it, longing for her own room at her childhood home filled with similar fabrics and softness. It had been close to a year since she'd slept on a feather bed with real satin sheets and a duvet that didn't smell like it was made from a yak. Independence was nice, but so was luxury.

The driver looked at the pair in the rear mirror with a smirk but drove through the streets overflowing with horse-drawn carriages, autocarts and those on foot, without comment. A short drive along the St. Lawrence River brought them to a formidable brick home with modern lights flanking a huge mahogany door. "Lovely, of course," Marguerite commented. "Where is Jacques now?"

"He had an engagement to attend this evening. He wanted me to assure you that he would call on you tomorrow at your father's home." The driver pulled to a stop, got out, and opened the door for the ladies. They stepped from the autocart and walked to the front door. It opened before they touched the knob. An automaton stood at attention, beckoning they enter.

"M'lady, your father awaits." Its voice had none of the sweet inflection or lilt of Outil's, but his gear work was magnificent and his metal shiny and new.

Marguerite walked past, taking him in, followed by the grand foyer beyond. Outil replied, "Thank you," and followed. Fresh flowers stood on delicate tables lining the walls of a round room with a vaulted ceiling. Windows lined the top of the space, each covered with a rainbow of stained glass. An elegant staircase clung to the wall, winding its way to the second floor.

"Your room is at the top of the stairs. I will show you there if you will please follow me," the bot croaked before stomping up the stairs in a very ungraceful fashion. Marguerite looked at Outil, who rolled her metallic blue eyes. The gesture was so human and so appropriate for the moment; Marguerite burst out a little giggle as they ascended the stairs behind the clomping bot.

"*There* you are." Her father's voice filled the rotunda and bounced off the gilt ceiling. Marguerite looked down at him from halfway up the stairs to the second-floor balcony. This welcome was decidedly less warm than the previous one. She was going to have to figure out how to apologize for ignoring his orders without giving up her hard-earned independence.

"Yes, here we are," she answered and walked down the stairs.

"Faulks will show you to your room. Please rest and change for dinner. We have much to discuss, and I'm hungry enough to eat a brass elephant, so we'll dine early."

"Yes, sir." Marguerite's voice dripped with sarcasm, but her father didn't seem to notice. After all these months successfully navigating life on her own, she found it ridiculous to have someone telling her how to dress and when to eat.

The room at the top of the stairs was gorgeous. Deep, ocean blue draperies flanked floor to ceiling windows. The bed filled most of the floor with four posts, a duvet that matched the curtains, and a mountain of pillows. Outside, Marguerite had a view of the city gardens and the river. It was truly glorious.

Her father's bot, Faulks, opened the doors to a towering wardrobe in one corner of the room. The trunk from her school and all of her books sat at the other side of the room. "These were brought in for her Ladyship this afternoon. We apologize for the lack of selection and possibly ill-fitting styles; we will do our best to update your wardrobe as soon as possible."

"That will do." Marguerite waved the bot away and flopped on the bed in a very unladylike fashion. Faulks didn't react. He nodded his shiny silver head and clomped out of the room. Outil shut the door. "Ah! This bed is like a cloud!" She spread her arms out and closed her eyes. "Outil, see if there is anything decent I can stand to wear tonight. I suppose I have to do *something* for Father."

Outil sifted through the contents of the closet and pulled out a light blue dress of fine linen and helped Marguerite dress for the evening. They left the room together and made their way down the stairs. "Best keep to yourself tonight. Father doesn't like automatons with opinions."

"Yes, m'lady," Outil answered.

The dining room was through the main lobby and around a corner. It was just as opulent as the rest of the home. Her father sat at one end of a huge table with only two place settings. He rose when she entered the room.

She decided on the spot to be kind to him. After all, she already knew she wasn't going to do anything he said. She might as well let him down easily. If there was a relationship to be saved without ruining her plans, she would save it.

"Hello, father. This is a wonderful home." She offered her hand and curtsied slightly. He took it and kissed it, a broad smile spreading under his mustache. She noted that it had much more grey in it than the last time she'd seen him.

"This is the daughter I've been longing to see." He beamed again and gestured for her to sit. As her father sat across from her at the end of a very long table, a human servant entered the dining room and served them the first course, a creamed soup with tiny bits of truffle and carrot.

"My dear, I want to tell you that I am not as horrible as you might think. I was took ill when I heard you'd run away. And when I got news of *The Triumph* going down, I was even more devastated."

Marguerite had to bite her tongue to keep from saying something sarcastic about him not caring enough to actually come help her; instead sending Madame Pomphart and a slick suitor. They'd traded letters a few times over the past few months, but only in the form of checking in to make sure the other was still alive.

"Now that we are together at last, and your *schooling* is out of the way, we should revisit our plans and start over fresh," he said with a smile.

To anyone else, that would sound like a perfectly lovely way to reconcile, but Marguerite knew it was a thinly veiled way to let her know he was still in control and had come to clean up the mess she'd made of her life. She opened her mouth to rebut him in the kindest way she knew how, but he didn't give her a chance to speak. "First things first. We are going to have to find you a suitable match here, since you seem to prefer it to France. I purchased this home with the idea of staying here until you are settled, then passing it along to you and whomever the lucky man is you choose. I hear that's how it is done here in the new world."

Marguerite was actually touched by his effort to meet her halfway, but she paused before speaking, "Thank you, that is very considerate, and yes, that is how it is done here in New France. But what do you mean you *bought* this home?"

"I also spoke with Captain Laviolette today. He is quite taken with you, but I made it clear that my aspirations for you are much higher than an aership captain who can't keep his own ship from blowing up." He was playing cat and mouse. She was obviously the mouse.

"I know you don't approve of Jacques, but I don't care. I'm not ready to get married, Father. We are not engaged; he is just a dear friend. Perhaps when I do decide to marry, it would be to someone like him, but for the time being, do not ignore my question. What do you mean you *bought* this house?"

"Well, if that is your attitude, then it's just as well that I've leased out the estate in France. I'm here to stay, my dear. There is no reason for us to be apart. We are the only family left to each other." Marguerite's heart dropped. This could ruin everything. She would have to put her plan into action first thing in the morning if it was going to work. Otherwise, her father would embed himself into the society and start dragging her around to balls again.

She thought of the last ball she attended and shuddered. She'd rather risk her life in the aether.

Chapter Six

Marguerite rolled over and dramatically pounded the bed with her fists. "Men make me *furious*, Outil. Who do they think they are? They can't plan my life for me."

"If you will excuse me, ma'am, I am not sure I understand why you are so upset this morning."

"I was up half the night thinking of all my hard work being thwarted by the men who claim to love me."

"I am sorry, but I don't see how anyone is thwarting you, m'lady." Outil pulled open the curtains to let the sunshine fall on Marguerite's bed and spill down to the floor. "Jacques thinks he can tell me when and where I can serve, and my father just moved halfway around the world to try and salvage my love life."

"I believe your father moved here to try and salvage his relationship with you, m'lady. And Jacques is correct about the rules of the Royal Fleet. You cannot serve on the bridge unless he calls in many favors, and that would not be favorable for anyone."

"But I could still serve on the ship. Why does he think I spent this whole year at school if not to serve on an aership? He thinks he can keep me here safe and sound while he goes off and has all the fun, but he is dead wrong." Marguerite sat up and swung her legs over the side of the bed. "Come, we're going to the school. I can't wait for the post to determine my future either. All I must do is get my test scores and my own post. Neither my father nor Jacques need to know."

"Yes, ma'am."

Outil set to work taming Marguerite's hair while Marguerite continued to grumble about men in general. Eventually, she was presentable, and the pair set off down the street, a breezy Montreal spring welcoming them. At the school, Marguerite proceeded straight to the dean's office. She knocked firmly on the door three times. "Yes?" A voice from the other side answered.

Marguerite walked in and pronounced loudly, "Dean Beaumont, I am Lady Marguerite Vadnay here to speak with you about my future at this school and as an aership pilot."

The stout man with the neatly trimmed beard and immaculate dress stood slowly but didn't look up from his papers immediately. Marguerite had always admired him from afar for his high standards of dress and decorum; however, she'd never had to speak one-on-one with him before. She was starting to feel uneasy with his silence, when he finally put the paperwork down and looked at her properly. Then he motioned for her to take a seat across from him. Outil took her place standing behind Marguerite's chair.

"Yes, of course. What seems to be the matter then, Lady

Vadnay?" He asked, looking at her fully now, taking in her strange flight suit and perfectly styled hair.

"The problem is that I am ready to go out and do something with all the information I have learned in this good institution, but there seem to be a few things standing in my way."

"Such as?"

Marguerite hesitated a bit, "Such as my test scores. I need to know if I passed my exams or not."

"Right, well, you will receive a notice by mail when those scores are made available."

"Of course. But, you see, I can't wait that long. There is a ship leaving in one week that I would like to volunteer to serve on."

"Ah, the pirate operation. Yes, I've had a number of young ladies offer to volunteer for those posts. However, I do not think it is their excitement or skill in battle that is fueling their readiness to serve king and country, but rather an interest in the captain of the ship. Plus, I cannot refer young ladies to a combat mission of this type. The admiral would laugh them away. It is a man's job."

Marguerite gritted her teeth and took a deep breath. This man was of a higher standing than most military men his age. He was educated and would not be intimidated by her anger or, she guessed, her title. She decided to change tactics.

"Of course, M. Beaumont. Do you suppose you might be able to, at least, pull my file and recommend a course of study or employment to best suit my skills then? I'm very earnest about securing my own future before settling into a marriage."

He regarded her for a moment and sighed. "I suppose I could take a look—but only as a favor to your father. I heard he is in town to check up on you. I was hoping to make his acquaintance."

Marguerite had to force herself not to explode. Favor to her father? The whole situation was infuriating. As the dean rose to retrieve her records, she took another deep breath and spoke as evenly as possible.

"Of course. I'd be happy to introduce you." She forced a smile and realized this could be her chance to get what she wanted.

"That would be lovely. I was invited to your home once when I was back in France. Oh my, it was decades ago. You may not have been born yet. Unfortunately, I was unable to attend. I am quite curious to see your father's collection of military machinery." He continued to flip through papers in a long and deep drawer as he spoke.

"Well, he hasn't brought much of that with him, but he did bring a new autocart from Paris."

"Excellent." He pulled a stack of papers from the heap and turned to her. "Here you are then." He sat back down and started reading through her reports and exams. Marguerite had to fight the urge to fidget as the dean flipped page after page, nodding his head and humming a bit. She knew she'd done well in all her classes. Her professors had remarked on her hard work and dedication, as well as her previous knowledge of most subjects. Still, she couldn't tell what the man in front of her was thinking.

He paused on a particular page. He squinted at the paper, his eyes repeating the same pattern as he read it a second time. And then a third. He looked over the top of the paper at her and then back at the page again. "Uh, huh. Interesting."

Drat! He's read about my crash. Marguerite tried to keep her face from falling, but it was not easy. "Yes?" She finally ventured to speak.

"It says here you scored perfect marks in every ballistics exam, including the practical and marksmanship?"

Relief flooded her heart. "Yes! I have quite good aim."

"I'm guessing your father gave you a head start?" He smiled knowingly over the paper.

"Yes, yes he did," she lied. The dean didn't have to know that all of her target practice as a girl was done without her father's knowledge.

"It's a pity you failed your practical flight examination. You will have to retake that before you will be allowed to fly anything for His Majesty. And yet, I was just speaking with Admiral Auboyneau and he was asking if I knew of someone with your particular skills. Granted, I'm sure he did not have a lady in mind when he asked, but I could possibly mention your name and see what he thinks. I believe the position he needed to fill was on the new ship they commissioned for this pirate raid all you ladies are so keen to go on."

Marguerite let a genuine smile spread across her face this time. "Oh, would you? That would mean so much to me."

"Just between us, you passed your final examinations with top marks." He smiled at her conspiratorially.

"Excellent!" She clapped her hands.

"Don't let word get out that I told you any of this. The last thing I need is a line of pupils at my door asking for their results and special favors. I am curious about something, though, Lady Vadnay."

"What is that?" Marguerite's mood was much lighter, making her happy to indulge the dean a bit.

"How is it that a lady of your standing wants to work on a battleship? You could have your pick of suitors on either continent, and if you retake the flight exam, you could have a private ship to fly at your leisure. I'm not quite sure I understand your aim here."

"It's quite simple, really. I want more than what is handed to me. I want to see the world, earn my keep, and use the brain in my head. A lady can't very well do that from a chaise lounge in a palace on either continent."

The dean nodded and tapped his desk with his fingertips. She could tell he wanted to say something else but was hesitant.

"Thank you for looking into—" she began.

"Are you aware that he truly loves you, and only you, m'lady?" he interrupted her.

"Excuse me?"

"Captain Laviolette. He also has his pick of eligible ladies of fine birth—of all births, actually—but his heart belongs to you. I've known Jacques for many years. He has not always been a faithful or completely, shall we say, faultless man. But since meeting you, he has made himself a better man and has dedicated himself to you and your happiness. He speaks highly of you and your goals to anyone who asks. I just wondered if you knew that."

Marguerite was speechless. She nodded a bit and stood. The dean stood as well. "Thank you, sir. I appreciate your time and insight. I will keep all of this in mind. Might I call on you later to inquire as to the position on the ship?" She struggled to keep her voice even.

"Don't trouble yourself. I will send a pigeon in a few days." He opened the door for her and Outil.

"One other thing." Marguerite had almost entirely forgotten. "Do you suppose I could retake my flight test this week? Is there any chance of that? As a special favor?" She smiled prettily.

"I'm sorry. We really can't do that. I'd love to, but really, I can't. There is another test in two weeks time. If this position doesn't work for you, then we'll have you set to retake then. Never fear, m'lady. You will not go to waste in New France. We will keep you engaged."

Engaged. Marguerite shuddered at the word but smiled and thanked the dean again before leaving. Once they were safely out of earshot, Marguerite turned to her bot, smiling. "That went rather well, don't you think?"

"Yes, m'lady. Very interesting. Congratulations on passing your exams."

"Oh, I knew all along that I would pass. It was just a matter of finding out for certain. Now all I need to do is make things good with Father. And that begins with new clothes. Where shall we spend our money today?"

The two spent the afternoon patronizing two dressmakers and a corsetiere. The result was a much more refined Marguerite and an Outil with very little energy in her reservoir.

"Father, we are home!" Marguerite cried as she entered the towering double front doors, leaving Outil to pay the driver. Faulks came stomping into the hall. "Welcome home, m'lady."

"Where is Father?"

"In his study. Will you be dining with us tonight?"

"Of course." Marguerite hurried past the bot, anxious to show her repentance by attire and to discuss her plans with her father. She found him in the study, as Faulks had said. Only he wasn't reading. He was fast asleep in his armchair, a copy of "The Hundred Years' War and its Follies in Weaponry" lying precariously on his lap. She regarded him for a moment. He looked so much older like this. So grey, and so very lined about the face. Her heart softened a bit as she regarded him.

"Father?" She asked quietly.

"Huh?" He jumped from his sleep with a start. The book slid from his legs and to the floor with a loud *thud*. Marguerite bent to pick it up. "My dear, what are you doing? What are you wearing?" He seemed confused, still on the edge of dreams and reality. She set the book on his bureau and spun so he could fully appreciate her new emerald green dress.

"I have a waist, Father. Aren't you happy?"

He rubbed his face and smiled in admiration. "You look amazing. Thank you. What is the special occasion?"

"Just that I missed seeing you smile when I came into a room, and I have good news."

"Of course. Please, sit down and tell me about your day."

Marguerite sat on the edge of a comfortable chair and leaned forward. "I have spoken with the dean of the school, and he has told me that I passed all of my exams. I even scored perfect marks in some of them." She smiled triumphantly.

"Well, then." Her father hesitated. "I suppose that is wonderful news."

"Yes. It is. It proves that I have more than just fluff in my head."

"I never thought that of you." He leaned forward, his face earnest.

"I have proof that it isn't true now, for anyone who does." She sat back and folded her hands in her lap.

"What is the next step for you then?" Her father stood and picked the book up off his bureau. He placed it carefully on the shelf.

"That is precisely what I wanted to talk with you about. I have a few opportunities ahead." Marguerite formed her words carefully as she watched her father align the book spines on the shelf with the precision of a watchmaker.

"Go on," He spoke without looking at her.

"Father, the last time we tried to make plans together, it ended badly. I would like to avoid that this time, but I'd also like to retain my independence." The words came out in a rush.

Lord Vadnay turned and regarded her now. "It ended badly because you ran off in the night."

"Yes. I know. No need to bring that up. Except that I would like to avoid a repeat performance."

"At least we agree on that." He took a seat across from her and sat forward listening intently. "What do you have in mind?"

Marguerite had to take a moment to compose herself. It occurred to her that this was the first time her father had asked her that—what she wanted. She took a deep breath. She didn't want to mess this up. "You know that I want to fly. And that I have the intelligence and strength to serve in His Majesty's aerguard."

"Marguerite, dear. If all you want is to fly, I can buy you a dirigible. We can get your papers in order, and you can fly to your heart's content."

"That's just it. I fear I will never be happy with my own little dirigible. I want to be part of something. I want to—well, I suppose I want to help people." Marguerite's words surprised her. She thought about what she'd said as she watched her father mull it over as well. Did she mean it? Or was she just saying this to get her way?

After probing her heart a bit further, she decided she did mean it. Working alongside Jacques to save *The Triumph* had been the highlight of her life. Losing Vivienne had been the worst moment of her life, but she knew she'd helped countless other girls that night. She wanted to do that again. She wanted to make a difference. "You want to *help* people?" Her father was still considering her sincerity.

Marguerite decided to explain what she had only just discovered herself. She'd never told him what she had been through before. The short telegraphs merely assured him of her safety and happiness. Sitting in the library with him now, she felt it was time to open up and recount the whole story. How she'd fought pirates, saved passengers, taken charge of evacuation, and helped to destroy the ship to keep it from falling into enemy hands. Her father sat at attention, his brow furrowed, taking in every word.

Marguerite's hands were sweaty and her heart racing as she finished her tale. A piece of hair had fallen out of place and covered one eye. She tucked it behind her ear quickly without thought to her appearance and waited for his reply.

"That's what I want, Father. Not necessary hand-to-hand combat, but I want to make the world a better place. I want to serve in the aerguard, and I want to help France."

Lord Vadnay shook his head and looked down at his feet. He splayed his fingers, pushing the tips together as he leaned forward, forearms to knees. He didn't speak. "Father?" Marguerite braced herself for an explosion of temper.

"You are just like her," he whispered.

"Like who?"

Lord Vadnay sat up and looked at his daughter, tears in his eyes. "Like your mother. She wanted adventure as well. She wasn't quite as bold as you, and she was never dedicated to helping others. She just wanted out of France. I, on the other hand, wanted a beautiful companion and lots of children running free on the estate." He pulled a hanky from his waistcoat and wiped roughly at his face. Marguerite didn't know what to say. She'd never seen her father like this before.

"I fought with her about it for years. She ran off once, but then she came back." Marguerite thought of the letters she'd found in the trunks of the estate back in France, her mother begging for forgiveness.

"So, I brought her home. We were happy for a while, and you were born, making our joy complete—or so I thought. But she grew restless again. She blamed me for her isolation and dull life. She called me a jailor. She lost interest in you, and all things eventually. I was afraid she would harm herself. I consulted doctors and specialists. They prescribed all kinds of ridiculous tonics and therapies. Then one day, she was gone. You were just shy of two years old, and she disappeared into the night."

A lump formed in Marguerite's throat. If only she'd known this story a year ago, she might not have run off into the night.

"At first, I resolved to find her and drag her back. It was my right as her husband to do so, but I knew it would just lead to more of the same, so I gave up. I focused my attentions on you. Such a tiny little thing with no mother to care for you now. My heart turned to you and there it has stayed." He wiped at his face again and cleared his throat.

"I had no idea." Marguerite stood and walked to her father's side, gently laying her arm on his shoulder. He was suddenly strong again. All emotion swept aside.

"I know. I didn't see the need to bring that kind of shame to your pretty head. The trouble is all my doing. I should have faced the truth long ago. You are your mother's daughter."

Marguerite felt taken aback at this statement. "I am not."

Lord Vadnay laughed out loud and patted her hand. "I don't mean to say that you would torment me to such extremes, but you have tormented me some."

"Yes, I have, but had you told me of her and how she broke your heart, we may have avoided a few things in the past year. We might not have wasted so much time being angry at one another."

"Yes, well, that is all in the past now, isn't it?"

"Where is she now?" Marguerite wasn't going to let this point fade into the background. Her mother didn't die like he said she had. "It's a fairly terrible thing to tell a child their mother is dead when in reality, they are just off gallivanting somewhere."

"I don't believe she is gallivanting anywhere. I told you she died because I believe she has. After she left me, her choices were not conducive to a long life. I tried to keep up with her for a few years, but it soon became evident that this was pointless."

"But you don't know for certain?" Marguerite felt silly and small asking this question, like a child clinging to a favorite toy.

"No, but I have compelling evidence to suggest as much. When we return home to the continent, I will show you all the documentation I have and some likenesses that were painted before you were born. It's time I did at least that much for you. For now, tell me what you plan to do."

He smiled at her, and she hesitated. This was a lot of information to consider all at once. Then again, she finally had her father's attention. He wanted to hear her out. He wanted to support her. She could push him to answer more questions about his shadowed past, but that could push him far away again. She felt his smooth old fingers hold her own young ones and felt a rush of warmth in her chest as she looked at his lined face, then Marguerite told him her plan.

Chapter Seven

The letter came by street post three days later. It had been a long three days, but also quite enjoyable for Marguerite. Her mind had been hovering on the possibilities the next week would bring, but her heart was resting in lazy days spent with her father.

He begrudgingly agreed to support her scheme, even though it was dangerous and altogether unbecoming for a wealthy young girl to pursue. This made their time together even less strenuous. They spent time in the library of their new home. They took the autocart out for drives every afternoon, and one day they even hired a private steamship to take them up the St. Lawrence River for the afternoon.

Marguerite was true to her word and invited Dean Beaumont to tea. He and her father got along swimmingly. This helped to ease the burden of guilt she carried when she thought of leaving him once again. At least he would have a friend to chum around Montreal with for a bit.

The evening after the boating holiday, an automated pigeon dropped in through their aermail slot carrying a rolled parchment bearing Marguerite's name. She just happened to be walking through the entryway when the clicking and cooing mechanical bird landed on the guest perch and dropped its cargo on the table.

"What a sweet little thing you are." Marguerite patted its shiny grey back and pulled an oil can from the table's hidden drawer. She gave the bird a couple of pumps of oil in each wing then bid it farewell, as it hopped to the swinging exit window and flew back into the street.

"Outil!" Marguerite shouted, "It's here!" She eagerly peeled off the wax seal and unrolled the thick off-white paper. Her automaton came up behind her and placed a shining silver hand on each of Marguerite's shoulders, peering over to the words below. "What does it say, miss?" the bot asked quietly. Marguerite read quickly then let the paper snap closed again in her hand. She turned to face Outil, biting her lower lip.

"What is this racket?" her father cried.

"Father, I have an assignment on *The Renegade*!" She was breathless with excitement.

"I'm hoping that's the name of an aership?" Her father puffed into the entryway, Faulks and a human servant trailing a safe distance behind. "It is!"

"And is it Laviolette's ship?"

"Yes, I believe it is."

"And this is what you wanted?" His voice was lower now, despite the acoustics in the vaulted room.

"Yes, Father. It is."

"Well, then, I suppose we must celebrate." Marguerite shoved the letter in the pocket of her dress and threw her arms around him in a very un-ladylike embrace. He grumbled and grunted and patted her back, then started barking orders at the servant to prepare a feast for dinner that evening.

"Would you like to invite Captain Laviolette to join us? Give him the good news?"

"No." Marguerite didn't hesitate for a moment. She felt a longing for him deep in her belly, but she would rather see her plans through to the end than give into a moment of girlish silliness. Besides, she hadn't told her father that Jacques was completely against this plan of hers.

"Suit yourself. I will invite a few of the neighbors, and we will make a party of it. Outil, you will assist Faulks today," he said.

"Of course, sir." Outil looked to Marguerite for a moment. Marguerite nodded her head. She got the distinct feeling that the bot had something to say but couldn't do so in her father's presence.

"I'll come find you later," Marguerite added.

"Very good, m'lady."

Marguerite found herself alone in the great foyer. She reached in her pocket and squeezed the thick creamy paper in her hand. She gave a little hop for joy, then called out to her father, "I'll be back in an hour. I'm going to go officially register."

"Good, good," he called out from somewhere deep in the

house. She gathered her cape and hat and strained to open the massive doors for herself. She took a deep breath of the springtime air and set off. No time to lose. At the registry a girl, not much older than Marguerite, greeted her with a tired expression. Marguerite produced the paper in her pocket and slid it across the glossy wooden counter.

"Hello, miss. How can I help you today?"

"Lady Marguerite Vadnay reporting for duty," she beamed.

The girl took the piece of paper with one hand and looked Marguerite over. "*Lady* Vadnay?" she questioned. Then she opened the paper and stared at it for moment before looking back up. "Assigned to *The Renegade*?" Her disbelief was palpable.

"That is correct. I'm the new second officer of ballistics."

"Ballistics?"

"Yes. See, right there." Marguerite reached over the counter and pointed to the assignment on the paper before spreading her fingers wide and adding: "Boom!"

Her antics did not amuse the girl. She verified Marguerite's paperwork, showed her to the outfitting station, gave her a very itchy uniform and a small trunk for personal items, then she showed her to the door.

Chapter Eight

Marguerite awoke to grey all around her. Clouds blanketed the normally bright spring weather, and a constant drizzle tapped on the floor to ceiling windows and dampened her spirits—but only a bit. She bounced out of bed and commanded Outil.

"Today is the day! Are my bags ready?"

"Yes, m'lady." Outil indicated a small trunk at her feet.

"Seems ridiculous, doesn't it?" Marguerite stared at the little box with handles. "To have come from so much in France to so little, and yet, I'm so much happier."

"I am truly grateful for your happiness, m'lady," Outil said.

"What was it you wanted to tell me the other day, Outil? I feel like I haven't seen you at all lately."

Since Marguerite received her commission, she had been busy with her father's party and preparations at the office of military affairs. Then she'd wound up spending all day the day before with Jacques. It had been wonderful. Just like the old times, even though Marguerite felt she may burst with the news of her job on his ship. He hadn't mentioned it, so she figured he hadn't seen the ship's manifest yet. All in good time. She knew he could have her removed from service if he wanted. As captain of *The Renegade*, he had the right to choose his crew. Marguerite hoped he left that duty up to his first mate and wouldn't take note of her until they were well on their way.

Outil hesitated a moment then asked, almost shyly, "M'lady, it's just that you never let me see what your actual assignment was on the ship. You folded up your missive before I was done reading."

"Oh, dear Outil. All you had to do was ask. I've been assigned as the second ballistics officer. Even though my eventual goal is to work on the bridge, I'm quite happy with this assignment. You know I'm an excellent shot and my knowledge of weaponry, both old and cutting edge, is quite extensive. It's a perfect fit, don't you think? So much better than the galley. Ugh. I can't imagine spending my whole voyage below deck preparing ship food for a bunch of aerman!" Marguerite finished her speech and began to dress for the day. Outil remained silent.

"Outil, aren't you happy for me?" Marguerite was suddenly annoyed by the bot's silence.

"Yes, m'lady. It's just that, I believe there is more to this mission than what he has told you."

"Whatever could you mean by that?" Marguerite snatched her military issued underthings from the bot and pulled them on only to throw them back to the floor. "These are horrid. I refuse to wear them. They will wear the hide right off my thighs. Give me the silks from Paris."

Outil obeyed and retrieved the light pink silk underthings. She helped her mistress dress, as she continued to explain. "It's nothing he has said directly. It's just a few clues I have picked up on while listening to your conversations."

"What clues?"

"I have also done more research into the foes we will be facing, m'lady." Outil pulled at the waist cinch of Marguerite's flight suit. Unfortunately, she had to wear the military issued suit.

"And what did you find?"

"They are more than just the common Mediterranean corsairs that attacked our ship. These seem to be a ragtag group of outlaws from several countries, most originating in the Caribbean and the British Colonies. The news I could gather on them suggested England might even have backed them."

"Well, that's neither here nor there." Marguerite waved Outil's concerns away with her hand. "Pirates are pirates no matter where they come from. All of them are wicked law breakers."

"If England has backed them, they will be a much more formidable opponent," Outil protested. "They would be considered Privateers and will be protected by maritime and aerlaw. That greatly limits your options for stopping them and avoiding war."

"What about Jacques? What clues are you referring to?" Marguerite changed the subject as she sat at her dressing table and waited for Outil to plait her hair. "Nothing in particular. I just get the feeling that he didn't want this commission, but that he didn't have a choice. You realize that a man of his ranking doesn't get much say, if any, in where he is assigned to serve?" Outil expertly pulled a stiff bristled brush through her dark, wavy tresses and began to weave them up and back out of her face, forming a neat arrangement at the back of her neck.

"Yes, but he knew that when he signed up." Marguerite admired Outil's work and turned to face her mechanical friend.

"Forgive me for saying this, m'lady, but he also didn't know you when he signed up."

"Outil, unless you have something of substance to tell me, I think we are finished with this conversation." Marguerite was tired of Outil playing the devil's advocate. Plus she didn't believe her bot could actually intuit or research more about the situation than she already had. True, she'd been busy with studies the past few weeks, but not that busy. If there were something more that Jacques wasn't telling her, she felt certain that she would have noticed it.

"Very well," Outil meekly stepped back from Marguerite's chair as she rose and headed for the door.

"Bring my trunk downstairs, will you?"

"Of course, m'lady."

After a quick meal, Marguerite bid her father farewell.

"Be careful, young lady." He had both hands on her shoulders; his face just inches from hers. "You are my greatest blessing, my greatest joy, and my only true treasure. It pains me to see you go, especially in this fashion. Are you certain you won't stay with me? We could have so many lovely days on the river and in the countryside."

"Oh, father. Of course, I will be careful. And you know that I would lose my mind if I had to sit here, idle and aging, as we took in the scenery together. I will make you proud while I'm saving the world, and bring home a uniform dripping in medals."

"Just bring home a uniform without any gunshots in it, eh?" He pointed to her neckline. "And cover that up, for goodness sake."

Marguerite reached up and felt a bit of pink silk peeking out from beneath the scratching blue wool. "Right." She blushed.

"Take care my girl. Remember that I love you."

They embraced only for a moment, long enough for Marguerite to whisper: "I love you, too."

And then she was off. The autocar delivered girl, automaton, and small case to the landing just off the St. Lawrence River at the Port of Montreal. The drizzle had stopped, and the sun threatened to break through any moment. Everything was damp and glistening, despite the grey light of morning.

Marguerite gasped as she took in the spectacle before her. It was so much grander than she remembered. So many more ships than back home in La Rochelle. Gleaming new dirigibles and aerships anchored side by side with older, more weather-worn vessels. Fishing rigs and ancient cargo ships filled the river below. There were people and officers and crates everywhere. Marguerite couldn't help but think of the first time she'd arrived at a dock like this, just a little more than a year ago with her friend Vivienne. Bittersweet emotions flooded her chest. What an adventure that had been. She allowed herself to miss Vivienne for just a moment, and then she turned to Outil.

"Here we go, Outil! Which ship do you suppose is *The Renegade?*"

"It seems fairly obvious, m'lady." Outil lifted a shining silver finger and pointed up river. Amidst a circus of ships in the air and the water, surrounded by busy bots and workers, was moored a gleaming black and silver aership of epic design and proportions.

"Yes, you are most likely correct." Marguerite agreed, and the two set off.

Despite the aership's massive size, it was a sleek and practical design. The body was slim and very pointed at either end. The stern and bow both sported razor sharp ramrods—for puncturing envelopes— Marguerite guessed—and the lower decks only showcased very small portholes and weaponry access. The whole ship gleamed like an autobot, bright silver in the morning sun. The envelope was painted black, and the royal seal had been emblazoned on the giant swaths of fabric making it look like one enormous flag.

If there was any doubt left in her mind, large letters were painted in black along the back edge of the ship: *Renegade.*

Marguerite turned to grin at Outil as they approached the ship. There was a flurry of activity beneath. Aermen and soldiers chatted and checked off lists. Lifts ran up and down as fast as the crew could load and unload them. Marguerite looked for someone in charge but was at a loss. Almost everyone had a uniform, and no one looked like they were in charge of new arrivals.

Across the crowd she suddenly spotted Jacques. He was

wearing his finest uniform, hat and all, and was shouting orders to those surrounding him as he approached a lift. The men cleared the way and let him enter with a few crates. He slammed the door, accompanied by a smaller man with a newer looking bot, and the lift pulled them off the docks and into the air. Jacques carefully surveyed the scene below him as he rose.

"Hurry, Outil! Hide me!" Marguerite ducked behind the bot. If he saw her in uniform, he would pounce at once. Her lunch with Jacques the afternoon before had been so wonderful; Marguerite had pretended that none of this was about to happen. She'd allowed herself to just enjoy his company. He did not propose; she did not argue. It was bliss.

Being at the docks and watching him ascend like a king to a floating throne, left a pit in her stomach. She had to keep her head down and her wits about her, at least until the battles were over.

"It is safe to come out," Outil said softly. "And I believe we must speak to that man over there. Marguerite looked up and saw a man with a paper and quill calling out names and pointing people to different areas of the dock. The pair made their way through the crowds of humans and bots to the frantic man who seemed to be in charge. He was speaking to a younger boy, maybe fourteen years old, and directing him to his station. Marguerite wondered at such a young lad going off to fight on the open seas. Then again, she was but three years older than that. She had no room to argue.

"Hello, I'm Lady Marguerite Vadnay," she said much too loudly at the man's face. He winced a bit and adjusted his spectacles. "I'm sorry, but you'll have to go to the end of the line—er, um, m'lady."

"What line?" Marguerite looked around her, but all she saw were throngs of men and bots. Until she realized that part of the throng did indeed form a serpent of bodies winding back away from the man with the papers. "Oh, dear. I'm ever so sorry."

"She can go in front of me," another young lad with sparkling blue eyes and a red dusting of shaggy hair spoke up. He smiled at Marguerite in obvious appreciation. "I don't mind giving way for a lady to pass." He held his hat in two hands and gave an awkward bow.

"Aren't you a dear?" Marguerite rewarded him with an appreciative smile.

The organizer grumbled but flipped quickly through his pages. "Just hurry yourself, m'lady. Let's see, ballistics?" He looked at her and the paper, alternating a few times.

"Yes, that is correct."

"And this is Outil, the automaton?"

"Yes." Marguerite nodded. "Alright, you are to report to the first officer of ballistics to the left of the ship, there where they are loading powder and such. Officer Vuitton. Safe voyage."

"Thank you ever so much."

Marguerite gave a little dip herself and was off to meet Officer Vuitton. Behind her, she heard the voice of a young man squeak, "I'm Louis!"

She turned to look at the red-headed boy. Just as she suspected, he was yelling at her. She smiled and waved. "Safe voyage, Louis!"

"Enough," the organizer grunted. "Louis what?"

As their conversation faded behind her, Marguerite focused her sights on the ballistics team. They seemed a sturdy bunch, each one hauling, at least, two crates to a lift and returning to the pile to get more without hesitation. An older man with sandy brown hair peeking from under a first officer's hat was calling out orders and hauling the odd crate himself. Marguerite approached him triumphantly, bursting with pride at having found her position.

"You must be First Officer Vuitton?" she chirruped.

The man stopped, a bulky crate in hand, and regarded her with annoyance. "And may I presume you are Lady Marguerite Vanday?"

"Yes, sir. You may."

"Thank heaven." His voice was heavy with sarcasm as he turned and continued to load crates of ammunition. "Get yourself and that bot in gear and give us a hand here. You may be a lady, and we'll make sure you are treated as such, but you have volunteered to serve His Majesty, and right now His Majesty needs his ship loaded as quickly as possible. That goes for all of you!"

He hollered at the rest of the crew who had stopped to stare at Marguerite and Outil. They jumped back into action and Outil followed suit. She stepped up to the dwindling pile of crates and picked up four to add to Marguerite's personal trunk and carried them to the lift. "Now *that* is what I'm talking about." Officer Vuitton cried. "You work as hard as your bot, m'lady, and we will be in business."

Marguerite huffed over to the pile and grabbed the handles

on either side of a crate. She jerked back, trying to lift it, but only succeeded in getting it balanced on her knees. Outil was back in a flash and helped her get the crate into her arms securely, and Marguerite proceeded to the lift. Hers was the last box on before the lift was yanked far over their heads.

"That's it boys, and er … um … Lady. Take five minutes to rest and grab a drink. Last load in fifteen minutes. You—" He pointed at Marguerite. "Walk with me." He set off at a quick pace heading down to the end of the dock. Marguerite scrambled to keep up, Outil at her heals. They caught him a few paces from the edge of the water. He clasped his hands behind his back and looked up at the massive schooner above. "Beautiful, isn't she?" he asked.

"Yes, sir. Quite."

"I was told that you know a thing or two about computations and weapons?"

"Yes, sir." He turned and looked her over carefully.

"I was also told your bot is capable of much more than the average automaton?"

"Yes, sir."

"Has it a name?"

"Yes, *her* name is Outil."

"Huh, fitting."

"Outil, it's been reported that you answer to no one but Lady Vanday here. Is that correct?"

"Yes, sir," Outil's sweet feminine bot voice sounded out of place given the situation.

"Well, we have to get a few things straight while you are on the *Renegade*. This is a military operation. We have a mission to accomplish and as ballistics officers—yes, I consider the bot my officer as well—you will be answering to me. Got it? You must do as I say when I say it, or you could very well die. I didn't want to bring a rich girl and her pet robot on this trip, but they assured me it would be worth my while."

"Of course, sir. We wouldn't dream of—" Marguerite started.

"That's enough. I don't need an explanation or any pretty compliments. I just need you to know that what I say goes. Not to be indelicate, but there is one more matter we must discuss."

Marguerite tipped her head, curious.

"You will have a bunk to yourself, but it will be in the ballistics hall. You will not be allowed in the other ballistics bunks and neither will your bot. You will lock your door each night, and your bot will be in your room with you at all times. You will not flirt, flounce, or otherwise use feminine wiles to gain favor, access, or exceptions. In return, I will make sure you are treated with the utmost respect. Are we clear, m'lady?"

"Clear as crystal." Marguerite clenched her fists and gritted her teeth.

"That should be yes, sir," he said.

"Yes, sir," she managed to sputter.

"Last but not least, it was brought to my attention that you have special favor with our captain. I hope I do not need to remind you that in the military, even though he may be my commanding officer, you are still my second in command and under my jurisdiction. I would appreciate it, for the sake of our comradery as a ballistics crew, if you would please keep your personal affairs to yourself."

"Yes, sir." Marguerite sucked in through her nose and out her mouth before opening it to speak, but Officer Vuitton was already heading back up the dock.

"I'm sure we're going to have a *lovely* time together," he called over his shoulder. Marguerite stomped after him. "Outil, help me pick up some crates, would you?"

"Yes, ma'am." Marguerite swore the bot giggled as she said this, but bots didn't giggle.

"I'm losing my mind," she muttered to herself. "Completely losing my mind."

Chapter Nine

On board, Marguerite barely had time to take in the amazing view from the deck before she was ushered below to help load the supplies and ready the ship for departure. The stairwells were much tighter than on the *Triumph,* and there weren't any of the hand-crafted wooden embellishments she enjoyed on that ship. This ship was made for nothing but war and efficiency. Everything was forged from aluminum alloys—gleaming in silver and bronze. She descended three flights of stairs before reaching the belly of the beast where she was shown to the main meeting room for artillery. Crates of ammunition were stacked on the floor, leaving hardly any room for all those assigned to maneuver in the tight quarters. In the center of the space, behind locked metal gates, one whole wall was lined with guns and knives, just like in *the Triumph.*

Marguerite stared at the possibilities in front of her. She knew exactly which weapons she preferred to shoot, which would feel balanced in her hand, and which would be hard for her to manage. She memorized their positions, from the giant long-range musket ballers to the air-powered dart slingers, and all the pistols in between. This was her new job.

She felt torn between excitement at such a remarkable array of weapons at her disposal and the memory of what it meant to actually use one—to be hit by one. She reached up and rubbed her shoulder without thinking.

Vuitton was there, barking orders again.

"Gentleman, and Ladies," he tipped his now bare head at Outil and Marguerite. "We are on a very important mission for His Majesty, King Louis XIV."

"Long live the king!" the men around her shouted in unison.

"Long live the king," Vuitton repeated. "You have a particularly delicate job on this voyage. We are to maintain the weaponry, keep track of the ammunition stores, calculate battle efficiency—if there is a battle—and if need be, provide the captain with support in hand to hand combat. If any of you do not feel like you can provide these types of services for His Majesty, that's rather unfortunate. It's too late to back out now."

A few of the men laughed at this. A few laughed while they looked at Marguerite and Outil. This crowd response did not go past Vuitton's watchful eye. "Gentleman, I'd like to introduce you to my second officer, Lady Marguerite Vadnay, and her automaton companion, Outil. Ladies, please join me." He motioned for them to leave the crowd and stand on an ammunition box next to him at the front of the small space filled with bodies.

Marguerite couldn't be sure, but as she passed through the

group, she thought she felt someone's hand on her backside. She jumped, but in a split second, decided not to pay them any heed. That's probably what they wanted, to see her squeal and squirm like a little girl. As soon as she stepped a bit farther, she heard a yelp behind her and turned to see Outil squeezing the hand of a man she'd just passed.

"I'm sorry. It was an accident," he whined.

"Enough, Outil. I'm pretty sure he learned his lesson," Vuitton ordered. Outil dropped the man's hand, and the ladies made it to the front of the room without further incident.

"Lady Vadnay comes to us with glowing references, battle experience, and a brilliant head on her shoulders. Outil is more than just a labor bot. She is highly intelligent, stronger than all of you put together, and able to crush your hands if you step out of line. So there will be absolutely no disrespect to my second officer or her companion. Am I clear?"

"Yes, sir!" the room cried in unison.

"Good, because the next person to disrespect either of them will be thrown overboard without a chute. Am I clear?"

"Yes, sir." They all cried again.

"Lady Vadnay will be referred to as Officer Vadnay on board. Her orders are as good as my orders. You will obey without incident. She will be in charge of maintenance, inventory, and calculations. I will assign a team to her momentarily. Outil will be in charge of assisting Officer Vadnay and any extreme, heavy work that needs doing. This does not mean that you will grow fat and lazy on my watch. This also does not mean you will order this bot around. This is not your bot. She does not belong to any of you.

She answers to me, Officer Vadnay, and King Louis. Is that clear?"

"Yes, sir!"

Marguerite tried not to, but she couldn't help smiling a bit at this man's ability to control a crowd. She tried to take mental notes on his stance, his tone of voice, anything that might set him apart from your average aership officer. She needed to learn fast and learn well.

The rally broke apart at Vuitton's word, and everyone got to work. "We sail in one hour!" He cried, and everyone cheered. "You two come with me." He had Marguerite and Outil outfitted with parchment and autopens and set them to work cataloging the ammunition. It was a tedious job, but it kept Marguerite from having to deal with any more wandering hands or carrying any more impossibly heavy crates.

The time passed quickly, and before she knew it, the audio pipes lit up. Marguerite nearly jumped out of her uniform when a familiar voice thrummed through the works and echoed in her compartments.

"All hands on deck! This is Captain Laviolette. We are pulling anchors now. All hands on deck!"

Marguerite looked up at Outil, who had been bent over a stack of retractable harpoons. The bot shrugged and pointed to the others filing out of the room to join the crew on deck. Marguerite shook her head and mouthed, "*No!*" She couldn't risk Jacques finding out she was on board yet. He'd toss her off with an anchor and be done with her in front of the entire city. It just wouldn't do. She bent back over her catalogue and continued to make careful marks on the thick cream paper.

"You too." Vuitton's voice was louder than necessary in the small space. Marguerite jumped. "Excuse me?"

"All hands on deck means you too. Come on, get to it." He stood by the stairway, the last of the men chugging up the stairs in front of him. Marguerite sighed and lay down her writing utensils. Outil followed suit and took up behind her mistress on the metal stairs. They were steep, and Marguerite's muscles ached by the time she reached the top, but her heart bubbled and burst when the excitement of the deck and the expansive view overcame her.

Men and bots, plus a few women, were everywhere, hoisting weights and coiling ropes as a fine mist from the gray clouds around them settled on their clothes and faces. They were all singing a working song in unison.

Upon the air, we'll fly our flag
Upon the currents merry,
And over shore and over land
We'll float our big brass belly!

Sing Hey! Sing Ho!
Shine up your gears
and fill the envelope!

Sing Hey! Sing Ho!
Toss off your fears.
The dawn is full of hope!

Renegade!!

Marguerite almost forgot to watch herself amidst this chorus of joy, dew, and sweat. Then she caught sight of Jacques across the deck, monitoring the progress and talking with another man of high rank. She quickly ducked behind a stack of flour sacks still waiting to be moved to the galley. Outil followed suit. "M'lady, do you mean to hide from him our entire journey?"

"No," Marguerite hissed. "But I don't want him to see me when he can just pitch me over the side into the St. Lawrence without guilt."

"Hey there, lass! Give us a hand?" A merry crewman signaled for her to grab a rope he and four others were already pulling on. "Just coil up the extra there in a neat pile while we pull it on deck, will ya?"

"Of course," Marguerite was more than happy to be given something to do other than hide. She grabbed the wet rope—as thick as her arm—and started to coil it at her feet as neatly as possible. Outil stepped up next to the small group and pulled the rope with both hands so effortlessly the humans stumbled to the sides from the slack in it.

"Well, now! That's a bot I could live with!" the man cried and slapped Outil on the back.

Having found themselves free from their burden, the others moved to help Marguerite coil—it was more than clear that she needed the help. The work was done in quick order, and the ship began to drift higher into the air, leaving Montreal far below.

A cheer went up from the onlookers left at the port. Marguerite ran to the port side rail to watch the river and city shrink beneath her. She couldn't suppress a gleeful smile and a bit of a yelp. Others soon joined her and began to wave and shout *Au revoir!* to those below. A loud roar burst through the cool morning as the engines came to life. A surge of steam shot from the stern and a horn sounded. The deck went wild with cheers. The *Renegade* was on her way.

Outil joined Marguerite and pointed to three smaller war vessels of an older make that had also lifted their tethers and were following closely. "What do you suppose they are about?"

An aerman standing next to them answered, "Those'll be our partners for this trip. Gonna take more than one ship ta bring in the cargo King Louis's sent this time."

"Seems a bit much, wouldn't you say?" Marguerite questioned.

"Oh no, my darling. You've obviously never encountered the southern buccaneers. It will take heaps more than this small fleet to stop them. There are also war vessels accompanying the supply lines. I only hope the Brits don't get involved—those bloody technology stealing parasites." The man spit over the rail and made an obscene gesture in the general direction of England.

"Oh, my goodness." Marguerite instinctively placed a hand on her face at the vulgarity. Outil immediately stepped between the two.

"Sorry, ma'am. Meant no offense."

"Quite alright," Marguerite replied, but Outil didn't move. Overhead a loud *whoosh* caught their attention and the entire crew still on deck looked up. A huge sail was unfurled and caught the morning breeze, urging them to the east as the envelope full of helium pulled them toward the aether. The engines kicked in, and suddenly the ship turned port side. They began to pick up speed, headed straight for the Atlantic.

The air was suddenly filled with the sounds of Jacques's voice. "Welcome, crew! I hope you brought your air legs and your iron spirits. This will be a harrowing voyage, but hopefully one with historical outcomes. We will be joined by our sister ships, the *Henrietta*, the *Steam Lily*, and the *Grapple*."

Marguerite looked around for the source of the voice, but couldn't see Jacques anywhere, so she relaxed and leaned back against the flour sacks to enjoy the ride. "The *Grapple* sounds like a proper name for a warship." Outil observed. "I'm not certain about the *Henrietta* and the *Steam Lily*, however."

"They ought to hire someone with a bit more imagination to christen these lovelies," Marguerite agreed while Jacques continued with his rallying speech.

"There is no finer fleet of aermen, women, and bots in the world! There is no chance for failure as long as we stand together. The lawless will fall, and we will return triumphant at the end of this campaign. Too long have the buccaneers and corsairs, even British privateers, assaulted our kinsmen and stolen our technology and goods. Today we fight back! Today we exact revenge! Today they fall!"

A cry went up from the crew, so loud that Marguerite had to cover her ears. She looked to Outil, who stood at the ready, and wondered for a moment if this was, in fact, a wise journey to have undertaken.

Chapter Ten

The *Renegade* rose high above the earth as Marguerite and Outil descended deep into its belly to continue their assignments. Marguerite felt particularly proud of herself for having not only secured this position, but also for doing so without Jacques finding out.

They gathered their lists and autopens and began cataloging and testing all the weaponry and ammunition. Marguerite found she thoroughly enjoyed this kind of work. She thought it would be tedious at first but quickly fell into a routine of polishing, oiling, testing and inventorying each item. She longed to fire some of them but knew better than to ask Vuitton for that privilege.

Meals were fast and small, but she was delighted to find that they were made up of more than just the dreaded salt meats and beer. Fresh fruits and vegetables accompanied fresh eggs and warm bread, and of course, salt meats and beer.

Her cabin was small, but it was her own. She dutifully locked the door and changed for bed while Outil powered down in the corner. She curled up on the small pallet and only wished for her silk covered feather mattress for a moment before she drifted to sleep.

The next day started in much the same way. Marguerite felt happier than she had in months. She was *finally* getting close to accomplishing her goal of being an aership captain, and she found that life on the aership suited her.

She and Outil were finishing up with a carton of ignitable grease pellets when the ship suddenly lurched forward. Since leaving port the trip had been very smooth, and Marguerite could hardly tell they were moving at all from the lower decks. Everyone stumbled and a few called out, but Marguerite flew right off her feet and landed in a heap of ammunition crates.

"Ow!" she cried. Outil was instantly at her side to offer her an arm, as were four other crewmates, smiling and shy. "Why, thank you all." Marguerite reached up and took the arm of the most attractive man within reach.

"It's a bit rough at times. Not usually that rough, but you'll get used to it, Officer Vadnay." He smiled wide, revealing dark yellow teeth and a few black holes where teeth of any color should have been.

"Oh, my!" Marguerite tried to hide her surprise at the contrast between his horrid mouth and handsome face. "I'll be ready next time. Thank you." Outil rolled her robot eyes and went back to her job.

"All stop," Vuitton came through to their compartment.

"Ship is at an all stop, prepare for orders." He continued into the next set of rooms and repeated himself. Marguerite let go of the man's arm and turned to another. "What exactly does that mean?" He was not nearly as handsome, but his teeth didn't show while he talked or smiled.

"Means something's prolly not right with the riggin's. I figure we're only about forty miles or so out of Monty, so it's prolly just a precaution." The sounds of shuffling and boxes moving were interrupted by a strange, new sound. It was light and steady, the sound of wings flapping.

Marguerite turned to see an automated pigeon flapping around the small compartment. Its wings beat frantically as it flitted about the small space. A few men swatted at it; others jumped out of its way. She laughed at the scene until she had to duck suddenly as the out of control bird sailed right for her head.

Outil was still standing close enough to reach out a shining arm and snatch the bird out of the air. However, she wasn't fast enough to do it before it emitted a formidable blob of gear grease right on Marguerite's head. "For the love of monkey wrenches!" she cried. "Who let this blasted bird in here?"

"Someone looking for you, miss." Outil held the bird out in one hand, its mechanical eyelids blinking with a *click click,* and its body still twitching from flight. In the other hand Outil held out a small piece of parchment.

"What is this fuss?" Vuitton asked as he rounded a stack of crates.

"Lady Marguerite is being summoned to the bridge, sir," Outil said.

Vuitton leaned in closely, measuring each word as he said, "If this is some kind of lover's spat, you best nip it in the bud and get back down here to work."

Marguerite's stomach filled with rocks as she read the neatly written paper. She'd recognize the penmanship anywhere. Even the best autopen in the world couldn't hide his scrawl. Jacques had found her out.

She wanted to lash out, to set Vuitton straight. They were absolutely *not* lovers. Instead, she nodded. "Yes, sir. Come on Outil. Let's get this over with."

"Oh, no." Vuitton took the paper from her hand. "This says, Second Officer Vadnay. It says nothing about your bot. We need Outil's help getting all these crates to their cannons before it's time to use them."

"But sir ... "

"I'm sure you'll be just fine walking up there on your own. Now snap to it! Don't keep the bridge waiting!" Vuitton dismissed her with a wave of his arm. Marguerite was both furious and frightened. *What if he was angry? What if he was already turning the ship around to take her home?* She couldn't bear the wondering, and the long walk up the tiny stairs, through the upper deck, and around to the bridge was infernally long.

The *Triumph* had boasted a captain's deck and a bridge, high above the body of the vessel, attached precariously to a structure that housed the giant round envelope. Marguerite remembered her first journey in the small banging lift, where she'd eaten her first real meal in days with Jacques, surrounded by an epic view of the oceans below them. She did not doubt that this meeting would be just as memorable. The envelope for the *Renegade* was much more sleek and streamlined for speed and war, making it impractical to house the bridge in the air. Marguerite could hear the wind howling and rain slapping the deck above her as she walked through to the fore of the ship. At least she didn't have to see him completely disheveled and wet.

The *Renegade* housed its bridge in the fore, just below one of its enormous razor-tipped ramrods. Windows lined the front most portion of the hull, allowing the officers to see what lay before them without having to subject themselves to the elements.

She finally reached the opening to the busy area. A crowd of men and two women—neither of whom were very pretty, Marguerite noted with satisfaction—were scurrying about with tools and maps and goggles, intent on their work. She stared at them and suddenly wasn't so keen about her assignment. *This is where I belong. Not down in the belly with the explosives and people missing their teeth.*

She touched her hair self-consciously and looked at the black gun oil stain on her fingers. A young man approached her and glanced at her grease-streaked hair, then the rank on her uniform. "Can I help you, Officer?"

"Yes, I am Officer Vadnay, I believe Captain Laviolette requested my presence?" she tried to sound confident, even though she felt sheepish and nervous.

"Yes, ma'am. I'll go find him."

The boy hadn't turned completely around before Jacques was upon them. When she saw his face, stern and furrowed, Marguerite couldn't move. *What was he going to say?* She'd lied to him less than forty-eight hours earlier. She'd hidden her plans from him and even kissed him passionately goodbye when Outil hadn't been looking. She began to panic. *What had she done?*

Then he smiled his beautiful smile at her, all of his teeth white and sitting exactly where they should be, his eyes twinkling and his tone merry. "Ah! The lovely Lady Vadnay." He bowed low. The warm welcome was worse than if he'd immediately berated her. Something was not right. Maybe he was ill? Except he looked healthy as ever and even quite dashing in his captain's best. The rest of the bridge turned to look at the exchange and watched curiously.

"Imagine my great surprise when I saw your name on my ship's manifest this morning. What an honor to have a *lady* of your standing aboard the *Renegade*." He smiled again. "I believe you are serving in ballistics?"

"Yes, Captain."

He sounded genuinely pleasant. Maybe he wasn't mad at all? Maybe he was happy to see her. She pushed aside the doubt and smiled.

"That doesn't seem like the right place for a *lady* to be serving on a warship." He stretched out the word lady again and scratched his chin. Marguerite didn't like the way he was saying *lady*.

"Oh, but I scored excellent marks in ballistics. They made me second in command."

"Yes, I'm sure they did. Excellent."

"If you have something else in mind, Captain?"

This could be it! She thought excitedly. *He's not mad, and he's going to invite me to work with him on the bridge! He knows as well as anyone that I am cool under pressure and a crack shot. Plus, I know my way around the instruments, and I'm a quick learner. This is all just a show for the rest of the crew.*

"Actually, since you mentioned it, I do have something else in mind. Come with me. Henry! You have the bridge. I need ten minutes." He smiled again, only Marguerite realized this time that his smile did not meet his eyes.

He took her arm, not gently, and steered her back through the hall and down a tight corridor. It was too close to walk side by side, so he was pressed against her and forcing her to walk quickly in front of him. If she hadn't been so confused about the direction events were about to take, she may have said something snarky to him about excuses to get close. She decided instead to try apologizing. Surely she owed him that.

"Jacques, I'm very sorry. It's just that I thought you'd be upset … "

He held up a hand to silence her then pulled them both to a stop at a speaking port on the wall. He pressed a button and spoke into the screened circle opening. "Marshton, are we in place?"

A squall answered back, "Yes, Captain."

"Good. I will be there in five minutes with the package." He flipped the button off and directed Marguerite to a door across the way. He reached around her and pushed down the brass handle while shoving it open in one quick movement. His second movement was to shove Marguerite inside as well.

The room was obviously private quarters. A bed sat in the middle. Made neatly, covers tight, pillows just so. A comfortable chair sat in one corner and a wardrobe in the other. A little table flanked the chair, and a large table in the middle of the room was covered in maps and sextons, a gleaming brass auto compass, and a pot of ink. Everything was neat and tidy and in its place. There was no sign of anyone having ever been in the room except for the mess of maps and charts on the table.

She turned around and glared at Jacques. "This is *your* room," she hissed.

"Of course it is, I need to speak with you in private, and this is the only room on the ship where we will not be disturbed."

"I do not know what your game is, sir, but that kiss the other day was not an invitation for a private meeting in your bed quarters!"

Jacques laughed at her outburst. "How did it end up that you are now cross with me? Aren't I the one you lied to, mislead, and made a fool of in front of his first officers and bridgemates?"

Jacques donned a false voice and flipped his hands in the air as he said, "Oh, Captain, how good of you to place Lady Vadnay in the ballistics team. Good show of faith in the Lady despite her lack of aviation skills. Oh, Captain, how lovely that your little *protégé* is joining us. I'm sure she will prove good company for long nights at sea. Oh, Captain—"

"Enough! I said I was sorry. I didn't mean for you to look a fool. I only wanted to have this adventure with you. I needed to get off land, Jacques!" She put her fists on her hips and held her place.

"That's exactly the problem. You only ever think about yourself. You never consider the positions you put other people in. It's always what will make you happy or what will keep you from feeling bored."

"That is not true!" Marguerite folded her arms and felt a bit like a child, but she couldn't help her lower lip sticking out a bit with hurt.

"Oh, isn't it, though?" He put one hand on his forehead and pushed his hat back then rubbed at his hair. "What did you think anyone else would gain from any of your little adventures? Hmm? Is your father so sick of you already? Does Outil actually want to be out at sea risking her life with pirates? How about Vivienne?"

"That's not fair. You didn't even know her." Marguerite's pout was turning into a fury. Tears boiled in her eyes, threatening to fall. Her nose felt tight, and it was getting hard to breathe.

"I knew her well enough, and I know you. You probably didn't even take the time to research what this voyage is actually all about or why I'm leading it, did you?"

He had her there. She hadn't asked anything when they'd summoned her, or when she'd spoken to Dean Beaumont. She supposed she could have probed a bit deeper, but that was beside the point. He was attacking her. "No. I didn't need to. We are going after pirates and to protect the king's fleet of supply ships."

"Why do you think His Royal Majesty would put a barely aether-worthy aerman who blew up his last ship—one of the finest ever built for king and country—in charge of a fleet of ships headed into such an important mission?"

"I … I thought it was because you are so good at what you do," Marguerite stammered. She hadn't thought about this either. "Besides, your name was cleared in the inquisition. It wasn't your fault the *Triumph* was lost. I don't see what this has to do with anything." She flipped at the map corner hanging off the little table and tapped her foot with impatience and discomfort.

"Exactly. You don't see. You don't want to see, and you don't care to see anyone but yourself. The reason they gave me the commission is because no one else wanted it. They all have families, Marguerite. The whole goal of New France right now is to settle, serve and survive. Once a soldier takes a wife, they have one year reprieve from service to start their family and build a home. Everyone there has taken a wife and land and started a settlement. I have half a crew of babies, because there's not a single soldier to be found who isn't supporting a wife and child now. I have no wife. I have no child. Therefore, I have no say in where I am assigned. I go wherever his majesty's whim takes me. This time it's on a suicide mission."

"Surely it's not as dangerous as all that," she insisted. "You have plenty of arms and support and bots. The armory on this dirigible alone could take down the Palace of Westminster."

"Yes, we will outnumber them, outgun them, and outmaneuver them. Hopefully, we will bring the shipments back safely and take a few pirates down with us, but that is not my only assignment. And don't think that this mission won't be pocked with casualties."

Marguerite took a deep breath. "So, you're telling me that I am selfish for not marrying you and saving you from having to risk your life to fight pirates? And that I should forget all of my dreams, so I can settle down and have your babies? And that is not selfish?"

"Marguerite!" He put both hands on his head and closed his eyes, a sure sign he was losing his temper. Then he took a deep breath and began to pace in the tiny space, turning tightly, obviously straining himself to come up with the next words. He stopped suddenly. "Do you know what the southern buccaneers do to women when they capture them? If you're thinking they kill them, you are wrong. They never kill women. They take as many prisoners as possible, men and women. The men are given a choice—pledge allegiance to the pirate captain, or be marooned on an island or tortured, depending on the captain's fancy that day. Women, on the other hand, are forced to *serve* the pirates, and I don't mean in the galley, or being sold as a slave in the islands. I would rather you be stuck at home miserably caring for babies than ever have that fate be a possibility."

"You exaggerate to scare me. I've read nothing so heinous in the journals. " Marguerite met him mid-stride and got as close to his face as she dared, just to make certain he knew exactly how she felt. "You have always wanted to control me. You say you love me, but you don't. It is all about control, and that will never happen."

In one swift move he wrapped an arm around her waist and pulled her into a kiss. Marguerite pushed back, but he didn't let her go. He put both arms around her and kissed her like his life depended on it. Then just as suddenly he let her go, keeping one hand on her waist.

"That is very true. I will never be able to control you, and despite what you think, I never want to. I'm trying to tell you that I may not come home from this mission, but I'm going to make certain that you do. I do not have control over your choices, but I am still captain of the *Renegade,* and I have complete control over who serves on my ship."

Chapter Eleven

Jacques left no time for her to question him or disagree. He opened the door and pulled her by the hand back into the passageway, marching forward so quickly she had to jog to keep up. They came to a ladder midway down the hall that appeared to lead to the deck above. Jacques hit a button on the wall and a trap door atop the ladder slid open. Rain began to pour onto their heads and into their eyes. Marguerite was in such a state of shock the only words she could manage were, "Where are you taking me?"

"Somewhere safe. Up you go." He grabbed her waist from behind with both hands and practically threw her toward the opening. Marguerite squealed out loud and grabbed the top rung. It was slick with rain now, and she barely caught it. Her left foot found purchase on a rung a tad farther down but, at least, she didn't fall. She had no choice now but to climb. Jacques was already climbing below her, his head nearly in her backside. She knew she couldn't win a hand-to-hand fight with him. Not even a foot-to-face fight would come out in her favor.

She pulled herself up grudgingly into the rain and wind. Two very small deck hands were there to help her up. She could see another aership hovering just above her head, a ladder dangling from the side. Its brown oval envelope was kissing the black envelope of the *Renegade*.

Jacques was behind her in a moment. He shielded his face from the deluge and pointed to the ladder. "Tie her down, lads!" The two boys quickly jumped to attention and fastened the dangling ends of the rope ladder to the deck of the black warship. "I'm sure they will have adequate necessities for you on the *Henrietta*," Jacques said.

"The *Henrietta*? You are putting me on the ship with the worst name in the history of aerships? Jacques, how could you?" Marguerite stomped her foot. Rain ran over her face and hair, beading up over the pigeon grease and soaking her uniform through.

"Only because I love you!" He shouted through the rain and wind. "Now go!" The two deck boys snickered. Marguerite gave them dirty looks.

"What about Outil?" Marguerite protested as he steered her to the ladder, much more gently this time.

"She is needed here. I will send her to join you as soon as possible."

"You can't do that! She is my property! Plus, I can't go alone! You are being completely unreasonable!" She hadn't felt this close to throwing a complete tantrum since her father had told her she was going to boarding school back in France.

"Some would argue with you there, my dear, but we don't have time to fight about the finer points of bot slavery. If she really is your property, and you really want to help the cause, then as the King's servant, I am commandeering her for the time being."

"But, Jacques!"

"Captain Laviolette, please."

"I'll go with her, sir!" One of the deckhands offered. Marguerite glared at him through the rain. She recognized his face and scruffy red hair peeking out from under his rain-soaked cap.

"Louis?" she asked.

"You know him?" Jacques said. "Very well. We don't want the lady to go without all of her servants. Keep an eye on her, Louis, And help out on the *Henrietta* as best you can. Take a turn in the nest and give Captain Butterfield my best."

"Yes, captain!" The boy saluted and scurried up the ladder to the deck of the other ship. "I have to get back to the bridge. We have precious little time to prepare. Get up that ladder now, or I'll strap you to a parachute. I doubt the Iroquois will deal with you as kindly as I do."

"Jacques!" she cried.

"Go!" He pointed again.

To the left, she saw her small trunk being hoisted off the deck by a rope on the *Henrietta*. She watched it whip and twirl in the wind and rain. Everything she loved was in that box, her new goggles, her extra flight suit and a book of aernautics she wasn't quite done studying, and three more pairs of pink silk underthings. She watched in anxiety until it was pulled to safety on the smaller ship.

She tried to give Jacques one last look of hatred, but she found her heart didn't have the energy to hate him or to fight him. She knew he would keep his word to put her in a parachute or worse, the brig. He had to. He couldn't let his men see him taking orders from a woman he wasn't even engaged to.

She took a few steps to the ladder and began to climb. The wind continued to blow rain into her face. The wooden rungs were slippery, and she was grateful for her water resistant boots. The soles had been painted with a tar-like concoction that made them excellent for walking a wet deck, or climbing a slippery rope ladder from one aership to another, thousands of feet above the earth. The ropes stretched and twisted slightly. The higher she climbed, the less stable she felt. Her body bobbed to either side every time she took a step. She looked down and saw the space between the two ships was just enough that should she slip or let go, she would plummet all the way to the St. Lawrence sprawled below her, or to the trees flanking the shores. She found herself freezing up about halfway to the *Henrietta*. Her arms shaking and her feet stuck to the rung. She shut her eyes and took a deep breath, water dripping into her mouth.

"You wanted this," she reminded herself out loud. "You wanted adventure. What's more adventurous than a forced ship transfer in the midst of the aether with no harness?"

Then with her eyes closed, she forced herself to take hold of the next rung up. She took another deep breath and pictured the rope ladder in her father's stables back home. She'd loved to climb it when she was a child. It was never soaking wet and hovering this high over nothing, but she remembered herself scampering up it just like Louis had. She tried to harness that child inside of her.

"Come on! You're nearly there!" Jacques cried.

His voice rose through the storm, bringing her anger back with it. Marguerite was in this position because of him. Determined not to let him see her falter in fear, she reached up with her other hand and then willed her feet to follow. The ladder wobbled, but she made herself keep going, hand over hand, foot over foot, until she had a nice rhythm.

"There you are, sassy britches." A raspy female voice surprised her. Marguerite's eyes popped open to see she had reached the starboard side of the *Henrietta*. A portly woman with wild grey hair sprouting out from underneath a deep blue tricorn hat reached over the side and grabbed her arm, practically yanking her off the ladder.

"Hold on, there!"

Marguerite scrambled not to lose footing as the woman's surprising strength overwhelmed her. Marguerite hit the deck like a wet rag doll and slipped as she tried to gain footing.

"You're safe with me as long as you don't cross me!" The woman hollered, then leaned over the deck and shouted below while waving her arm in a huge circle overhead. "We got her, boys! Safe flying!"

A faint cry of "Safe flying!" came from below and the

Henrietta lurched away from the *Renegade*.

"Alright then. That wasn't too painful. Get yourself below and get dried off. Report at the mess hall in thirty minutes for a meal and debriefing."

"I'd love to, but I haven't any idea where to go or how to get dry or—" Marguerite was cut off unceremoniously.

"Pierre, and you, Louis?" The woman pointed at the red headed boy who grinned at Marguerite. "Pierre, take them both below and show them to the aft quarters."

"Yes, Captain Butterfield," the boy shouted and saluted.

"You are the captain?" Marguerite asked incredulously.

"Right now I'm soaking wet and cranky, and yes, the captain. So if you don't want to see my temper, you'll get yourself below before I send ya back without a ladder." She waved an arm at Marguerite.

Marguerite wasn't sure if she should salute or run or just walk backwards without taking her eyes off the stout, wiry old crone. She chose an awkward curtsy, realized it was the wrong choice when Captain Butterfield laughed out loud and decided to turn and walk quickly after the boys.

Below deck on the *Henrietta* was even more cramped than the *Renegade*. As soon as they lifted the hatch to enter the lower levels, a great waft of animal, human, and machine gear smells hit her nose. She took a few steps into the dense air lit by old-fashioned yellow lights and felt the ship take off at full speed ahead. No doubt they were trying to make up for lost time in the great embarkment adventure. She swayed and grabbed the rails to steady her, too late realizing they were also covered in dirt and gear grease.

"Oh my word," she mumbled to herself as she followed the two boys down the steep, single file staircase while wiping her hand on her uniform. They descended another staircase and then proceeded down a long hallway, the smell of animals growing stronger with every step. Marguerite couldn't take it any longer. "What on earth is that smell?" She plugged her nose with two fingers; pinky raised daintily in the air.

"Oh, that's Fifi," Pierre called over his shoulder. He looked to be about the same age as Louis, twelve, maybe thirteen. Both boys bore the marks of a hard life—thin arms and legs, messy hair and dirty faces, but both boys seemed happy enough to be on this stinking ship.

"Who is Fifi?" Marguerite called after them as they trotted ahead.

Pierre came to a quick stop. "Here's your bunk, miss."

She couldn't' take the impertinence any longer. "It's Lady Vadnay, or Officer Vadnay, if you please."

Pierre looked confused. "Oh, I'm sorry m'lady, er, officer. I was told you lost your rank and was being kept here till they could court martial you or some such."

"Court martial? No. I do not think so." Marguerite knew how quickly gossip could spread, in a small town, in a girl's school, and on a ship. "I'm here only until we get things sorted out with Captain Laviolette. Never mind. I don't need to explain to either of you. Now, where is my room?"

She leaned against the two boys, moving them away from the open door, and her heart sunk as she saw the tiny room with four bunks and three chests at one end, her soaking box of belongings at the other. She sighed audibly, "And who am I to be sharing this room with?"

"Oh, the galley gals, I suppose. You'll be workin' on the farm, though, miss." Pierre caught himself, "I mean, lady."

"The farm?" This was just getting to be a bit much.

"Aye," Louis answered this time. "The *Henrietta* is famous for her floating farm. It's one of the reasons I offered to come with ya, m'lady. I wanted to see it for myself." He looked suddenly sheepish then. "I hope you don't take offense to that. I'll be here to help you out as well."

"It's right down here, come on. I'll get you to a washroom and a clean towel while we're there. Laundry's right by the farm." They continued down the narrow hallway until it opened into what Marguerite guessed was the aft of the ship. A glass dome of triangles lay overhead. She remembered seeing part of it on deck, but with all the drama, she hadn't paid it much mind.

The rain beat on it now making the chamber echo and ring. The smell was almost overpowering, but she truly couldn't believe her eyes. Surrounding the large skylight were artificial lights, fired up no doubt to compensate for dreary sunless days such as this. They cast yellow light on an amazing array of plants growing below. Walls, floors, and benches were covered with food producing plants of every shape and size, and in the center stood the biggest Abondance milk cow Marguerite had ever seen. Her body was a deep red with patches of white on her legs and friendly cow face. She wore a leather strap and bell for a collar that dinged when she swung her head to look at them. The smell told Marguerite this had to be Fifi. A makeshift fence of copper piping held the cow in a stall with plants arranged all around her to nibble on like some sort of bovine buffet. A pipe extended from the deck above, allowing rainwater to gather and pool in a bucket attached to the floor for the beast to drink from. She stood chewing happily, and paused only to *moo* at them for a moment as Marguerite inspected the vast room filled with plants of every variety.

"What an ingenious idea!" Marguerite forgot to hold her nose or the fact that she was freezing cold and soaking wet as she pushed past the boys, opened the waist high gate, and proceeded to give herself a tour of the farm. "This is as fine a greenhouse as I've ever seen, even in France. It's a bit dusty, and the materials could be updated, but the design is pure intelligence put to work."

She identified several varieties of citrus trees, berries, pole plants, and even melons. One whole section was dedicated to greens of every kind, and grape arbors grew from containers fastened to the walls, dancing and twirling across the beams of the deck above. A pond of light-colored fish swam at the end opposite the cow, chickens pecked and scratched at the floor around the pond, alternately pooping and flicking scratch into the fish. Marguerite followed the line of the pond to pipes at one side and a pump that appeared to distribute water to all of the greenery, and then alternately, it caught the runoff and returned it to the pond.

It was the most amazing thing she'd ever seen, but as she took a deep breath, as she was used to doing when she wanted to appreciate something fully, she nearly gagged on the smell of Fifi.

Marguerite walked up to the beast and entered her pen.

Having grown up with free reign of a working estate in the country, Marguerite knew a thing or two about all things flora and fauna. She examined her from all angles, patting Fifi on the soft white forehead and rubbing her back. Then Marguerite made her way around to the steaming pile of manure that lay on the floor at the lovely animal's hind quarters.

"Who is in charge of mucking this stall? This is atrocious. No animal should have to stand around in this, and humans shouldn't be forced to endure the smell! It's absolutely wretched on every level."

At that moment Captain Butterfield walked in, picked up a flat-ended shovel and threw it at Marguerite's head.

"For goodness sake!" Marguerite cried as she caught the shovel with two hands saving herself and Fifi from a nasty blow. "I don't think that was necessary."

"You are," Captain Butterfield said with a smile.

"I am what?" Marguerite asked.

"In charge of the cow." Captain Butterfield laughed heartily then turned to leave. "Get to scooping."

Chapter Twelve

When the two boys were finally done laughing behind their hands at the soaking wet *lady* holding the shovel in front of them, they showed her the trap door for the excrement. If she hadn't been completely mortified, the contraption might have impressed Marguerite. It had a lever she could step on that retracted a space in the floor right next to Fifi's small pen. She could then shovel with both hands while her foot held the door open.

Pierre demonstrated and then handed the shovel back to Marguerite, who reluctantly took it from him and demonstrated a quick mastery of the chore. A bell rang overhead. Pierre stood to attention and turned to Louis. "We better get going. That's the deck boy's call."

"I'm assigned to help Lady Vadnay. I'm staying right here." Louis stood tall and immovable at her side.

"Suit yourself," Pierre answered, and then he ran off, placing one hand on the top of the fence and vaulting over it in a single bound. Louis immediately reached for the shovel and took it from Marguerite's hands.

"The laundry is over there, m'lady. I'll finish up here while you get a towel and swap clothes." He blushed a bit as he smiled.

"Well, thank you, Louis. That is very kind of you." She started to walk toward the door opposite the fence they'd entered in but stopped and turned to the small boy who was now furiously scraping refuse out to sea. "Are you certain you don't need to be somewhere else, Louis?"

"Captain Laviolette ordered me on this ship to help you. Those are my orders, and I plan to follow them." He put the shovel to his side like a musket and saluted her with two fingers to his forehead.

"Well, lovely then." Marguerite turned and left Louis to shovel without a second thought.

She found the laundry easily enough. It was a tiny room directly opposite her bunk on the other side of the ship and was filled to bursting with two women, two large copper pots of boiling water, and several overhead-drying contraptions. One woman stood on mechanical stilts while hanging rags to dry high above the other woman who was stirring a pot of grey suds. Marguerite wondered what they could possibly have to wash so early in their journey, but decided not to ask.

Both women took one look at her wretched state and motioned to the stack of dry towels without a word. Marguerite thanked them and turned to leave, toweling her rain-soaked hair as she went, when one called out to her. "One towel per person.

Washing day is recorded on your bunk door."

"Thank you!" She called and hurried to her bunk to change. Excellent. She would have to find somewhere to hang her soaking garments, or she would be stuck in these clothes for another week or so. When she'd followed the boys to Fifi, she remembered seeing a passageway that looked like it cut through to the other side of the ship. The last thing she wanted was to cut back through the farm and end up having to help muck cow dung, or worse, before she was dry.

She found the passage and only had to deal with a handful of shipmates giving her strange looks on the way to her bunk. She quickly closed the door and prayed that none of her new bunkmates would show up before she got herself decent again. The tiny space was like being locked in a closet. She thought of her old governess locking her in the cellars and shuddered. Small dark spaces were not her favorite.

She opened her chest and was relieved to see that her clothes were still dry. She peeled off the wet wool suit and hung it on an empty peg on the wall, then carefully took off her pink silk under garments, threw them on the floor, and hurried to replace them. She put on a new flight suit, and then debated what she should do with her undies. They weren't soaked, but they did need to lay flat to dry.

"Drat," she swore. "If Outil were here she'd know what to do." She rubbed her head vigorously with the towel and laid it over her trunk to dry. Marguerite cursed Jacques then as well. He was such a bastard for putting her in this position. There was no other word for him. True, he could have sent her home, or given her a chute and thrown her over the edge of the ship, but this was only a miniscule step above complete abandonment. She gritted her teeth and stomped her foot for good measure. She was going to get even.

In the meantime, she decided to try to determine what bed was not being used and laid her things out there. Only, none of the beds had been used yet. They were all made up tight, untouched. She sighed in frustration and just picked a bottom bunk to arrange them on, then resolved to get back in time to put them away before anyone else returned.

Back at the farm, Louis had finished cleaning up the mess and the whole place smelled measures better. He had found a brush somewhere and was in the middle of rubbing down Fifi, who appeared to be enjoying the whole affair immensely. "Well then, Louis. You've done a fine job here. She's a lovely Abondance, isn't she?" Marguerite walked to the pen and leaned in to pet her. Fifi stomped her foot and threw her head away from Marguerite's hand. A stout woman with bright red hair piled high on her head came panting and chuffing into the farm. She spotted Marguerite and Louis and pointed at the pair.

"You the new help from the *Renegade*?" she asked. "Yes, ma'am, I'm Lady Vadnay, and this is Louis," Marguerite answered.

"Right, well you are both going to come help me. I'm *Lady* Cook, and I need at least six more hands to get evening meal on before we hit the preparations for tomorrow's rounds." She rolled her eyes as she said *lady* in a mocking tone.

"Oh no, I am not a galley worker. I'm sorry. I'm an officer and a Lady, and I do not prepare food." Marguerite was firm in this point. She stood her ground, hands on her hips. Fifi mooed long and low as if to mock the aristocrat pouting by her pen.

"You may have been all those things on land or even on the *Renegade*, but here on the *Henrietta*, you're nothing but what Captain B. says you are, and today, that's a galley hand. Now get those lovely little aristocratic hands off your hips and help me fill these baskets with greens or you'll get no supper and quite possibly the chute." The little woman picked up two baskets from a pile near the door and tossed one unceremoniously to the floor at Marguerite's feet.

Marguerite knew the woman was right. The law of the skies was not the way of things on land. All that mattered up here was your title according to your captain, and neither of her captains was interested in promoting her anytime soon.

She had no choice.

She bent over and picked up the basket. Louis put down the brush and climbed out of the pen. Fifi mooed again.

The rest of the day was much the same. She cut her hand trying to learn to peel carrots; she stubbed her toe while carrying a pot of potatoes and water from sink to stove, and she ended up covered in grease when the ship lurched to starboard and a pot of lard tipped and tumbled off a shelf.

She had to admit that the meal was quite good, considering they were several leagues above ground and even farther from civilization. However, the after dinner clean-up nearly did her in. Even with Louis running circles around her, helping in any way he could, she felt beaten and bloody and even more determined to make Jacques's life a living hell if she was ever to see him again.

She made her way back to her bunk in low spirits and with a bedraggled appearance. She heard voices coming from all the rooms she passed. Some had doors open, some closed. Some were merry, most sounded tired. It was a crew of mostly women and boys. The *Henrietta* was a galley ship, which meant it prepared food and carried extra supplies for the rest of the convoy. This saved space for the other vessels to carry larger weapons and more men for battles. At supper each night, the *Henrietta* coasted over the other ships and dropped food from a parachute system. In the morning, the ships floated over her deck and returned the shoots and empty containers.

Marguerite hadn't ever spent much time in the kitchens of the estate where she'd grown up. She took for granted the fact that hot meals showed up on her dinner table and at her bedside at regularly scheduled times. Even at the school, she didn't think much about where her food came from or whose hands had prepared it. She looked at her own hands. They were white and shriveled like ghostly prunes. Nicks and scrapes here and there lent shocking peeks of blood. To add insult to injury, three of her nails had broken to the quick. She felt wretched.

Ahead of her, the door was open to her bunk. Merry voices drifted down the hall and met her ears. She hesitated; worried that she hadn't arrived soon enough. What would they say about her underthings? Just when she thought the day couldn't get much worse, she was now convinced it would.

She decided to meet the problem head on.

Marguerite marched up to the open doorway; head held high and mangled hands on her hips. Their laughter and chatter stopped suddenly when Marguerite appeared. She looked them over carefully before speaking. The three girls sitting on bunks before her were a mixed bunch. Two were mousy with thin watery-brown hair and upturned noses; obviously sisters, but not twins. One sister was broader through the forehead, looked a bit more care worn, and even while sitting down was a head taller than the other.

The third girl was sitting on the bed Marguerite had claimed earlier. She had tight black curls falling in lovely ringlets to frame a creamy brown face. Marguerite was instantly jealous of her hair. When she saw Marguerite, her soft brown eyes grew wide at first, and then narrowed in mischief. "Oh, good! Our roommate is finally here," she purred.

Marguerite instantly identified her as a new pain in her side. One of the many girls her age whom she could not abide but would have to endure. A troublemaker, a bully, a nasty heart in a pretty package. She bristled as she realized the girl was holding her now dry pink satin underclothes up to her own body and smiling like a cat with a mouthful of canary.

"I'm ever so grateful for the gift you left on my bunk. I haven't had pantaloons so fine since I left Paris. Ooh la la!" The girl posed and threw her amazing hair over her shoulder. The other two girls laughed quietly. Marguerite took two steps into the room and stared down at the pretty face with the jolly expression.

"Those are mine, and I'd like them back please," she said. Then she braced for a fight. Back at school and even on the ship ride to New France, every confrontation with these kinds of common girls came with a fight. But Marguerite was used to it now and even though she was exhausted, she was ready to put this horrid person with perfect curls in her place.

"Oh, I'm sorry. I didn't realize you claimed this space. I don't see your name on it anywhere." The girl's eyes twinkled as she smiled a wicked grin. Marguerite leaned over and snatched the pantaloons from the girl's lap before the girl could react. She pulled open the waistband and flashed her monogram in the girl's face. *LMV* was stitched in meticulous, scrolling letters across the soft, silky fabric.

"Lady Marguerite Vadnay," she said with steely defiance. "Now please remove yourself from my bunk and hand over my camisole." The girl flinched.

Ah ha! Marguerite thought, *I got her. She's afraid of me. I am scary!*

"Alright, alright." The girl stood, forcing Marguerite to back up to make room for her in the small space. She tossed the camisole onto Marguerite's head and scampered up to the top bunk in one quick move. "Calm down. I'm just having a bit of fun with you, *Lady Marguerite Vadnay.* I'm Lucy; that's Rori and Audrey."

Marguerite didn't know who was who, but the sisters raised their hands simultaneously and smiled. She felt suddenly off guard. She wasn't sure how to respond. It took her a moment to register the fact that it had been a very long time since a girl other than Outil, who was actually just a bot, had been nice to her.

Chapter Thirteen

Two more days passed as the ships flew at top speed to the aid of the convoy from France. Rain continued to pound down on the fleet, and high winds pushed them forward at top speeds with minimum fuel needed. The smaller ships tossed back and forth relentlessly, making Marguerite airsick for the first time in her life. If she could just get above deck for a breath of fresh air, she would feel better and get her legs beneath her, but there was no such luck. The high winds and dangerously cold temperatures meant that even the deck boys spent as little time out there as possible with the unrelenting storm.

Even if she could have escaped for a morsel of air not laden with the smell of cow and fishpond, she didn't have time. The *Henrietta* was a hive of activity at all hours, and she didn't have a moment of free time from morning wakeup call until she fell into bed at night.

If she thought her hands were a wreck on the first day, she wept over them as she tried to sleep the third night. Her fingers ached from cracks and cuts, and all of her once manicured nails were now gone, lost to shredders and peelers in the kitchens. In a matter of days, her hands had gone from those of an aristocrat to the maws of a dirty washerwoman.

Her bunkmates continued to be kind to her. In fact, almost everyone on the ship was kind, with the exception of Lady Cook, who'd insisted Marguerite and everyone else in the kitchens call her that after Marguerite had arrived and announced her title. Marguerite still wasn't sure how to handle these women who were kind and even funny. She tried to smile as much as she possibly could and otherwise kept her mouth shut.

She had much more important things to think about than getting along with common aerwomen. Like how to get back at Jacques. It wasn't enough that she had resolved never to have a thing to do with him again. Her anger had blossomed into schemes of revenge. She wanted to annoy him. She wanted him to feel like she felt—helpless, humiliated, and small. The fond memories she held for him were being persistently mashed to a pulp by the autohammer she used to tenderize the meat every night, and she made little effort to remember what it was she loved about him.

She should have been cataloging weapons, testing trajectories, and preparing for war. Instead, she was scrubbing pots and pans, chopping leeks, and brushing a cow that hated her. At least Louis had stuck around to help her with the manure. Fifi loved him, but every time Marguerite tried to get close, the beast flipped her with her tail or head-butted her, and just this morning she'd kicked her square in the stomach, quick as a whip. Marguerite had never seen a cow move that fast in her life.

She rubbed her still sore ribs with her aching hand. She seriously considered sending a note to her father asking him to come get her, but then she dismissed that thought immediately. She wouldn't be able to bear his smug I-told-you-so laugh once he had her safely back in the luxury of his grasp. No, she was going to tough this out and get even, and make them all see that she was made of stronger stuff than they all thought.

In the meantime, she was going to have a good cry. She turned her face into her pillow, took a deep shaking breath, and let the tears fall. She tried to stay silent so the other girls wouldn't hear her and bother her—she didn't want to deal with anyone right now. She knew at least two of them were asleep, as she heard the soft lady-like snores of tired girls. But when she accidentally sniffed a bit too loudly, she heard the bunk above her squeak as Lucy shifted and then slid down the ladder like a spectre in the night.

She sat on the edge of Marguerite's bed and put a hand on her shoulder and whispered, "Are you alright there?" Marguerite wanted to swat her hand away and tell her to cog off, but she took another deep breath and tried to calm herself instead.

"I know it's hard being out here. I imagine you aren't used to this kind of life. Anyone with drawers as fancy as yours hasn't spent much time doing the kind of work we do on the ship. Are your hands ok? You're on galley duty, right? That can be murder on the fingers. Hang on a second." The girl stood up and started rummaging in her trunk then returned and sat on the bed again. "Let me see your fingers."

Marguerite reluctantly pulled her hands from under her rough wool blanket, wiped the tears from her face, and held them out. Lucy found them in the dark and pulled them toward her and let them rest on her knee. Marguerite could hear her opening a jar in the dark, and a pale red light from the hallway lit a silhouette of Lucy's lovely curls.

One by one, she rubbed an ointment on Marguerite's poor fingers and palms. It felt amazing. Lucy was careful and quiet and didn't push too hard on any of the cuts. "I heard Fifi got you in the gut today?" she asked softly.

"Yes," Marguerite finally whispered.

"She is a nasty, nasty cow, that one. Only likes men. Typical woman." Lucy finished with one hand and picked up the other. "Does that feel better?"

"Yes." Marguerite sniffed, emotion threatening to bubble out again. "Why are you being so nice to me?"

"Why not? You're a human being, aren't you? You seem pretty miserable, and I don't like to see anyone in misery."

"But you don't even know me or why I'm so miserable," Marguerite protested

"Does it matter?" Lucy asked as she finished with the last hand and set it on Marguerite's bed. She screwed the cap back on her jar and stood to put it back in the trunk, leaving a cold spot on the bed where she had been sitting. Marguerite realized she didn't want her to go.

"No, I suppose it doesn't matter." Lucy sat back down. "Do you want to tell me your story?"

"There's not much to tell. I'm a fool stuck in a man's world, trying to find a way to get out." Marguerite realized how utterly pitiful that statement sounded and instantly felt self-conscious. She didn't realize how huge the pity party was she was throwing for herself until this very moment.

Lucy laughed quietly, "Aren't we all? Listen, let me tell you my story and you can tell me yours. Then we'll call it good for the night, yes?"

"Deal," Marguerite answered.

"My parents were wealthy merchants in Paris," Lucy began, "but they thought living in New France would be an excellent adventure, so they packed my brother and me up, bought a dirigible, and took everything we owned to the skies. Everything was fun and exciting, until we got to Montreal. My father had made a deal with a land agent for a shop in town where he was going to set up an importing business. Only the agent turned out to be a crook, and we lost everything we had. Father went to work at a brick factory and mother did what she could here and there, cleaning or sewing for wealthy families. We lived in a tiny cottage on the outskirts of town, and when the pox came through, well, I was the only one who made it. How about you?"

Lucy told this story like it was reporting the events of a very dull day. Not a hint of sadness in her voice.

"I am so very sorry," was the only thing Marguerite could think of to say.

"Don't be. It was about six years ago. The nuns took me in and took care of me. They tried to marry me off this spring, but I told them I wasn't having any of it. So they got me a post on this ship. It was the best they could do for a penniless orphan. So far, so good. I love flying. I can't wait to get out from under the deck. It's driving me crazy to be locked up down here."

"Where do you serve?" Marguerite asked, anxious to change the topic.

"Crow's nest is my favorite, I have a good eye with a glass, but this week I'm on chute duty. I help pack the goods for the other ships at meal time, and I collect and service the chutes when they come back in the mornings. Doesn't sound like much, but it's a full time job. Lots of patching and cleaning to be done. What is your story?"

Marguerite sighed and began her tale. She tried to keep it short and absent of melodrama, especially considering the events Lucy had just relayed. There was no competing with losing your whole family and having to strike out on your own. At least, Marguerite had known somewhere in the back of her heart that her Father was always there should she need him. There was always plenty of money and family, and if nothing else, Outil.

Outil! How Marguerite missed her bot! She wondered quickly where she was, what they were having her do and if there was a competent smithie on board to help her oil her gears.

"I can't believe he took your bot," Lucy said. "Kicking you off the boat is one thing, but commandeering your bot is completely out of bounds. It's definitely his right, but you'd think someone who knows you and is worried about you would, at least, send you with your bot. What do you think he's up to?"

"What do you mean?" Marguerite asked.

"Well, he must have something planned for her, right? Some reason to keep her?"

Marguerite hadn't thought about this. Why *had* he kept Outil? Was it really just to help around the *Renegade*? Outil was strong and excellent with gearwork. She took orders without complaint and was able to fly any vessel with only a short introduction. Still, Jacques knew just how much Outil meant to Marguerite. Lucy was right, he was up to something. "Whatever it is, it's just one more reason I'm going to blast him into the next aethiosphere as soon as I can get my hands on him."

Lucy laughed. "Somehow I have a feeling Captain Laviolette knew you would react this way and is going to avoid you for quite a while after this."

"Don't worry, I won't let him ignore me," Marguerite growled. A light came on in the hallway, followed by a bell. Their bunkmates rolled over and moaned. Lucy sprang to her feet and opened her trunk. "What's that sound?" Marguerite asked.

"All hands call. We must have made contact with the shipment from France, and I bet the news isn't good. Get dressed and report to the mess hall," Lucy sounded like she'd been flying all her life.

Marguerite sat up, weary to her bones, and willed herself to swing her legs out of bed and put her flight suit back on. The other girls did the same and all four of them stumbled down the corridor, joining the rest of the ship in the mess.

Captain Bonnifield stood on a dirty brown crate of yams in order to see above the throng. All in all, the ship had a crew of about fifty people crammed into the small mess. Marguerite guessed a few were still at the bridge and in the engine rooms on deck. The rest standing here looked tired and disheveled. She wondered for a moment what she looked like. She hadn't seen herself in a mirror for three days. She touched the knot of her hair on the top of her head self-consciously. Without Outil here to brush it and tie it up for her, she'd done the best she could with a piece of twine she'd nabbed in the galley, but she was sure she looked no better than the other girls around her. Lucy seemed to be the only one who looked as fresh and ready as if she'd just woken from a sweet dream on a feather bed. Marguerite made a mental note to ask her the secret to keeping her hair tame and her face from puffing up like a balloon.

"Gather round. Push in, make room for everyone!" Captain Bonnifield called.

Marguerite felt the people behind her push in, forcing her to move closer to those in front. The effect of all those bodies so close was a room that smelled almost as bad as Fifi's stall. "Good, good. I'm sorry to have brought you here at this late hour after a hard day's work, but we have made contact with the *Royal Armada,* and they are, in fact, being besieged by pirates as we speak."

Lucy bumped Marguerite with her elbow and whispered, "I told you so."

"We are now seven ships to their three, and we are under a strict no light policy. If your bunk has a porthole, your power has already been shut off. The *Henrietta* is even now being tacked into a safe spot on the winds behind the skirmish where we can continue to provide food, support, and aid to our fellow countrymen. Captain Laviolette of the *Renegade* has spoken with Admiral Lautrec on the *Dame de Guerre,* who has escorted the shipments this far from France, and they have relayed to us that this battle will be over by the morning. In the meantime, I expect you to be prepared for anything. Sleep in your uniforms. If the bell sounds three times, it is all hands to the ready stations, five times, all hands to deck. Dismissed." The round little woman jumped down from her box and walked quickly through the crowd toward the bridge.

"She's such a funny little Captain," Marguerite said. "I'm not sure I've ever met a woman like her in the military."

"Oh, she's not in the military, this isn't a military vessel. Didn't you know?" Lucy explained.

"No, I didn't realize." Marguerite felt foolish once again.

"Captain Butterfield is a privateer. She operates as a free agent for whoever pays the best price. She owns the *Henrietta* outright and has sailed her all over the world. I think she's amazing." Lucy beamed as she watched the round lady walk out of the room.

"That explains a lot," Marguerite said as she thought about Fifi and the unprecedented farm operating in the aft. She couldn't wait to get back to Montreal and talk to her professors about the possibilities of improving on the idea. Imagine, fully self-sustaining ecosystems in the air. Marvelous!

The girls were still chatting as they made their way back to their bunks. Marguerite felt better, body and soul, as she lay down on the hard mattress again and covered herself with the rough blanket. She felt Lucy climb the ladder and settle into her own bed above. As the three girls wished each other goodnight, for the first time since arriving, Marguerite joined their tradition and whispered through the dark, "Sleep well."

"You too, Lady Dungslinger," Lucy giggled.

"Very funny," Marguerite smiled and fell instantly asleep.

Chapter Fourteen

The morning call came far too early. Despite her rough surroundings and tiny space, Marguerite dreamed she was at her Father's house in Montreal, lounging in her lovely feather bed. Outil had just arrived with tea and a pastry for her breakfast.

Then a siren wailed, and she was back to reality. The sights and sounds, and especially the smells, of the *Henrietta* crashed in all around her. But today was different. Today there would be action. She jumped from her bunk, nearly knocking her head on the rail above her, and dressed quickly, making sure to grab her new goggles. She put them over her head like a headband to help hold her hair back. "Off to the races then?" Lucy asked. "We're only a gust of wind away from your beau."

"Yes, I am well aware of that. I have a lot of things planned for today." Marguerite replied.

"Oh, *things*, eh?" Lucy wiggled her eyebrows.

"Yes, many, many things. Do you think it might be possible to borrow a chute and a box or two?"

"You're not thinking of dropping into the middle of the battle are you?"

"There may not even be a battle, Lucy, especially considering the size of our fleet. I doubt any pirates would be brave enough to take us on. No, there will probably be a parlay and much strutting, flexing of cannons, and then the pirates will fly off with their envelopes between their legs."

"True that. But what do you want a chute for?" Lucy asked while climbing down carefully from her bunk.

"I don't want to explain right now. Do you know where I might find one?" Marguerite dug through her trunk as she spoke.

"It may be possible if you know the right people. We have loads in storage toward the aft," Lucy answered.

"Excellent. I'll see you in a bit then." Marguerite knew her new friend wanted her to expound, but she didn't have time. There was much to do. She smiled and headed out to the farm. Louis was there already, brushing the cow and whistling a merry tune.

"Good morning, Louis!" Marguerite smiled in genuine happiness at the boy. He certainly was reliable.

"Good morning, m'lady. If I might say, it's good to see you in such fine spirits."

"We have pirates to deal with today, Louis—and captains," she added the last bit under her breath.

"Yes, ma'am. That we do."

"Have you had your breakfast yet?" Marguerite feigned concern.

"No ma'am. I haven't. I like to get down here to Fifi and make sure she's taken care of first, and then I feed myself." He rubbed the cow affectionately.

Marguerite noticed that he had, indeed, freshened her water and put out new food for the beast. "Well, you are just a dear, Louis. Why don't you run along and take care of yourself now. I will finish up the nasty bits today." Marguerite indicated the waiting pile of manure.

"Are you sure, m'lady? I don't mind doing it all, but I am a bit hungry. Dinner was sparse for deck boys last night, and I'm not used to all this green fruity stuff." He waved an arm at the garden before him.

"Of course. Hurry on now and get a baguette before they are all gone." She smiled at the boy who beamed up at her and only felt a tiny bit of guilt for her not-completely-sincere intentions.

After thanking her far too profusely, Louis ran off toward the mess and Marguerite took stock of the situation. She grabbed an apple from a barrel and munched it as she studied the pipes and pots and especially the cow. "Right then," she told herself as she threw her apple core to the chickens that attacked it greedily.

She grabbed a sturdy looking basket from the pile for harvesting and lined it with a gunnysack. Then she picked up the shovel from the corner and set to work scooping up the foul smelling sludge. With her first scoop, Fifi mooed in angst and swung a foot toward her. But Marguerite was ready for her this time and jumped out of the way. "Oh, no you don't," she said.

A huge *BOOM* shook the ship and lady and cow both stumbled. Marguerite braced herself on the fence and had to gulp hard and breathe deep to get a hold of herself. She knew it was probably just a warning shot, but visions of rough corsairs and a rollicking ship falling to pieces began to flood her mind. Remembering the sight of Outil carrying Vivienne's limp body as the *Triumph* was thrown about like a rag doll made her shudder and panic.

No. She thought. *I can do this. I wanted this. It is not a proper battle. There won't be any sort of battle.* She braced for more fire and scooped quickly, then wrapped the remaining edges of gunnysack over the top of her disgusting treasure and prayed no one would question her on the way to the chute room. Fifi mooed angrily at her as she left. "Go milk yourself!" Marguerite hissed back.

The chute room wasn't hard to find. It was just below the kitchens in the belly of the ship. It was dark and a bit musty smelling. She only received a few strange looks as she passed her shipmates in the small passages with her smelly package. Marguerite heard Lucy before she saw her. She sat sewing a chute next to an older woman and laughing her merry giggle, despite the stress of the moment. Marguerite set her basket down at the entry and hurried to Lucy's side. She tried to sound official.

"I have a special delivery for the *Renegade*, Miss Lucy. Could you assist me with delivery?" Lucy put down her sewing and looked up at Marguerite with a conspiratorial smile.

"Of course, Lady Vadnay." The two walked casually to the pile of crates, and Lucy picked one up.

"No," Marguerite stopped her and pointed to another crate that looked to be on its last leg. "That one."

"I'm not sure it will make the landing," Lucy questioned.

"Exactly," Marguerite said. Lucy shrugged and handed it to her just as another *BOOM* sounded in the distance. This time, the ship did not shudder and rock, however.

"What on earth could they be shooting at? The sun isn't even up yet." Lucy wondered out loud.

"Those are traditional warning shots, probably from the *Renegade*. Captain Laviolette is letting them know we are serious about defending ourselves." Marguerite took the crate back to her basket by the door, far from the other women. She picked up the gunnysack carefully and slipped it into the wooden box, then hammered the lid on securely. Lucy walked up to her carrying a fresh chute.

"Breakfast drop is in fifteen minutes. We always send special morning rations if there is a battle possible. You're going to need this too." She held out the small tangle of canvas and ropes.

"Oh, no I won't." Marguerite grinned. "All I need is a bit of chalk or charcoal. Ah!" She spotted a chunk on the main work table. She snatched it up and wrote *Special Delivery, Captain Laviolette* in block letters across the sturdiest plank left in the whole box.

"My goodness, what is that smell?" Lucy asked as Marguerite examined her handiwork.

"It's a delicacy Captain Laviolette requested for the morning of battle." Marguerite smiled as the other women caught wind of the crate and turned up their noses. Then she whispered to Lucy, "Remember, no chute." The breakfast delivery began to arrive just in time to stop anyone from questioning the peculiar package.

Lucy nodded and laughed, then put the package in the midst of the shuffle as Marguerite headed for the deck. For a moment she hesitated, rethinking her joke, but she knew there was no danger this morning. Negotiations would be first, and then a battle only if the pirates were completely crazy and they couldn't come to an agreement. She couldn't imagine any small band of pirates being foolhardy enough to take on an entire fleet of French warships. More likely, they would bargain for their own safe release rather than demand any booty or attack.

She continued up to the deck. It had been far too long since she had seen the sky. Even if it was still full of clouds and pouring rain, she needed to be outside. She needed to smell the ocean air and to feel fresh wind on her face. The trap door she'd entered the first night on the *Henrietta* was easy to find. She grabbed a deck-boy jacket and flipped the hood over her messy up-do. She pushed open the door and prepared for a deluge of water in the face.

To her surprise, all was calm and clear. The sun was just about to break on the horizon to the east, making the whole world a gorgeous pink color. The clouds had all but disappeared, and a moderate wind blew up from the south. Marguerite's spirits instantly lifted. She filled her lungs with cow-free air and smiled as she pushed off the black waterproof hood.

The scene was as close to magical as Marguerite had ever seen. Ships of all sorts bobbed and drifted on the winds. It was clear which belonged to King Louis, with their flowing black envelopes and bright silver crests. The brown support ships with the *Renegade* were notwithstanding. There were three warships in total, flanking three cargo ships. A little ways south of this great bobbing conglomeration was another group of four ships, hodgepodge affairs, nothing like the foreign vessels that attacked her ship last year. These aerships looked to be at least a decade old, patched with various parts from other ships, and crawling with crew.

Small, dark bodies moved over the decks and rigging of each ship, like ants on an abandoned picnic. She flipped down her goggles and adjusted the scope mechanism for a better view. They were definitely preparing for something, but Marguerite couldn't tell if it was battle or retreat. She couldn't imagine how in the world the pirates could think of taking on nine royal ships and bring back any bounty to speak of.

She flipped her goggles back up as Pierre scampered past, hauling a rope as big around as his leg. "Mornin' miss." Two other boys scampered to help him.

Marguerite nodded and then asked, "Only one warning shot this morning, Pierre?"

"Yes, miss. I doubt there'll be a fight today with the whole fleet together now. The *Renegade* is at the head. She's been chosen to lead should the rogues lose their brains."

Marguerite noted the *Renegade's* position was closest to the pirate vessels, but she agreed with Pierre, there would most likely not be a fight making this the perfect time for her to get off the *Henrietta* and get back on the ship she was commissioned to. She felt bad leaving Lucy and Louis, but she needed Outil, and she had words for Jacques.

As Pierre scampered off, Marguerite took note of the assets

on deck. If she wanted to be of use and get herself off this ship, she was going to need a plan and some materials. There were ropes aplenty, random tools, mops, brooms and—ahh! An escape ship!

The *Henrietta* kicked in its propeller and began to head for the *Renegade* to make its morning drop as Marguerite quickly assessed the small aerdinghy. There wasn't much to it. It was older than she was, had the tiniest speck of a motor and no envelope, no retractable glide wings, and the rudder was broken. How in the world was this supposed to save anyone?

She tinkered a bit with the engine and then checked the fuel tank—completely full. Then she realized it had an intake funnel for rainwater. Excellent. She checked to make sure no one was observing before she adjusted the throttle and pulled the start cord. The little monster coughed and chortled to life, then roared like a lioness awoken from a nap too early.

Marguerite slammed the off switch and ran for the hatch, ignoring the stares from the deck boys. There wasn't a moment to lose. She barreled past other girls rushing to their duties, all the way back down to the belly of the *Henrietta*.

"Lucy! I need a chute after all, a big one!" Lucy looked up from her position at the drop hatch. Her goggles were askew, and her perfect hair flipped wildly in the wind. Marguerite noticed her box was second to last in line to go out.

"Hang on," Lucy said to her coworker, then made her way to Marguerite's side. "They are over here."

Marguerite could see the *Renegade's* deck coming into view through the hatch. She watched as the first crate was dropped and its chute popped open, guiding it softly onto the deck below. One by one the little crates were popped out in succession, like a giant dandelion being blown into the wind. "It must take a lot of skill to get them in just the right spot," she commented.

"Yes, it does," Lucy pulled a large pile of folded canvas from a bin. "These ladies have been precision dropping for years. This is the biggest chute we have. Don't lose it or get cow dung on it, or whatever it is you're planning."

"Will do. Thank you, Lucy." Marguerite gave her a genuine smile of appreciation.

"And be careful! I want to visit your fancy house in France and meet your bot, Outil. Can't do that if you're dead, you know."

"Of course! Au Revoir!" Marguerite cried as she raced back up to the deck. Her legs burned from climbing all the stairs, and she was completely out of breath by the time she reached the little ship again. She began to secure the ropes of the chute to the hooks and holds of the aerdinghy, and occasionally she peered over the edge to the *Renegade* below.

By now its imposing black envelope was bellied up to their own brown one again. The two ships snuggled in the breezes like friends seeking shelter together. The parade of food was nearly complete, gauging by the size of the stack of crates on the deck below. A hand touched her softly on the back. Marguerite jumped in surprise and whirled around. "Excuse me, m'lady, but what are you doing with the old dingy?" Louis stood there with wonder in his eyes—or was that fear?

"Nothing, Louis. Get back to work and nevermind me."

"But, I'm sorry, m'lady, if you're planning to do what I think you are, those knots won't hold you for two blasts of wind." He indicated her neatly tied bows around the edges of the cockpit.

"Oh, well, I suppose that's good to know," she mumbled, unsure of what type of knot she could tie in its place. She was much better with machines and gadgets than she was with everyday nonsense such as rope.

Luckily, Louis was quick in both hand and mind. He deftly removed each tie and resecured them with much more complicated twists. "Excellent!" She patted him on the back and pulled her goggles back down and her hood up. She pulled the engine cord and climbed into the driver's seat. There was only room for four people total. Such a useless rescue ship, she thought. The seat cracked and groaned with age, making her wonder about the stability of the entire vessel. Nevertheless, she tested the throttle again, and when she was happy with the state of things, she gave Louis a huge grin and shooed him away with her hand. He made as if he were going to climb in behind her, but she shook her head forcefully and yelled, "No!"

This was her idea, her scheme. Should it go awry, she wasn't going to have anyone else hurt because of it. She'd already dragged enough people into deadly disasters in the past. She was willing to risk her own life to face Jacques once and for all, and to retrieve her bot, but not anyone else's. Besides, all she had to do was drop and drift a bit with the aid of the small motor, and she would land on the deck of the *Renegade*.

A gust of wind caught her chute, whipping it up and forward. She shoved the chute out of her way and checked over the side of the little ship again, just in time to see the second to the last box plummet without a chute and hit the deck with a loud *SPLAT!*

"Ha!" She laughed out loud as she watched the deck hands scurry out of the way. She adjusted her scope and easily made out the figure of Captain Laviolette standing near the "special delivery" in his finest uniform, wiping at a cow dung stain and cursing. She could also still make out her charcoal message on the single board still intact on the pile of exploded cow dung.

Serves him right, she thought.

The chute strained against the wind again. She had to get going; things were picking up. She looked back to Louis and started to pull free the latch hooks that held the dingy to the ship. She motioned for him to help her with the back ones, but behind him she saw Captain Butterfield stomping toward them. "Go!" She yelled as she climbed over the seat to reach the hooks herself.

Louis stayed, however, and popped the last two without worry for his own demise. Then he called out to her, "Don't die, m'lady!"

She twisted back into her seat and fastened the harness just as the last hook came free, and the ship plummeted into open space.

Chapter Fifteen

*T**his was a terrible, terrible idea.* Marguerite chided herself as she dropped like a rock out of the sky.

She revved the engine and pulled hard on the throttle, trying to get some forward thrust. The parachute whipped and whistled, occasionally hitting her in the head as it flipped in the upward wind. Then just as quickly, it caught on a gale and popped open, slamming Marguerite hard into her seat.

Terrible idea! She repeated as the little ship bobbed a few times, and then headed right for her target, the deck of the *Renegade.* Except that her target was moving.

By the time Marguerite had secured her chute and cut the aerdinghy free of the *Henrietta*, they were already done with the food drop and sailing up and away from the larger ship, which was now sailing toward the pirate ships.

Excellent, Marguerite thought. *All I have to do now is steer this little disaster of a ship to the giant moving target ahead of me. Easy as winding a gear.*

Except that the wind blowing her toward her mark was also blowing her mark away from her. She pulled hard on the rudder, and then remembered it was broken. She pushed with all her strength on the throttle. It kicked in a bit more power, but not enough. If she was lucky, she would make it to the aft deck—but only just. As she drifted helplessly, the wind picked up again. A huge gust blowing her higher in the air and forward in the right direction. She shoved on the rudder again. This time, something clanked, and it gave way sending her soaring a good fifty feet higher than was necessary.

"Oh, merciful gears!" She cried out as the chute deflated in the upward motion and she began to plummet again. Her engine continued to spit out full power, pushing her forward, but the chute wasn't catching now. She was rocketing straight for the giant black envelope of the Renegade.

Marguerite quickly inspected the round hull of her ship and counted her lucky stars. There was a chance she wouldn't puncture the giant bag of explosive gasses, but only a small chance. She held on tightly and closed her eyes as the black balloon rushed up to meet her tiny wooden capsule and her bottom left the decrepit seat again.

This is it, she thought. *This is how I die.*

But impact was not as explosive as she'd feared. In fact, it was quite lovely. She sank deep into the giant oval shaped balloon and was instantly bounced back into the aether. It was an exaggerated copy of the way it had felt to jump on her father's bed when she was a child. She would land on her backside and rocket back into the air, landing on her feet on the floor. Only, this time, she felt her chute catch the wind again as she arched up and began to soar back down toward the sea. She had just enough time to catch her breath and open her eyes before she realized that she had been too liberal with her throttle and the *Renegade* was now nowhere in sight. Instead, the patchwork riggings of a pirate ship were dead ahead.

"Clogged cogs and steaming cylinders!" She yelled out loud and covered her face. Even though the chute slowed her descent, she was still coming in too fast. It was not going to be a soft landing. The aerdinghy hit the rigging, just above the deck on the smaller of the three pirate ships. Marguerite hit the controls of her dingy with a loud *crunch, and* the ship ricocheted off the ropes and posts and then hit the actual deck. Marguerite heard another loud *whack* and the sound of wood splintering as she was thrown about her tiny cockpit like a wet noodle in an autocart spoke.

A few more *whacks* and *clangs* and a final, nasty knock on the head, and Marguerite and her ship came to a sudden stop, leaving her bruised and bleeding and dizzy. Her head felt like someone had boxed it repeatedly with a monkey wrench, and she had somehow managed to land upside down.

Rough hands grabbed her and shoved her harness slack as they unhooked it; then they dropped her unceremoniously to the ruined deck floor. A piece of splintered wood jammed into her side, and she cried out in pain. "It's one of them she-fliers!" a voice cried out. "Get her up and outta here." Marguerite realized suddenly that these were not the strange voices of foreign corsairs, but English-speaking men with British accents.

While the British had always groped and fought over the best French tutors for their children, believing fluent French was a sign of culture and sophistication, the French never bothered with learning English. To Marguerite it sounded short and clipped, an ugly language lacking emotion. Still, she enjoyed reading some of the English authors in their original texts, and occasionally there was an interesting article published on engineering in England, so she'd taken the time to learn enough to understand. But she wasn't anywhere near fluent enough to bargain her way out of this mess.

A loud man barked next to Marguerite's ear as he pulled her to her feet.

"Send word to Captain Douleur. We'll throw her in the brig till we get orders. In the meantime, clean this blooming mess up!" Her head throbbed, and her vision was still blurry, but things were starting to come into focus. Whoever was supporting her took her by both arms now and held her in front of him.

"Ain't you a pretty little suicider then? Musta done something stupid, or you're just plain crazy, to be assigned the first strike against the meanest pirate rig in the Atlantic. Eh?" She blinked at him and tried to make out his face. Her goggles were still firmly in place, however, and she realized one reason she couldn't see was because they were fogged up with the foul breath of the man examining her.

"Those is nice glasses you got there. I think I'll have them for me self." He reached out and plucked the goggles from her face and looked them over carefully. Marguerite could see clearly now.

He was a hulking British man covered in soot and grease; hair cut short—a sure sign of recent lice. She shuddered and stood on her own two feet. She tried to shake off the dizziness. Her knee and her shoulder ached, but she was fairly certain nothing was broken.

"Captain says she's taking us in. Battle's on boys! To your stations!" The man had let go of Marguerite and was now trying to shove the goggles onto his own massive head, but he only succeeded in getting them pinched onto his brow. "What do I do with her?"

"Tie her to the mainsail and get to work! We'll use the parts from her ship in the catapult. Them Frenchies are going to regret the day they took us on!" A great cry went up from the men all around her. The big man pulled Marguerite, stumbling, toward a post that traveled up into the envelope of their ship. She couldn't help but think what an interesting design it was but her thoughts were jerked back to the present as he yanked her arms behind her and around the pole then started fastening them with a rope.

This was a disaster, an absolute and complete disaster. All the warnings Jacques gave her about what buccaneers did to women began to flood her mind. Even obscure tales she read as a child of tongues being torn out and bodices ripped open raced through her thoughts and bludgeoned her heart. She had to stay calm. She had to think. Panicking would only get her killed. "Ah!" she cried out in pain as the pirate yanked too hard on her arm, in turn hurting her throbbing shoulder.

"Come on, Jo!" another man cried. "I need you on the ship cudgel!"

"Right, I'm coming!" He hurried with her knot and then

grinned in her face. "Don't worry pretty little French lovey, I'll be back for you in a jiff."

Marguerite shuddered and watched as her beloved goggles trotted away on top of the oaf's head. The ship began flying some sort of maneuver. It spun around and flanked its sister ship. The deck crew made quick work of her wreck, tossing any bulky, unusable pieces overboard and organizing the rest near rustic catapults. Other men brought up buckets of goopy liquid and set them next to the catapult operators.

Marguerite looked out beyond the scene in front of her and saw the *Renegade* was closing in quickly, with its razor sharp battering bow. The rest of the King's ships stayed behind as the *Renegade* flew directly at what appeared to be the main pirate ship, right in the middle. But the pirates made quick work of the situation, maneuvering up and around the *Renegade*, like a matador dodging a massive, flying bull.

The air was filled with auto pigeons carrying notes back and forth between the warships. Each ship had wireless telegraph, but there was no telling if the pirates could intercept the transmissions. The birds were much more secure and reliable in a close battle like this.

Marguerite would have been fascinated by everything happening around her, except that she kept trying to wiggle her hands free, and was completely unsuccessful. Watching the ships square off to fight while she kept at her ropes, she realized that the *Renegade* was going to miss its target and was now trying to regain footing as the pirates prepared to fire on her when she passed.

Air cannons roared through the driving winds and men stood at the ready, dipping debris in the buckets of liquid and securing it to catapults. As the *Renegade* drew near, she could see the crew of its deck making similar preparations. Then a man aboard the ship Marguerite was tied to brought out a torch and walked along the line, lighting each catapult's load on fire as they aimed toward the *Renegade*

"Oh, grease and gears," Marguerite swore. Fire was just about the worst thing you could have hit an aership. She willed the crew of the *Renegade* to see the smoke and glowing flames and steer clear.

Her thoughts were answered by Jacques' vessel making a quick bank to the right, away from the ship she was on, and a blast of cannon fire from the aft of the *Renegade*. The pirates returned fire, but it was too late. Their flaming scraps of rubbish drifted harmlessly to the ocean below as cannon blasts rocked the boat out of position. Marguerite jerked and shook with the vessel she was tied to, but in her heart she cheered for her shipmates.

Her shipmates. Outil and Jacques. What had she done? Where were they? How would they get out of this mess she'd caused? It worked once, so she tried again, willing the *Renegade* to turn and leave with the rest of the armada. She could figure out these pirates on her own. Maybe she could even steal a ship and fly back, catch up? "Oh crusty custard," she swore again. No matter how stupid she was, or how terrible the peril she'd caused, she knew Jacques and Outil would never leave her. They had seen her stupid dingy land on the pirate deck and even if they didn't know she was flying it, Jacques wouldn't leave a man behind.

Even if they did leave her behind, she knew deep in her heart that she probably wouldn't have the will to fight on anyway.

She wallowed in self-pity until she saw another of the French warships break off from the pack, safely gliding away from the fight to circle the battle at an unbelievable speed. It was smaller than the *Renegade*, sleek and shining silver in the morning light, but it didn't have the obvious weaponry of the *Renegade* either. Still, it was wicked fast and tore around the pirates, blocking their maneuvers.

Now that the small ship had cut them off, Jacques fired up his surplus motors and surprised the farthest ship out with his own burst of speed. The razor sharp tip of reinforced brass raced right for the hull of the smaller ship. Deck hands scurried to retreat, but it was too late. The huge spike ran right through the center of the body of the wooden ship.

The noise of metal and wood crashing together carried over the high winds to all in earshot. The smaller ship stayed lodged on the spear of the *Renegade* like a sausage recently forked for dinner. Men cursed and scurried to reload their now empty weapons. Marguerite stared in wonder. She'd assumed the sharp points were meant for puncturing envelopes, but she supposed this worked as well.

The smaller, faster French ship spun to attention and flew to the *Renegade*'s aid as the remaining pirate ships did the same— only not to help. The pirates raised red flags on all three ships. Marguerite had read enough to know this was a bad sign. It meant they were out for blood; no survivors would be taken. Her ship turned and sailed toward the *Renegade* as well. Marguerite guessed that these pirates thought they would fly up alongside the huge warship and blast it, maybe even board it, and have the day. But even with her short time on the ship, she knew there was enough fire power on the *Renegade* to take out several little scrap metal fliers like the one she was on, fire or no fire.

The small French ship flew to the envelope of the skewered pirate ship and tied on, a prime position to tap the gasses and leave it hanging helplessly until its weight pulled it to the ocean and beyond. As the pirates with their red flags drew nearer, the *Renegade* threw up its white flag, calling for negotiations. The men around her cheered, "They surrender!"

The man who appeared to be in charge struck out at the closest of his deck mates and clocked him good in the face. "You idiot, that's not a flag of surrender; that means they want to talk. They've got us by the gears right now. One poke from that little ship up there and the entire crew of the *Lolly* will be shark food."

"Well, what we going to do now?" asked another man.

"We wait till Captain Douleur makes a move. If the red flag stays, we attack, if she flies the white, then we gots to sit back and wait till they be done talking."

Marguerite watched as the main ship drew nearer. The ship she was on was now close enough for the men on either vessel to give each other dirty looks. Side by side, the *Renegade* was obviously the far superior ship. She searched for Outil's face, or even Jacques's, but couldn't see them among the deckhands. They were probably on the bridge.

Someone on the *Renegade* spotted her and cried out. "They've got one of our own tied to the main sail!" She realized she was still wearing her French flight suit. It was the first time she felt grateful for it since the scratchy thing had been issued.

"Call the captain!" Another man on the *Renegade* called out. "He'll want to know!"

Oh, I bet he'll want to know. Marguerite thought.

"Truce!" a pirate called out in English.

She looked to the largest of the pirate ships, and sure enough, the red flag was gone and a white flag was taking its place. All she had to do now was wait. She tried to sink down to her bottom. Standing against the pole was becoming very tiresome, and her leg still ached from the crash. Men ran around her in all directions, preparing for whatever came next. Some had weapons drawn, some ale. Some were laughing while others looked fierce, ready for blood. As she slid down the pole, she wiggled her hands and twisted them around again, hoping the new angle would provide better leverage for slipping free.

She was right. The bony part of her left hand popped against the tight rope. Pain shot up her arm and brought tears to her eyes, but her hand slipped out of the tight ropes providing space to release the other hand as well.

Ha! Take that you goggle thief! She thought.

She kept her hands behind the pole and shimmied back to standing while she began to calculate her options. Three men in front of her, a good ten feet between the two ships, ropes, bits of debris—she could do this.

She took a deep breath, tried not to think about the pain in her head, shoulder, and leg, and now hand, and charged forward with every ounce of strength she had left.

Chapter Sixteen

The first clue that Marguerite's plan wasn't going to work was when she grabbed the rope in front of her at full speed, and her shoulder and hand exploded with pain. As small as she was, the weight of her body was too much for her injured arm. The crew of the *Renegade* saw her attempt and cheered while the men around her flew into action.

She slid lamely off the rope and held her shoulder with her good arm trying to find another way to get back to her ship. A pirate ran for her with both arms open, but she easily ducked under him and grabbed a board with a nail in the end left from her wreck. Swinging wildly with her good arm at anyone else attempting to come near, she made it to the port side. Trouble now was that she knew she wasn't strong enough to jump the distance between the ships, and she couldn't take her eyes off the pirates in front of her long enough to even climb up and ready herself.

Someone on the *Renegade* tried to throw her a rope. She snatched at it with her injured arm while shaking her board with the other, but missed, allowing the pirates to jump back in the fight. She swung her board as hard as she could and connected with the beefy man wearing her goggles, but it wasn't enough to stop him. He grabbed her weapon and threw it over the side of the ship as if it were as easy as plucking a sweet from a baby. A smaller man grabbed her from the other side and spun her around so that her back was pressed up against his belly as he pressed a knife to her throat. The crew of the *Renegade* cursed and shook their arms as she was dragged back, away from their reach.

Marguerite's heart pounded in her chest, her whole body hurt now, and the edge of the blade was scraping at her skin, cutting a little here, a little there. She couldn't help the fat tears that began to roll down her face as she watched the *Renegade*'s helpless crew watching her.

What had she done? How could she have been so foolish? She thought of her earlier anger and childish thoughts of revenge. She wished she could take them all back. Of course, Jacques hadn't behaved himself either, but her blunders far outweighed his heavy-handedness.

Just when she thought it couldn't get worse, a familiar face in a captain's hat pushed through the crowd to the edge of his ship. He walked purposefully, probably on his way to meet with the pirate captain. She watched him go, wishing she could call out to him, but knowing he wouldn't hear. And then someone from the crowd grabbed his arm and pointed him in her direction. He stopped and looked directly into her face.

Jacques's expression was a mixture of sorrow, anger, and fear. It hurt her heart more than anything to see him looking at her that way. She tried to convey with her pleading expression and tears how sorry she was to have caused so much trouble. She was so close to being with him, and she realized she did want to be with him. Not just on the *Renegade*, but actually with Jacques. And now she couldn't reach him, and he would have to risk his life to reach her. All she could do was continue to walk backwards and cry.

Jacques turned and spoke to the man next to him. The man ran into the throng, and Jacques continued to stare at her for a few more moments, his eyes large and fixed, his jaw clenched as the pirates tied her arms and legs and forced her into a sitting position in one of the catapults facing the *Renegade*. She knew him well enough to know that he was very angry, and not just at her. He was about to do something rash to the pirates holding her.

The dish she sat in was deep, and her legs stuck out at an odd angle. There was no way to wiggle out without free arms. A small, nasty looking man with rotten teeth grabbed a bucket of the sticky looking liquid they had covered the debris in, and climbed onto a crate just behind her. The men in front of her began to yell and shake their fists as Marguerite felt the first drops of cold liquid hit her head and run down her face leaving a film of sludge behind.

Jacques balled his fist and slammed it on the railing. Then he cupped his hands over his mouth and called across the void in English, "You damage one hair on my aerman's head, and I will skewer all of you personally."

His aerman. Was he trying to hide exactly what she meant to him, or was he letting her know her place? At least he didn't tell them to go ahead and burn her, that she'd caused him more trouble than she was worth.

"Keep your knickers on!" The little man yelled back, "We'll wait on Captain Douleur's answer. And then we'll burn her!" He laughed maniacally and waved the torch over his head, coming dangerously close to Marguerite's now flammable body. The man Jacques had spoken to earlier was back at his side, and Jacques nodded as he spoke. Then he turned to Marguerite again and mouthed the words *je t'aime*, before he moved back through the group on his deck and disappeared.

I love you.

He'd said it. He still loved her. She felt a flash of hope, before it instantly turned to second-guessing herself. He could have said a number of things that looked like je'taime. Things that would make more sense, like I hate you, you ruin everything, why did I ever think we could marry and live a happy life together, or you are a disaster. All of which made more sense than him loving her right now. He was gone, she could only assume to meet with Captain Douleur, and she would just have to wait to learn the outcome of that meeting.

The wind blew relentlessly as the minutes turned into an hour. Marguerite's thoughts drifted from worry to complete despair. She rallied a few times with thoughts of escape, but there was no freeing her arms this time. Her injuries and the extra tight binding kept her stuck in her misery. The sludge she was covered in smelled strongly of chemicals and eventually began to sting and burn her skin. Her arms were at such an angle that the pain in her shoulder was constant, almost unbearable. Marguerite was close to wishing they would just finish her off and be done with the whole ordeal. She sat with her eyes closed, wishing for her father, and her soft bed back in Montreal, not daring to wish for Jacques, when a familiar mechanical voice cried out from the *Renegade*.

Most of the crew had gone back to their work, a few stayed to watch Marguerite and her ruthless captors, and in the middle of them all, Outil appeared, shining as bright as the day she was built.

"Be strong, aerman!" the bot called out in French.

Marguerite was surprised by the informal address, at first, and then she realized that the pirates had no idea who she was, and if they did, it could turn the tables on negotiations in their favor. She tried to smile at her wise robot friend, but the chemical gasses burned her eyes, and she had to close them again. She heard shuffling and rumbling all around her, along with complaints, cusses, and thumps. Occasionally someone would poke or prod her or whisper something lewd in her ear. She ignored them all and kept her eyes shut tight against the fumes.

Suddenly she felt pressure at her ankles, and her eyes flew open. A man bent over her, cutting her ropes. Another was at her wrists cutting there. She clenched her eyes against the pain.

"You are one lucky lady, aerman. Quite the bargain struck for you. Must be a favorite of the captain. Eh?"

He poked her belly, and she swatted at him with her now free hand. She dared to ask in her broken English, "You are letting me go?"

"Oh, yes, lovely. We are letting you go. But we are still coming out on top." She wasn't sure she wanted to know what they meant. Once she was cut free, she started to try and climb out of the catapult, but they shoved her back down. "Now, how do you suppose she thinks she's going to get back, Jo? Can't fly, can't even hold a rope."

Marguerite looked up to the man wearing her goggles on his head as he said, "Only one way for it." He leaned in to trip the trigger on the catapult, but before he could, Marguerite reached out and snatched her goggles back, pulling his head down with them. His forehead smashed into the bucket of the catapult as it launched Marguerite and her goggles high into the air between the two ships.

For the second time that morning, she found herself flying helplessly through the aether, thousands of feet above the Atlantic Ocean. Marguerite decided she wasn't sure this particular type of adventure suited her at all. Maybe Jacques was right. Before she could finish exploring that thought, she landed with a painful crash onto the deck of the Renegade. A cheer went up, and battle broke out.

She kept her eyes glued shut, listening to the clang of grappling hooks hitting the opposite deck, the crack of gunfire, and the thudding of running feet. She tried to blink quickly to see where she could crawl for safety when familiar cold metal arms gathered her up from behind and carried her through the fray to the decks below.

"Outil!" she sobbed.

"Do not worry, m'lady. We have clean water at the ready.

You'll be good as new in twenty minutes."

"I'm so sorry; I didn't mean to cause all this trouble."

"Hush now. It is time to rest. Let the men fight, and the automaton clean."

"Where is Jacques? Can I see him? I need to apologize."

"If my guess is correct, m'lady, he is still aboard the other ship. I'm sure he's busy battling Captain Douleur."

"But, Outil, I've been so horrible. I caused this whole skirmish, and now he's in mortal danger," she sobbed the words out as best she could, but she couldn't finish. Outil opened the door to what must have been the washrooms. A blast of steam hit Marguerite in the face, and she could smell the strong lye soap.

"We'll have plenty of time to talk once we get you cleaned up. Hold on, this might be a bit hot," Outil said. Marguerite felt the bot take her goggles and pull her boots off her feet then lift her up and over the lip of one of the giant brass wash tubs.

She cringed and prepared herself for a scalding, backside first. But the air roared with explosion and the Renegade rocked dangerously from side to side. The water in the tub sloshed up to meet her prematurely, and Outil slipped and dropped her in. Marguerite had been so cold from sitting on the deck of the pirate ship, covered in wet who-knows-what, that she felt she might actually be on fire when the hot water hit her. Her whole body went under in the giant tub, and every nerve ending threatened to burst from the sudden heat. She pushed herself up to the surface as best she could, coughing and spitting soapy water.

"Oh, dear. I am so terribly sorry," Outil said as she climbed back to her feet and handed Marguerite a bar of soap.

"Gears and goblins!" Marguerite cried. "It's as hot as the river Styx!"

"Yes, and I have prepared a solvent that should do well to get the tar, and whatever else is in this mixture, off," Outil said. "Just keep your eyes closed, miss." The ship rocked again, and the sound of battle raged on above them. They heard the Renegade's secondary engines roar to life and felt the ship lurch and sway back into movement.

"I need to get these clothes off," Marguerite ordered as she took the rag soaked in fuel and scrubbed furiously at her face. "We need to help." She winced with pain as Outil pealed the ruined flight suit off her injured shoulder; then she carefully removed everything else as best she could.

"I'm afraid your arm may be dislocated, m'lady." The bot carefully took Marguerite's favorite pink underwear and hung them in front of the drying ovens.

"Yes, I would agree. But this lye soap seems to be doing the trick." She used her good arm to reach up and rub the cake all over her head. "Oh, Outil, I don't even want to see a mirror for at least a month! Help me get this through my hair. Would you?"

The two continued to work on Marguerite's hair and body as the battle raged on. Being with her bot and safely able to scrub the events of the morning away was helping Marguerite recharge. She was considering all her options and determined to actually help this time. "At least this ship seems to have a bit more staying power than the *Triumph* did," Marguerite noted. By this time in the battle with the last pirates they'd encountered, the *Triumph* had been bursting to pieces.

"I'm fairly certain that the Renegade is doing most of the firing, m'lady. Officer Vuitton and I have been preparing rigorously the past few days. I found him to be a very intelligent commander. I can only assume he would be as intelligent in battle as well."

"Oh, Outil, I've made such a mess of things," Marguerite rested her head in her hands as the bot continued to work the knots and goo out of her hair.

"M'lady, you haven't done anything to intentionally hurt anyone. These are unfortunate circumstances. You could possibly—" the bot stopped short.

"What? Please, let me know what I could possibly do other than what I have done." She slammed her hands into the water and pushed away the other clothing floating around her.

"It was nothing." The bot sounded a bit afraid.

"Tell me, Outil. I order you."

"Very well. You could stop to think about the outcome of your choices before you act, m'lady. Especially when it concerns the safety of yourself and other people."

Marguerite didn't have time to lose her temper at the bot for her insolent comment. Just as she opened her mouth, a huge explosion rocked the ship, sending the water and women flying. As soon as they could get themselves back together, Marguerite cried, "Outil, get me out of here. I need clothes. I'm not going to die naked in a laundry tub!" She pulled herself out, grabbed a half dry sheet and wiped down, then pulled on her almost dry underwear. "I am *not* giving up my silks," she declared as Outil handed her a man's flight suit.

"This is the best I could find, m'lady."

"It's fine. Help me get it back on this blasted shoulder," she winced with pain as she pulled the suit back up to her chest.

"If you don't mind, m'lady, I think I can fix this," Outil said cautiously.

"What are you going to do?" Marguerite asked. "Just close your eyes and lean into me." The bot reached for her shoulder.

Marguerite took a deep breath and steadied herself against the cool hands of her automaton. The bot held her arm carefully, bending it at the elbow. She rotated it up and then outward with a quick jerk. Marguerite cried out in pain at the same time as a satisfying *pop* gave instant relief.

"You are horrible, Outil! That hurt like crazy, but it feels measurably better now." Marguerite grabbed the sheet she'd used to dry herself off with and tore one end into a long strip.

"Do you think you will need a sling?" Outil asked.

"Oh, no, this isn't for my arm. This is for my ridiculous hair." Marguerite wound the cotton around her head then through her hair and tied it all up on top of her crown like a wild turban sprouting tufts of wavy brown hair, like some sort of exotic plant. Then she slipped her feet back into her boots and cried, "Come on, let's go."

"Excuse me, m'lady, but where do you propose we go?" Outil asked.

Marguerite marched down the passage rubbing her shoulder, turban bouncing, explosions still roaring above. "Ballistics, of course. I need a gun. Preferably a big one."

Chapter Seventeen

The ballistics rooms were a hive of activities. Men, women and bots were rushing from one duty to another. Officer Vuitton was in the middle of it all, shouting orders and peering through a great scope pulled down from the ceiling. He pulled back from the eyepiece just as Marguerite walked in.

"Well, if it isn't Lady War-Maker herself." He slammed the telescope back out of head bashing way and jerked open the gate to the armory closet.

"I'm here to help," Marguerite said, head held high, maybe a bit too high as she took the guns and strapped them to her waist.

"I think you've helped quite enough. We all heard about your trick in the dingy this morning. I'll have you know negotiations were moving along just fine before you flew into the middle of it like a loon on fire." His words were harsh and critical, but he reached into the cabinet and rummaged around as he spoke. He picked up a medium sized flame musket, then thought twice, put it back and pulled out two traditional pistols in a holster and handed them to Marguerite.

"Take these and get on deck. We need sharp shooters up there, and you scored higher than any of this lot in marksmanship." He pulled out a gear motion rifle and an ammunition belt and gave those to her as well. Then he handed Outil a giant arrow launcher and a quiver of exploding arrows.

"Those will be a good fit. Now get up there and don't kill anyone in a uniform. And for the love of all that is greased and geared, do not blow up our own ships." He shooed both of them away like flies and started barking orders to his crew again. Marguerite tried to say something in her defense, but another explosion sounded, and Outil grabbed her arm pulling gently.

"Now's not the time, m'lady."

Marguerite nodded, "Right." And they jogged back down the passage to the stairs.

"Let me go first," Outil slipped past Marguerite once they reached the hatch and pushed up on the heavy wooden boards. The door swung open on its hinges, landing with a thud, and the noises of war exploded around them, no longer filtered by the ship's dense walls. Pirates and aermen alike fought on the deck of the Renegade. The two ships were still tethered together, but the Renegade's engines roared against the other ship, trying to pull away, but only dragging it along like a giant floating anchor. The smaller ship the Renegade had skewered was no longer hanging on the bow, but also wasn't floating anywhere in site. She could only assume the worst. The explosion was most likely the envelope being destroyed, but there was no time to check the waters below for debris.

Marguerite looked desperately for Jacques but didn't see him in the throngs. Maybe he was still on the other ship, the main one with Captain Douleur. She tried to pull on her goggles, but they stung her red and burning cheeks. She slid them down round he neck for safe-keeping and wondered if the English-speaking pirates realized the meaning of their captain's French name was pain. Either way, it certainly was fitting. Captain Douleur had caused her more pain already than she cared to think about and they hadn't even met face to face.

She looked for the other ship. It was high above locked in battle with the smallest of the French fleet. Then she scanned for the fleet.

They were gone. Not even the smaller support vessels were anywhere in sight. She noticed a French aerman ducked behind a few water barrels, reloading his hip shooter. She ducked behind the barrels, and Outil covered her while she questioned him.

"Where did the fleet go? Where is Captain Laviolette?"

"Captain's still up there," he paused loading his gun to point to the ships above.

"What about the fleet, where did they go? When did they leave?" She frantically tried to think of a way to get to the battle above.

"Oh, they caught the trade aethers back, and we stayed on to finish the job. It's what we were sent for anyway."

The man looked up from his job to address her and his face changed from concentration on his weapon to recognition.

"Hey, aren't you the lady who started this whole mess? Jumped the Henrietta's escape boat and bounced off the envelope?" It was not a pleasant statement at all. Rather, one laced with hatred.

Marguerite jumped up and started to jog to the next set of barrels calling over her shoulder, "No, not me! No idea what you're talking about!" But the soldier followed her.

"Yes, it was you. Your face is all burned up from the pirate fire mix, and you're the one with the fancy bot." He thumbed a hand at Outil as she fired on a pirate running at them.

"What does it matter? I'm here to help now. And you should too. Stop babbling and get to work!" Marguerite peered over the barrel with her rifle ready, trying to assess the situation and how she could best help.

"It matters because we were on the brink of settling all of this with a peaceable agreement. Then you fly outta nowhere and dive bomb their ship like some kind of crazy suicider, and the whole deal is off."

Marguerite winced at his accusations, but held firmly to her gun, took aim, and fired at a hairy pirate with a nasty blood-smeared sword. Her aim was true, and he fell to the deck. She took aim at another trying to attack a smaller boy cutting desperately at the rigging ropes.

The aerman kicked her in the backside. "What do you have to say for yourself? If you're not court marshaled you should be lynched in the least. I'd throw you overboard myself if I could." Marguerite and Outil both swung their weapons in his direction.

"That is quite enough," Outil said calmly.

The aerman took a step back but kept talking, raising his

voice, "Captain said as soon as *she* was safe, we should attack. We moved fifty barrels of fresh water and rum to their ships, plus a dozen bots, then they throw her over and all hell breaks loose. My best mate died in the first round. We been friends since we were kids, and it's *her* fault." He pointed at Marguerite and spat as he spoke. "So, no. I don't think it's enough!"

A pirate ran up behind the aerman. Marguerite moved her aim to the side and shot the man directly in the heart, then moved her barrel back to the aerman. There wasn't a way to get to Jacques, so she would do the best she could here, and try not to think about the aerman's accusations.

Outil spoke again, "I think you need to turn around and fight now, sir. Lady Vadnay will be dealt with by those in authority." Marguerite didn't look back. She threw herself into her job, shooting as best she could, her aim always accurate and her breathing steady. She was good at this. She could do this. She could help make up for her mistakes, make Jacques proud again.

Thinking about Jacques made her tear up again. She wiped her swollen eyes on the rough, too big sleeve, and refocused. The boys nearly had the ropes severed when the *Renegade* cut back its engines to save fuel, and the pirates were falling left and right on the deck. Those pirates who figured out what was going on were beginning to scramble back to their ship. Marguerite realized they would soon be free of them, but only for a time. They were too close for air cannons to work without damaging their own ship, so hand to hand combat was all that was left. Unless ...

"Outil, can you light your arrows?" Marguerite called to her friend.

"Yes, m'lady, but I don't suggest it this close to our own envelope." The enormous black balloon was only a few feet above their heads. "An accidental fire could be disastrous for us."

"But you have excellent long range capabilities on that weapon, right?" Marguerite asked. "Not particularly," Outil replied. "I'm much more effective at close range. I was not designed for combat."

"Hurry then, trade me weapons and light up an arrow." Marguerite stood next to Outil and forced the swap.

"But miss, I'm not certain that you should do that. Protocol calls for no fire to be used on board unless in dire circumstances."

"These circumstances are fairly dire, Outil. Light me up." She held up the cross bow with the arrow fuse first. "The boys are almost done cutting; we haven't much time."

As a small deck boy chopped at the last rope, the two ships drifted farther apart, straining the connection. The *Renegade*'s engines roared to life again in preparation for separation. Outil let out as much of an exasperated sigh as an automaton was able and used her finger to light the fuse.

"Excellent, cover me!" Marguerite ran into the battle, eye fixed on her target, Outil at her heal, blocking all of those who tried to harm her mistress. As the boy came to the last few centimeters of rope, Marguerite took aim and fired directly at the ship that had held her captive less than an hour before. A gust of wind caught her shaft and blew it off course; it exploded in the air above the deck harmlessly. But the pirates had now realized her plan and began to take action.

One of them called out to the others, "She's going to blow the envelope! Get her!"

Another cried, "Save yourselves!"

Pirates and aerman were everywhere at once, attacking her, jumping ship, throwing tethers, and calling out curses.

But the boy's knife was true, and now that she could factor in the wind, so was Marguerite's aim. As the rope between ships broke at last, Outil lit another round and Marguerite aimed and shot without hesitation. The small staff flew through the air in an arc against the wind. Perfect aim drove it right to the heart of the brown bag of gasses over the pirate ship's deck. The *Renegade* roared to life, swinging out and away from the other ship, just as the arrow exploded and the giant brown balloon went up in flames faster than a heartbeat.

"Yes! I knew it was hydrogen!" Marguerite cheered as the flames sent an updraft of heat, causing the two ships above to fly apart. With its envelope gone in a matter of seconds, the pirate ship and everyone on it dropped out of the sky like a rock. The crew of the *Renegade* gave an uproarious cheer, and the pirates left on deck dropped their weapons and fell to their knees in surrender.

"That was extremely lucky, m'lady," Outil said.

"It had to be done, Outil. There was no way around it. If they'd gotten away, they would have continued to pester us, and we would have lost more aermen."

"Yes, m'lady," Outil conceded. Marguerite was not pleased with her bot's reaction, however. She expected more praise. A pat on the back, something. She was trying to make right all the wrong she'd caused that day. A roar filled the aether around them, louder than the *Renegade*'s engines. It came from above.

The whole deck raised their eyes just in time to see the remaining pirate ship roar to life, a spout of flame shooting from its stern just before it shot away at a mind blowing speed.

"What on earth?" Marguerite wondered. She'd never seen anything like it before. No ship could travel that fast and no ship would have flames that large on board a gaseous craft.

"You!" A voice cried behind her. Marguerite turned to see Officer Vuitton marching toward her on the deck. She smiled triumphantly, awaiting his praise. Instead, he scowled and pointed at her with a stout determined finger.

"Lock her in the brig! I don't want to see her again until we are in New France at a tribunal!" Two officers flanking Vuitton came from either side and took Marguerite by either arm.

"What for? Why are you doing this? I just saved your ship from the pirates. Besides, you have no authority to do this. I want to see Captain Laviolette. Now!" She stomped her foot and shook her turbaned head.

"I would like to see him as well, but thanks to your ridiculous antics, he is no longer with us." Marguerite's heart dropped to her gut like a bird from the sky. "What do you mean?" she asked, bracing for the worst.

"Did you see that ship tearing out of here like a sinner from church? That's the *Dragon*. Fastest pirate ship in the Atlantic. No one knows how it operates or where they got the technology for it, and we were moments away from capturing her when, for the second time today, you ruined everything!"

"But what about Jacques? Where is Jacques?" She had to know. She couldn't wait another second.

"He is still aboard the *Dragon*; you fool. They have stolen our captain and our rum and half our supply of water." Her gut twisted over on itself. She had imagined a warm and loving reunion, now that all of the danger was behind them and the pirates thwarted. Since she helped in the final battle, surely all would be forgiven, and they could start anew. Especially now that she realized she didn't want to fly without him. She didn't want to do anything without him.

"You don't think he's—" she couldn't finish the sentence. She didn't even want to think of the possibility of not seeing him again.

"He's not dead if that's what you're getting at. Douleur will try to ransom him off, but I doubt King and country will go for that. So she'll give him a choice, be branded part of her crew or tortured to death. Laviolette isn't stupid. He'll stay alive one way or another." She leapt at this news. He wasn't dead. She could hold onto that. She did not kill him, so he was just fine. He could handle pirates. They just had to ransom him. He would be fine.

"Well, for goodness sakes, let's go get him and the rum and water, Vuitton! That is a simple mission."

"You, my dear, are the only thing simple around here. They are already halfway to North Carolina by now, and that is British country. We have no jurisdiction in that aetherspace. Our orders are to return to Montreal with the fleet. They are already several hours ahead of us, and we must catch them or pray for rain if we want to make it without dying of thirst." He turned to his men now. "Put her in the brig. I'm done with her. I don't care how good her aim is."

"You aren't going after Jacques at all? What happened to leave no man behind?"

"No, *m'lady*. We are not going after *Jacques,*" he said the name with a sneer. "The admiral will never agree to it. There are far more important things at stake here. Invading British aerspace and starting up a new war with those technology thieves is not worth the life of one man, no matter how fine a captain he is. If Laviolette wishes to return, he'll find his own way."

"You can't be serious!" Marguerite kept herself together for the better part of the harrowing day, but this pronouncement of idiotic policy was the last straw. "There must be some sort of provision for rescuing a fellow aermen. What if it were you out there? How is he supposed to find his own way?"

"Lady Vadnay, I'm hardly the person you should be angry about over this. I do not make the policy; I simply follow it. Captain Laviolette is no longer our concern, and it's your fault."

Chapter Eighteen

The brig was everything Marguerite feared it would be—a wooden bench to sit and sleep on, no window, a bucket for personal business, and bread and water for meals. She kept forcing herself to focus on the positive aspects of being locked up. Luckily she was the only aerman in custody. No pirates had been taken prisoner. They either fell in battle or escaped to their own ship. They also let Outil keep Marguerite's goggles, and Outil was allowed to bring her a book and a blanket. Plus there were only three days left before arriving in Montreal.

The only other problem was that Montreal was three days in the wrong direction, and the book was less than exciting—*The Mating Habits of West Indian Green Vervet Monkeys and Other Odd Creatures*. Marguerite read it cover to cover the first day. Then she spent the whole of the next day crying, which earned her a hankie from the guard on duty. By the third day, she gave up feeling sorry for herself and read the book again. She found little solace in the fact that mountain chickens were actually frogs and quite tasty roasted over an open fire, or that vampire bats would only drink one ounce of blood at a time and were meant to be called butterfly mice. All she desperately wanted to know was whether Jacques was alive or not and if he would ever forgive her.

Late on day three, while wondering if she could train a magnificent frigatebird to carry cargo, Outil stopped by to visit her. "I brought medicinal salve for Lady Vadnay," Outil addressed the half asleep man in the little wooden chair.

"Sure, fine," he snorted back without waking. Outil handed a little crock through the bars. Marguerite took it and eagerly rubbed it into her rough red cheeks and forehead.

"How are things going above? We must be nearly home," Marguerite said.

"Yes, the harbor is in view, m'lady." Outil answered directly, but she was watching the guard, who was not paying attention, out of the corner of her gleaming copper eye.

"What is it?" Marguerite whispered.

Outil held up a hand and continued to speak in a normal voice. "They will most likely escort you from the ship directly to the holding cells in town, m'lady. I have sent word to your father, and he should be there to meet us."

Marguerite wondered what it was her bot really wanted to tell her, but in the meantime, she played along. "Ugh! My father. I didn't even think about having to face him. What will he say?" She put her head in her hands and waited for Outil's next move.

"I'm certain he will be understanding m'lady."

A voice called from up the stairs to the guard sitting half asleep on his chair. He snorted and called back. "You're needed on level three for check in," the voice said.

"What about this prisoner?" the guard called back.

"Forget her. She's not going anywhere. Come on!" The voice was insistent.

The guard looked at Outil and then Marguerite and said, "No funny business." He jingled the keys clipped to his belt. Marguerite wondered if he was trying to make some sort of point about who was in power, or if he was just insecure and felt a little jingle might help ease his nerves.

She rolled her eyes as he tromped up the stairs. "Did you have something to do with that? What is going on?" She whispered, even though the guard was long out of earshot.

"I made a few friends while you were away on the *Henrietta*. I also worked closely with Captain Laviolette and was privy to a few conversations I don't think he intended me to hear."

Marguerite looked back at the stairwell and then nodded, "Go on, what does this have to do with me being incarcerated?"

"Well, it doesn't really, but I know you are worried about him, and I just thought you should know that I am quite positive he is not dead." Outil tipped her head and watched Marguerite's face.

"That is very nice that you are *quite positive*, Outil, but that doesn't actually get him home or get me out of jail. What did you hear?" Marguerite sighed in exasperation and sat back on her wooden bench, arms folded.

"I don't want you to think less of me, m'lady, but I heard a few things, and I read a few things."

"You *read* a few things? Outil, did you go snooping in Jacques's personal papers?" Marguerite was very interested now.

"Possibly. But only the ones he left sitting out in his room. He sent me there to fetch instruments a few times. I couldn't help but see a couple of wireless telegraphs from before we left Montreal," the bot actually looked sheepish.

Marguerite was on the edge of her plank now, "What did they say? Who were they from?"

"Both were from Montreal, some admiral there. At first, I thought they were written in code. But after the skirmish with the pirates, I realized they probably weren't."

"Outil! What did they say?"

"The first said: Capture the *Dragon* and bring her home. The second must have been in reply to a question of some sort. It said: Orders as follows. Use any means necessary to capture the *Dragon*. I also heard him speaking to his first officer about the *plan* a few times. It was obvious that whatever they were talking about wasn't common knowledge or the plan to escort the fleet home."

"So, you think they were referring to the pirate ship *Dragon*? Not an actual mythical beast?" She rolled her eyes. Her long days reading about monkeys had made her more snarky than usual.

"Lady Vadnay, I believe Jacques is alive and may have planned not to leave that ship, and I don't believe any of it was your fault. Of course, other things were your fault, but that's not important right now."

Marguerite returned her head to her hands. Her hair was still wrapped in the turban, but she smelled of chemicals, and in spite of Outil's cream, her face was still tender to the touch. She thought for a moment about what Outil was saying. It was a small bit of hope, but she wasn't sure if she should grab onto it. Was it enough to sustain her? If so, then what should she do with it? She felt her chest begin to tighten, and her eyes begin to water once more.

"M'lady? I know you don't want anyone to think that you are in love, or that you care for Jacques, or possibly anyone, deeply. But I want you to know that you are at your best when you let yourself care for those around you." Outil's words hit the very center of Marguerite's heart. Of course, the automaton, the non-human, was right. But Marguerite didn't want her to be right. She didn't want to be in love. It was too messy, too painful. But she also didn't want to think about a life without Jacques. She stood up and walked to the gate facing her bot. "Outil, you have to get me out of here."

"M'lady, if you just wait until we meet with your father, I'm sure he will find a way to have you released."

"No, Outil, you have to get me out now. It could take weeks to rectify this mess, and in the meantime, we will be losing more and more of our advantage."

"I do not understand, Lady Vadnay," Outil shook her metal head.

"We need two chutes, paper, and autopen, and I'll need a change of clothes. Wait, no. These clothes will be fine. Can you get the rest to me tonight? We will be disembarking in the morning, and by then it will be too late."

"Yes, I can procure those items, but m'lady, I don't understand what you intend to do."

"We're going to save Jacques!"

Chapter Nineteen

Marguerite sat waiting for her guard to fall asleep. She'd had this guard the first night of her stay. She was thrilled to see him return for the shift tonight because, while she had a terrible time sleeping on the wooden bench, he had no problem tipping his head back and snoring the night away on his hard chair. Just as she guessed, only a few moments after his snores reached a fever pitch, Outil came creeping down the stairs.

Marguerite met her at the cell door and waited patiently as Outil picked the lock with one of her tool fingers. The mechanism eventually *clicked* into place, and the door swung open quietly. Marguerite scurried out, leaving her turban in a wad on the bench with the blanket heaped next to it in hopes that the guard wouldn't be immediately alarmed should he wake in the night.

Outil locked the door again; the second *click* brought a snort from the guard, but nothing more. Then they raced up the stairs as quietly as possible. Outil led her to a deserted bunk room where she'd stashed their packs. Leave it to Outil to think of food and water. Marguerite was desperate for more than bread to eat, but she took the pencil and paper first and scratched out a quick letter to her father.

"We must drop this in the post bag before we go." One of the perks of being in the military was that there was no charge for posting letters from a vessel in service. Marguerite guessed the Renegade was still considered in service, and this was the best way to contact her father without raising suspicions.

"There is a drop slot on the way to the deck, but we must hurry. They will be changing shifts soon, and we don't have much time." Marguerite nodded in agreement and strapped on her supply pack and then her chute over the top of it. She would just have to wait a few more hours to eat real food. The two set off down a long corridor for the opposite end of the ship. Outil led the way and stopped only for Marguerite to drop her folded paper in the mailbag. She prayed that her father would understand, not only her cryptic missive but the reasons behind it.

They stayed quiet and kept their heads down. Most of the crew was sleeping soundly tonight, knowing a triumphant return home awaited them in the morning. There were a tense few moments when they came upon other aermen in the passages and thought they would be caught, but everyone was either deliriously tired or deliriously full of drink. All was quiet until they approached the hatch to the deck. They heard uproarious laughter and the sounds of singing above. "Oh, dear," Marguerite said.

Outil stuck her head out the hatch for a moment, and then returned. "I believe there is a celebration underway."

"Right. I didn't think about that. They usually have some sort of deck party the night of arrival. Blast it. Can we get out without them seeing us?"

"The only light appears to be coming from a barrel containing a fire at the starboard bow."

"Well, isn't that brilliant. Light up a fire on the deck of a dirigible full of explosive gasses. Where do they find these ninnies?" Marguerite paused, and then her eyes lit up with inspiration, "Outil! This is perfect. Run to the nearest pipecom and call in to the controls that there is a fire on deck. That should give us enough of a diversion to jump ship."

"Excellent point, m'lady. Only, I wish you'd reconsider this whole plan. I'm sure your father—"

"If I wanted my father to fix everything in my life, I never would have left home in the first place, Outil. Now hurry! I'd go myself, but I'm meant to be in a cell at the bottom of this beastly boat."

"That is true." Outil seemed somewhat defeated as she turned and trotted down the steps to the nearest pipecom. Marguerite could hear her soft voice reporting the violators to the commanding officers. Then she heard the rumble of agitation deep in the ship as the guards were awoken from their beds to deal with imbeciles. And finally, she heard Outil's footsteps softly padding back up the stairs. "We should go now, m'lady. Guards are already making their way to the starboard deck entrance," Outil whispered.

"Right," Marguerite replied with a nod. They crept up the stairs until they could see the raucous men and their foolish fire. They could just barely make out the trap door for the opposite side of the ship flying open through the dark, but they definitely heard when the guards began to shout at the wrongdoers. "Now!" Marguerite hissed to Outil.

They climbed the rest of the way out of their hole and headed straight for the side of the ship. Marguerite paused, her breath catching in her throat, as the cold air hit her face and the sight of Montreal so far below began to register in her mind. This was going to be a very long drop. Outil already had one leg over the side. "M'lady, you must go now, or they will see us, and you will be taken back to jail. We won't have another chance like this."

"I know; I'm coming."

"Would you like me to go first, or would you?"

"Together, we go together." The noises behind them were growing. It seemed the party goers weren't too keen on ending their celebration. "On three," Marguerite offered. "One, two ..." she threw a leg over the side as well. "Three!" She nearly shouted the last number; she was so nervous. And as she left the safety of the deck behind her, it occurred to her all at once that she had no idea how to activate her chute.

"Outil!" She yelled at her bot, but it was too late. Outil had drifted sideways and the rushing wind blowing up at them was deafening. The lights twinkling on the docks and reflecting in the river below her were growing nearer much too quickly. She knew there was no way to make sure she would hit the water. Even if she did, it wasn't deep enough, and she was falling too fast for a safe dive. She groped at the straps for anything, a button, dial, anything. There was nothing but a tiny ring. Outil's chute opened suddenly, black as the night. It caught the wind, and she shot up while Marguerite continued to fall like a cannon ball. The funny thing was, Marguerite thought she heard Outil yell, "Pull!"

So Marguerite grabbed the little ring and pulled as hard as she could. The ground below her instantly stopped shooting up to meet her. The black chute exploded open with a whoosh and carried her on the wind toward Outil and the wooded northern shore of the Saint Lawrence. She took a moment to close her eyes and breathe in the deep cool of the night air and calm her heart. This was going to work.

She watched Outil fall gently into the trees below, and she braced herself for the same. Her feet scraped the leaves harmlessly at first, then she dipped farther, and her legs began to catch on larger limbs. As she descended deeper into the foliage, she realized just how fast she was going. She tried to brace herself, but she was dipping lower into the forest and hitting trees left and right as she went. She tried not to cry out, but every time she bounced off her already injured shoulder, she couldn't help but squeal in pain.

Within seconds, her body tore through the woods at full speed, snagging on every branch and limb until she hit the massive trunk of a pine tree and slid straight for the ground. Her harness jerked her to a stop as her chute finally caught on a limb, leaving her dangling a good ten feet off the ground. "Isn't this lovely," she said out loud. "I am fairly certain that every landing I make is going to be a complete disaster."

"Outil!" Marguerite hissed through the darkness. "Outil, where are you?" After what seemed like an eternity of hanging, the bushes below rustled, and Outil stumbled free of their tightly woven branches. "Oh good, I was afraid I'd have to start screaming for help or some such. I can't quite reach a limb for leverage, and I can't unbuckle the straps. It's too tight with me hanging on it."

"I'm not entirely sure I know how to help you, m'lady," Outil called out. "Well, just climb up here and, I don't know, pull me to safety or something." Marguerite gestured with her hands in exasperation. "And keep your voice down. We aren't that far from the outskirts of Montreal. There's no telling who could be lurking out here."

"My ability to climb trees is not as refined as it should be, m'lady. I can try, but I think we'd be better suited with another plan," the bot whispered as best she could. "Have you decided what we are going to attempt to do next, m'lady?"

"I thought that would be obvious, Outil. We are going to go see Claude."

Chapter Twenty

Marguerite kicked her legs and tried harder to swing herself to the closest branch, but it was no use. She couldn't get enough momentum, and the branches were too far away on either side of her. "As much as I would enjoy seeing my creator again, I'm not sure how visiting Master Claude can help us in our predicament," Outil answered.

"Who else do we know in this wild place who has access to weapons, ships, and owes me a favor?" Marguerite tried squirming out of her harness once more.

"Forgive me, m'lady, but why does he owe you a favor?" Outil asked, hands on hips, gazing up.

"Well, because we grew up together. You are always in debt to your childhood friends, aren't you? And because he will owe me favors for the rest of his life for not making his feelings clear before he left France and ran off to marry someone else," she barked.

"But, m'lady, you don't want to get married." Outil sounded genuinely confused.

"That is beside the point. He is an old friend, and I can trust him. If we can find our way to his new home, we can use his supplies and communication devices and put together a plan."

"I suppose that makes sense." Outil picked up a formidable branch from the forest floor. "Maybe if I push you with this branch you will be able to reach the limb nearest you?"

"Did you happen to pack any weapons in these packs, Outil?" Marguerite asked as she suddenly stilled. "Yes, m'lady, a pistol each, why do you ask?" Outil carried her piece of wood to the base of the tree and lifted it up.

"Because you might want to get yours out. There is a man watching us from the bushes just in front of me."

Outil dropped the limb and had her pistol out in lightening speed. She stood between Marguerite's dangling form and the man who was now stepping out into the clearing to face them. He was very tall, and as best as Marguerite could tell in the dark, he appeared to be dressed in simple leather breeches and coat. She guessed they were homemade by the looks of them. He had a dark complexion and long black hair that fell at his shoulders. He also had a very large, very modern looking rifle strapped over his shoulder and a pair of goggles around his neck.

He held up one hand, indicating peace, but kept the other hand on the gun at his side. He stayed at the edge of the clearing around Marguerite's tree. She couldn't speak; she was so afraid. Two shots from the weapon at his side and both she and Outil would be dead. Actually, it would probably take four or five shots to get Outil, and she might get a shot off at him in the meantime, but Marguerite was a dangling duck, ready for the killing.

Outil was the first to break the silence. "Who are you, and what do you want?"

The man replied with a strange accent Marguerite had never heard before, "I should be the one asking who you are and what you are doing on my land."

"Your land?" Marguerite couldn't help but spit the words out. "This property belongs to King Louis."

"Oh no, it doesn't. Not as of four days ago. Your King of France signed a treaty with my nation, and this land belongs to the Iroquois."

"Iroquois? Are you a native then?" Marguerite couldn't hide her excitement at meeting a real, live native person. She'd spent countless hours poring over books about indigenous peoples discovered in all the new worlds around the globe. Her favorite, by far, were in New France. And now here she was, dangling above a heavily armed man, stepped right from the pages of one of her books. Except, he didn't seem backward at all. Other than his simple dress and uncut hair, he was altogether very modern. And handsome—she couldn't help noticing that, too. He cut an amazing figure by the moonlight; broad shoulders, bulging arms, a perfectly square jaw, and aquiline nose.

"I am Iroquois, and my people are native to this land, but we are not *native* in the way you suggest." His voice was proud and sharp. He glowered at them and repeated his question. "What are you doing on our land?"

"I'm ever so glad they signed a treaty. This is wonderful news. However, does that mean you are in league with the French officials? Or, rather, are you going to turn us in for trespassing? Because, I'd really prefer that you not. Maybe you could help me get down from this tree, and then we'd be happy to leave your land as quickly as possible."

"We have our own officials and our own laws. We do not need the usurpers of Montreal to handle our affairs for us," he sneered.

Outil uncocked her pistol and let the barrel shift to the ground. "We did not mean to land in this particular location, sir. We were disembarking the ship over there and caught an unexpected current."

Brilliant! Marguerite silently cheered Outil on.

"Would you be so kind as to help me cut my mistress down?" she asked.

"I could do that," he replied. "But I also want you to tell me what you want with Monsieur Claude."

"You know Claude?" Marguerite practically squealed. "This is wonderful!" The man lifted his gun a bit and widened his stance.

"Lady Vadnay, I'm not sure this is good news." Outil lifted her pistol once again. "It might not be the same Claude."

"Of course, it is the same Claude," Marguerite snapped." He's a famous inventor, the best in this part of the world. Everyone knows him because he can build anything. Also, because he has a horrible wife." Outil shot a quick look at Marguerite.

"What? I'm sure she is horrible. I mean, I hope she's not, but anyone who'd snatch a man up that quickly has to be horrible."

"I know Monsieur Claude of whom you speak. He is a great engineer and a friend to my people. We have made many trades with him in the past year, and he has taken care of our needs. It is in part because of him that we have our land back. If your intentions are not of the purest good, I will shoot you before I take you anywhere near his home." Marguerite was stunned. She knew none of this about her friend. They had exchanged a few letters over the past few months, but the post wasn't reliable by air or land, and he'd never mentioned anything about native relations.

"The last thing in the world I want to do is harm Claude. He is a dear friend of mine. We grew up together. I've found myself in a bit of a pickle, and I need his help is all. I know he's not far from here. Can you please just help me down and point us in the right direction?" A bird called from somewhere off to the left. The tall man cupped one hand over his mouth and repeated the cry perfectly; then she heard someone running from that direction toward them. Marguerite's heart almost burst with excitement.

More natives! I mean, Iroquois! If only they don't kill us, this will be the best day of my life! Another man, slightly shorter than the first, appeared in the clearing. After staring for a moment, he raised his eyebrows at the first man. Marguerite could only imagine what it must look like to see a woman in a man's uniform hanging from a tree and a bot with a tiny pistol pointed at them. The two men exchanged a few words in their language. The second man, also carrying a very modern gun, took a battle stance and pointed his own gun at Outil, then motioned for her to lower her own.

The first man swung his gun to his back and walked toward the tree, climbing the trunk like he did it every day of his life. As he reached the branch above Marguerite where her chute was tangled, he spoke. "I will help you down, and I will take you to Monsieur Claude, and he will decide what to do with you." He pulled a huge knife out of his belt and sliced through the harness with one swift movement. Marguerite fell into Outil's waiting arms, and the man scaled back down the tree without a sound, her chute in hand. He said something to his companion and then motioned for Outil and Marguerite to follow the smaller man through the woods.

Outil set Marguerite down carefully, and they did as they were told. The man behind them reached over his shoulder and grabbed the gun from his back, then used it to poke Marguerite from behind. She turned on him, surprised and angry at the rough treatment. "Is that really necessary? I am walking as you said."

"Give me your packs, and that gun." He poked Marguerite again.

"You really needn't do that." She gladly peeled off the heavy pack and handed it to him. Outil did the same with hers.

"That was for what you said about Madame Claude. She is a lovely woman with many gifts. He is lucky to have her."

Marguerite scowled. Suddenly the man didn't look as handsome as before, now that he was looking down on her with such disapproval. "I'm sure she is just wonderful," she replied.

"She is. And she doesn't get stuck in trees either." He poked her side with his gun, indicating it was time to move on. Marguerite swatted the barrel away and stomped after Outil and the other stranger. It hurt to stomp, but she did it anyway. Her whole body hurt. She needed a hot bath and a real bed. Also, real food would be very, very nice. Whatever kind of woman Claude had married, Marguerite hoped she was, at least, a good cook.

Eventually, they came to a clearing and a trail of sorts. Two strange contraptions sat off to one side, almost concealed by bushes, but the chrome and brass work sparkled, giving away their position. The first man pulled on a handle and rolled one machine out into the clearing. Now that Marguerite could see it more clearly, she realized it was like a mini autocart, but with only two wheels and a long seat connecting them. The smaller man swung a leg over the seat and straddled it like a horse. He pushed a few levers and slid his goggles into place as a small motor came to life, coughing steam.

"What is that?" Marguerite admired the fine workmanship and brass details.

It's a steamcycle. Get on," the first man said as he pointed Outil toward the machine. "Ride quietly and we'll get there quickly." Outil looked a bit taken aback. She turned to Marguerite, who nodded. They really didn't have any choice but to do as the men said and hope that they were telling the truth. The bot climbed on behind the first man, awkward and unsure of the movements. Marguerite had never considered that her bot hadn't been programmed to ride anything but an autocart or carriage. She'd have to talk to Claude about some sort of equine programming. It would be handy should they ever wish to ride horses, or these amazing machines again. The first man pulled his own matching machine from the bushes and pointed for Marguerite to get on first. "I'm sorry; I have no idea how to operate this thing," she said.

"You're not going to drive. I just want to keep my eye on you." His face was stone cold serious. Marguerite was suddenly grateful for her flight suit as she threw a leg over the contraption and looked for a place to hold on. The Iroquois man did the same, one hand on the steering handles and one wrapped around her waist.

"Oh!" she cried as he pressed close to her back. He was so warm, it felt so good, but it was so improper. "This isn't exactly ... " she started. But he flipped a few switches, and the machine roared to life. He pulled his goggles down, and they took off, moving faster than Marguerite had ever traveled over land in her life.

The trail before them was narrow enough that she could have reached out and struck a tree on either side of them, but they flew by so quickly she didn't dare for fear of losing an arm altogether. Instead, she closed her eyes and tried not to think about the strong hand holding her ribs, or the fact that the only thing she had to hold onto was that arm, or the fact that his clothes were handmade leather and so soft she didn't want to let them go. She also tried not to think about how warm the man was or the fact that he smelled amazing—an earthy smell mixed with strong spices and herbs she couldn't identify.

Jacques. Must think about Jacques, she chided herself. The night wore on for quite awhile. Eventually, the trail opened up onto a road, and as best she could tell, they were heading farther away from the city and deeper into the northwestern wilds of

New France. If she remembered correctly from his letters, this was the general direction to Claude's settlement. She had never been there, so she didn't know for certain. Eventually, she got brave and turned her head to ask, "How far is it?"

Unfortunately, when he leaned down to hear her over the engine noise, his ear and goggle strap brushed Marguerite's lips. His thick hair, flying in the wind, wrapped around her head and she was engulfed in his amazing smell. Marguerite's heart fluttered and swelled in her chest. She tried to stop from thoroughly enjoying herself, but she couldn't help it. Luckily the wind blew cold and fast in her face, keeping her from completely forgetting herself. His reply did not help her at all.

"We will arrive before the moon is set. You should rest your eyes. I will not let you fall."

Marguerite's heart fluttered. It had been so long since she and Jacques had been this close. And even then, they were never this close for so long. She reminded herself that she did not know this stranger at all. He could be one of those horrid scalp stealers she'd read about on the open plains or a mercenary with no conscience. What she really wished right now, more than anything, was that he was Jacques. That they were safe together on this amazing machine, flying away to explore some remote area of New France. She squeezed her eyes shut and sent up a prayer for his safety. He had to be alive; he just had to. And she would find him, no matter what it took. She turned back to the man's ear, her lips ready for the close contact this time; her heart steeled against unfaithful thoughts. "What is your name?" she asked.

"Otetiani," he answered.

"Pleased to meet you." Her manners kicked in out of habit.

"We shall see," his voice rumbled low through the noise of the steamcycle. Marguerite closed her eyes, pretended like it was Jacques holding her, and let exhaustion have its way. The steamcycle came to a sudden stop. Marguerite's eyes burst open, and she sat up, instantly aware of her proximity to Otetiani. The Iroquois man sat back and released her waist, then climbed off the cycle, balancing it with one hand. They were at a settlement. A modest single story home sat in front of a modest barn, and a rickety fence held a goat and a horse in the side yard. The door to the home opened, and an autolight appeared to illuminate the night. Outil climbed off the back of the other cycle immediately and walked up to the light. A familiar voice called out.

"Outil, what are you doing here?"

Marguerite jumped from the cycle as delicately as she could and ran to the light. "Claude!"

Chapter Twenty-One

Claude gathered Outil into one arm and Marguerite into the other. "Marguerite! How do you know Otetiani, and what are you doing here in the middle of the night? Is everything alright?" Marguerite was so tired and travel weary; she almost began to sob, but she remembered herself and took a deep breath.

"I only just met Monsieur Otetiani. Thanks to your reputation, he was kind enough to cut me out of a tree and give me a ride here." She nodded to the tall, dark man.

"These women were trespassing on the north shore. They claimed to be looking for you and seemed to be in a bit of trouble," Otetiani said. "I see it is true that you know them."

"Yes, thank you so much for bringing them here. Outil is my first sentient autobot, and Marguerite is my oldest friend. But, what has happened to your face? And your hair?" He held the light up to Marguerite and gazed at her rough red skin and matted hair with wonder. Marguerite touched her cheek in embarrassment and then tried to smooth back her wild tresses.

"It is a very long story. Suffice it to say, Outil and I can't stay very long, but we need a great favor."

Claude nodded, his face furrowed with concern. "Let's get you inside out of the cold and we can talk there." Marguerite realized he was right. It was freezing. She'd been cold for a week straight now, and the thought of a warm fire in a snug little home was very welcome.

"Make yourself at home. Louisa is sleeping, but I'll be in shortly. Let me take care of these gentlemen." She looked at the two natives and tried to match them with the word gentlemen. It was a stretch, but Claude using the word to describe them brought them up a few pegs in her mind. If he called them gentlemen, then there was no way they were scalp stealers or mercenaries. She wondered what her father, or any of the upper classes of France, would say if she walked into a ball with Otetiani on her arm. My, but he was handsome.

Outil put an arm around her mistress and gently coaxed her toward the front door of Claude's home. "Come, Lady Vadnay, Master Claude is right. You need to get out of the cold."

She took a few steps with Outil, then stopped and turned around. Claude was shaking arms heartily with Otetiani and his companion. They spoke in low tones, some in French, some in what Marguerite guessed was Iroquois. She walked up to the three men and curtsied low.

"Thank you, Monsieur Otetiani, for your service and kindness. It will not be forgotten." She smiled as prettily as she could and tried not to think about the state of her face, hair, and clothes. She was a Lady of France, and no matter how many court marshals she faced, she would still behave like one in good company.

"It was my pleasure to serve any friend of Monsieur Claude's, Lady Vadnay." His somber face broke into a crooked smile, and Marguerite knew it was time for her to leave before she swooned again. She nodded to his companion who nodded back, then she turned on a dime and marched herself into Claude's home.

The main room was bigger than she expected. The kitchen, sitting room, and dining room were all one large space. A fire was dying in the hearth of a rock fireplace that sat in the middle of the room. Outil immediately grabbed a few logs from a stack on the floor and stoked it back to life. Marguerite let her eyes wander over the simple, sparse furnishings. She noticed a rocking chair in one corner that looked more comfortable than anything else. Nothing was upholstered. Everything was handmade; she suspected by Claude.

She was correct; the chair was comfortable even though it wasn't soft. And the fire roared to life quickly. She heard a clicking sound and a whir from somewhere in the chimney. She got up to investigate and found a fan of sorts attached to the stone wall. A small box next to it was rigged with some sort of wiring and a thermometer. "Brilliant, as usual," Marguerite said.

"What is it?" Outil asked.

"Claude has rigged a thermostat and a fan into this fireplace so that it will blow the warm air back out into the room when it reaches a certain temperature. What will he do next?" The front door opened, and Claude walked in with his lamp. Marguerite heard the steam cycles roar to life outside and then recede into the distance. She couldn't help it. She made her way back to his side and hugged him again.

"Oh, Claude! It's so good to see you! I swear you've grown taller," she whispered in excitement. He was still the same height, but his face was tanned a deep brown, and his clothes were shabby and worn. He had the look of a man who spent many, many hours working out of doors. Of course, he'd grown up working outside, putting in long hours, but he still had the carefree smile of youth.

"It is good to see you too, Marguerite. But I swear you are much dirtier!" he teased. He smiled down at her, but as a voice came from the back of the house, his expression turned dark, and he immediately let his arms fall from about Marguerite's slim frame.

"So, this is the famous Lady Vadnay?" A female voice filled the room.

Marguerite turned to see a girl about her own age standing at the doorway of what must be their bedroom. She was small as well, but thicker in frame. Her light brown hair hung in an unkempt braid over her shoulder quite a ways, and beneath her white nightgown, her belly protruded in a huge, round bump.

"I've heard so much about you. You just can't imagine what a treat this is for me." Her words were welcoming, but her tone was annoyed.

Marguerite faltered for a moment, and then bowed to her hostess and smiled. "I'm ever so glad to make your acquaintance," she lied.

"Louisa, you should not be out of bed." Claude rushed to her side and put an arm around her, a worried look on his face.

"No, I really should have on my finest to welcome *Lady Vadnay* to our humble home, but as you can see, it is the middle of the night, and we weren't expecting you. I hope you will forgive us."

"Of course," Marguerite answered quickly. "There is nothing to forgive. We are so sorry to intrude on you at such a late hour, and in your condition." Marguerite indicated the woman's protruding belly. "Claude, I had no idea! I suppose congratulations are in order?" She kept her tone light and civil, but her heart clenched in a fit of emotion. Claude was going to be a father.

"It's quite alright. We've just had a few complications, and Louisa is supposed to stay in bed until the baby comes, but she keeps insisting on getting up." He laughed nervously.

"When we have important company like this, I can't very well stay in my bed and miss the fun or make them feel uncared for." She smiled at her husband, but the smile did not meet her eyes. "What can I get for you two?"

"Nothing at all," Outil was quick to speak. "We are quite well. Lady Marguerite will need a place to sleep for the night, and I will await daylight to recharge."

"Of course, she will," Louisa said. "Claude, dear, can I speak with you in our room?"

Marguerite sat down in the rocking chair as the couple left the doorway to talk privately. She rested back in the fine wood and closed her eyes as she heard bits and pieces of their conversation. Things like, "Who does she think she is?" and, "I suppose you are going to give her my bed? They are not sleeping in my baby's room," came from the behind the closed door in a shrill female voice. Claude's voice was much calmer and measured, but she heard him say, "She can't be expected to sleep in the barn like a common mule," and, "Of course I don't want to share the bed with her! Don't be obscene." At that, Marguerite looked at Outil and stood.

"Claude, we'll be heading out to the barn now so you can get some sleep. We can talk in the morning. So very sorry we bothered you tonight," she called. Claude came jogging out and put an arm on her shoulder, his face apologetic. "No, no. That won't be necessary. There is no heat out there, and we've run out of straw. The loft is warm and dry. There are no mattresses yet, but we have quilts and pillows to spare." He directed them to a ladder off the kitchen wall. "I'm so very sorry, Marguerite."

"Claude, stop. You had no idea we were coming. I'm just grateful to be here and to be safe. Thank you for having us. I've slept in far worse places over the last month. Believe me."

"Oh, I do," he said with a smirk. "I can't wait to hear your tale in the morning. Sleep well." Marguerite climbed the ladder while Outil chose to stand at the window in order to soak in the first rays of sunlight to recharge her battery. The loft was warm and dry as he'd said, and a stack of neatly sewn quilts sat in one corner. Marguerite set to work making herself a bed, and Claude eventually tossed a pillow and her pack up to her.

She thanked him and set to work peeling off her boots. She decided while she was at it, she would get out of the wretched flight suit as well. She tossed it in a pile by the ladder, along with her socks and boots. Outil would be able to wash them in the morning. In the meantime, Marguerite would curl up in this giant mound of quilts and sleep until she couldn't sleep any more.

Marguerite awoke to random voices and the sounds of pots being banged around. She smelled something delicious, but she was too tired to get up. After rolling over and sleeping a few more hours, she finally yawned and stretched at midday. She felt so much better; she almost forgot where she was, why she was there, and the state of her hair.

She rolled toward the ladder and noticed her flight suit was gone. There were no voices coming from below, so she wrapped up in a quilt and carefully climbed down the ladder to find out where her clothes were and if there was any of the source of that amazing smell left to eat. Just as she set foot on the wood plank floor, she heard a gasp. Marguerite turned to see Louisa, fully dressed now in bonnet and prairie skirts, standing at the fireplace staring at her.

"Good morning. I was wondering if you had any idea where my clothes may have got off to?" Marguerite smiled and tried to keep her voice light. Louisa did not.

"Your clothes have been burned. They were making the whole house smell of rotted animal carcass, and I just can't have that in my condition."

"Right. I'm so very sorry about that. Should you be out of bed?"

"No, I should not. But who else is going to wait on your needs, m'lady?"

"I have Outil for that. Do you know where she might have gone off to?"

"She's with Claude in the barn. But you cannot go out there like *that*." She indicated the quilt. "And I'd rather not have you traipsing around my home dragging my grandmother's handiwork all over the floor either." Marguerite adjusted the bottom of the quilt, pulling it off the floor and tighter around her shoulders. This was getting ridiculous.

"I'm sorry, Louisa, but what would you have me do? Hmm?" Marguerite was beginning to lose patience. Her stomach ached for real food, and her head ached from the rough week. She just wanted a moment of peace.

"I'd have you go back to France, marry a rich lord or prince, and stay there." Louisa's tone was serious. She hobbled to the kitchen and pulled a loaf of bread and a crock of cheese from the larder.

"I'm sorry, but I just don't understand why you are so venomous toward me. This is our first meeting, and Claude is one of my dearest friends. I was hoping you and I might be friends as well."

"You have a very funny way of showing your friendship. We are up here scraping by, day to day, trying to carve a life out for ourselves, while you sit down there in your fancy school with your bot and your riches, learning how to fly and generally making a mess of everything you touch," Louisa practically spat out the last words. "I've heard all the stories about you. He thinks you walk on water. He thinks you are the best thing since the steam engine. He thinks you are going to rule the world someday."

Marguerite couldn't quite believe the waves of jealousy this woman was emitting. She had met a few people in her lifetime that didn't like her, but this was a whole new level. And seeing herself through Claude's eyes this way was making her a bit ill.

"But I—" She tried to defend herself.

"But nothing. Let me tell you what I think. I know your type. You are rich, spoiled, and careless. You think about no one but yourself. Do you know what we could have done with the money you took from us? Money you didn't even need. Do you know that because we can't afford bots or even the parts to scrap one together, that I had to work the fields through my last pregnancy and that our first baby didn't survive? Did you know that this time around, I had to keep to my bed, and Claude had to harvest everything on his own when he couldn't trade for help? Did you know that we owe so much to the Iroquois Nation now that we will never be able to leave this place? I wouldn't be surprised if they showed up at the door and demanded our child next."

Louisa was red in the face now. Sweat trickled down her forehead, and she sucked in heavy breaths while she held the counter's edge for support.

"Listen," Marguerite said, "I'm terribly sorry. I didn't know about any of that. There are a lot of things I can help you with, but I think you need to lie down now. I can tell you the whole story, and we can start fresh. I can even have money sent here as soon as I can order it."

"Of course you didn't know." She slammed the bread down hard on the table. "Claude would never in a million years ask you for any help; he had to work his whole life to get away from you. A good friend would know that." She held her belly and grimaced.

"I really think you need to lie down," Marguerite tried again.

"Don't you tell me what I need." Louisa waddled past her, still holding her giant bump, and went back to the bedroom. After a moment of bewilderment, Marguerite's stomach won her battle of conscience. She didn't want to disturb the woman any further by following her around defending herself, and even if she was going to stand her ground, she needed food first. She went to work cutting off a piece of bread. It was perfect and fresh, made that morning. The cheese must have been from their goat. It was creamy and soft and smelled wonderful. She slathered it on thick and was about to take a bite when she heard Louisa cry from the back room.

"If you want to remain at my house, you'd better come here."

Marguerite took a bite, gathered her quilt up again, and tiptoed into the back section of the home. A small bed sat in the middle of a good-sized room. The bed was just right for two, but not nearly as big as her bed back home in France. In the center of it lay Louisa. Her breathing was still heavy, and beads of sweat dripped down her pale brow. Her whole face had turned ashen, and she squeezed her eyes shut.

"My goodness," Marguerite exclaimed. "I know you hate me, but won't you please let me fetch you something to ease your discomfort? I'm not completely useless, you know. I can fetch Claude or Outil."

"First, put that on." She opened her eyes for a moment and pointed to a dress that had been thrown on the end of the bed. It was light blue and had mud stains along the hem, but it was soft and just about her size. Anything was better than a quilt at this point. "Then you can get Claude, and he will take care of me."

"Are you certain you are going to be alright? You don't need a midwife or some such?"

"There's a wash house out back. You can heat water there, and there is soap and a tub for bathing. There's a cloth for drying as well." She moaned a bit and shifted on the bed.

"Is this for the baby? Do you think the baby is coming? I am in no way qualified to deliver a child."

Louisa took a deep breath and calmed herself then looked at Marguerite. "I wouldn't let you anywhere near me or my baby; it's for you to take a bath. You smell horrible, and I can't stand it another minute. I'll shut my eyes, you get dressed, and for the love of all that is a turned stomach, get cleaned up before you come back in my home."

Marguerite gritted her teeth, forcing herself to be civil to the sharp-tongued woman in front of her. She moved quickly to the side of the bed and dropped the quilt while slipping on the dress. Marguerite was tempted to leave *grandmother's handiwork* in a heap on the dusty floor, but she decided to have pity on the ornery pregnant woman, picked up the quilt and folded it nicely, then laid it on the end of the bed. She was about to leave when Louisa, eyes still closed, said, "You can keep that dress. It's no use to me now."

"Alright, but please, just know that I love Claude like a brother, and I didn't mean for any of those things to happen

to either of you. I will make sure you get his money back."
Marguerite was determined to show this woman that she didn't
know anything about her. She was a good person. She could do
nice things and think of other people.

The answer was half moaned whisper. "Pretty words aren't so
pretty when they are too late. Just go take a bath and tell Claude
to come see to me." When Marguerite didn't move right away,
Louisa added, "Please?"

With that, Marguerite walked out of the room, grabbed her
boots from the loft, and strapped them on as quickly as she could.
Then she grabbed her bread and cheese and slipped out the door.
Outside the air was warm and glowing with sunshine. She jogged
to the barn as quickly as she could and called in. "Claude? Outil?"

"We're here, m'lady!" Outil cried from somewhere deep in
the back. The space was the same size as her father's smithie shop
back in France. Yet only half of it was set up for machine work.
The other half was filled with the implements of a working farm.
Marguerite found her way through the parts and plows to the back
where Outil had called from, but she still couldn't see the pair.

"I think something is wrong with your wife, Claude. You
need to go help her." She stood next to an old autocart with one
hand resting on it. Claude's head suddenly appeared at her feet.

"Oh!" she jumped back in alarm. "What are you doing down
there?" He pushed himself out from under the car, covered in dirt
and bits of straw. Outil came out next.

"Sorry, we were just working on this old beast. Trying to get
it running before the baby comes. What did you say is the matter
with her?" He was brushing off his clothes furiously as he asked.

"Well, for starters she hates me. I don't know what you've been telling her, but she didn't like the sound of any of it. Second of all, she got herself all worked up into a big hissy fit and then started sweating and grabbing at her belly. She wouldn't let me do a thing for her. She said I smelled horrid and ordered me to bathe."

Claude's face was knit with concern. "Outil has been telling me your story. I really can't believe you, Marguerite. You've got more backbone than brains. But yes, I'll go see to my wife, and then we can work out a plan. We'll have you back in the air in no time." He started to jog toward the house. Then he turned backwards and shouted back at her. "You really should take a bath!" Marguerite folded her arms and made a very unladylike noise of frustration.

"I believe the wash house is this way?" Outil offered.

"Not you too. It's as if you all think I had a choice in the matter. Did you tell him I'd been imprisoned?" Marguerite pouted as she followed her bot.

"Yes, I did."

"And did you tell him I nearly died about five times in the last week?" she asked.

"Yes, I did."

"Outil?"

"Yes?"

"Do you think Louisa is going to be all right?"

"I do not know many facts about human childbirth, but I know it can be a precarious situation at times."

"I hope they are both all right," Marguerite said.

"As do I," the bot softly replied.

Chapter Twenty-Two

It took two full hours for Outil to work the last of the knots and pirate goo out of Marguerite's hair and for Marguerite to get back to her idea of cleanliness. She was disappointed to have to put on such a worn old dress after having taken so much care to scrub and primp, but it was better than nothing, and it was clean.

Marguerite emerged from the wash house feeling like a new woman. Outil left her hair down for the sun to dry, and they set off to see how Louisa was feeling and if Claude could help them come up with a plan to save Jacques. They found Claude in the shop working on a small engine on his bench.

"How is she?" Marguerite asked.

"Sleeping now. She is good. I talked to her and got her to eat and drink. She will be fine. We just need to let her rest for now."

"Claude, I hate to even ask anything of you, knowing what

I've put you through already. I'm sorry we even came." She meant every word.

Claude put down his tools and looked her in the eye. "I'm not sorry at all. I'm glad you came. It's time you two women met and got to know each other. Plus, I'd feel terrible if you were in trouble and didn't think you could come to me. You are family, Marguerite, always will be." He picked up his wrench and started tinkering again.

"But Louisa thinks … "

"Please," he sighed. "I need you to understand that she is not always like this. She is just overcome with worry about the baby. She only has one more week before it will be safe to deliver. We just have to get to that point, and I'm sure that once this is all done, she'll be back to her normal self. She is the sweetest person I've ever met, Marguerite. You'll have to come back, or better yet, I'll bring them both to visit you in Montreal." He smiled. *Always an optimist*, Marguerite thought.

"So what do you need from me? Because I have suggestions, but knowing you, you already have your mind made up," Claude asked. Marguerite decided to let the whole wife issue drop and move on.

"Well, we need guns, a ship, and a lot of ammunition."

Claude dropped his work and looked at her with raised eyebrows. "Sounds like you need the Royal Fleet. I don't have any of that here."

"But you could make it." Marguerite pressed. "Jacques said you just finished a commission for the Royal Fleet, a defense system or weapons?"

"Yes, I did, but it wasn't a very big job and only paid enough to get us through the winter, not to stock my workshop. Maybe if I had a couple of months, but there's no way I can do that in a couple of days."

Marguerite folded her arms. "Then what do you suggest? We can't go back to Montreal yet. They'll lock me up again. I am pretty sure I just got myself kicked out of His Majesty's service when I jumped out of the *Renegade*, and my father is going to kill me if I don't get myself killed first."

"Does he know where you are at least?" Claude asked.

"Yes. I sent him a note before we left the boat." She rolled her eyes at his insinuation that she didn't think to let her father know where she was.

"Don't you have any friends down there in the big city that have things like dirigibles and guns?"

"No. I've been spending all of my free time with Jacques when I wasn't in school with a pack of very unladylike ladies."

"I will vouch for her, Master Claude, the other aerwomen weren't very friendly," Outil added. Then Marguerite remembered sitting on the bunk with Lucy her first night on the Henrietta; how kind and helpful she was and her amazing hair.

"I suppose there is Lucy."

"Who is that?" Claude asked. "She served with me on the Henrietta—the ship I was on after Jacques kicked me off the Renegade. Do you have any auto pigeons, Claude? How fast could we get a message to Montreal?"

"I have something better than an auto pigeon. Do you think this Lucy could help you? Does she have an arsenal at her beck and call? And do you know what you are going to do when you get to wherever it is you are going?"

"The pirate Captain Douleur has captured Jacques and is known to live part time in Cape Fear, North Carolina," Outil added.

"Right," Marguerite agreed. "We are going to North Carolina. We will find this Douleur and get Jacques back."

"Captain Douleur?" Claude asked.

"Yes, why? Have you heard of him?" Marguerite pulled up a stool and sat down, hoping for good insight. Claude stood up and started digging through a box of parts under the work table.

"Marguerite, do you know how she got her name?"

"She? Douleur is a woman?" Marguerite asked.

"Yes, and that's not her real name. They call her Captain Douleur because she enjoys torturing those who don't bend to her wishes. Most pirates and privateers do so because they are sick of being mistreated by the royal services of their countries. Being a sailor or an aerman is not an easy life, and you make very little pay."

"Yes, I'm very aware of that fact. Go on," Marguerite added.

"Most pirate ships work as a democracy. If you are captured, you have the choice to join the crew or be dropped off at the nearest port, unless you are a bot, then you are sold. It's a better life for some men than anything they could do legally. All proceeds from plundering are split equally among the crew. The captain gets a bonus, but only because the biggest part of their job is keeping track of the books."

Marguerite gave him a funny look. "They keep books? Like

ledgers and bank notes?"

"It's a very simple, yet highly organized system with benefits the royal establishments can't offer. Pirates are not welcome anywhere in the New World except Cape Fear, North Carolina, and I hear there is a new governor in New York who is welcoming all ships to the harbor there as well."

"So what about Douleur, what is her story?" Marguerite asked. Claude stood up holding an odd shaped gear and a motor box. He opened another box and pulled out a small mechanical swallow.

"This is Hector, my Spanish swallow." Claude smiled and laid the bird out on the work table then proceeded to dissect Hector from top to bottom. "Outil, could you hand me that awl?"

"Yes, Claude." The bot scurried to get the tool and place it in his hand. Claude continued to tinker as he continued his story.

"Captain Douleur is not a normal pirate. She runs a huge crew, and she doesn't take prisoners. You either join her crew, or you die. She is also very battle savvy. She has a tendency to outmaneuver even the most sophisticated of ships with whatever ragtag vessel she's commandeered at the moment. She's an amazing shot, and she doesn't like French officers of any branch. Jacques got himself captured by the wrong woman."

"Well, I'm sure he would just join her crew, then escape at the first chance he could. I plan to be there to meet him." Marguerite leaned forward, fascinated by Claude's skilled movements.

"Oh no, see, that's the thing. She tracks all her men. When you join, you are branded with her mark. The first few *volunteers* who left didn't realize they had signed on for life. She hunted them down and either killed them or tortured them until they

came back. She runs the largest crew in the Atlantic. And because ,
she is fair with wages, no one tries to run away anymore. When
you're too old for service, she grants you leave with a new brand."

"She did have three ships at her command when we ran into
her. One of them was exceedingly fast—*the Dragon*. Have you
heard of it? Do you know how it works?"

"Everyone that studies pirate movements has heard of it,
Marguerite. I'm surprised you haven't."

"Well, I was busy this year studying mechanical engineering
and flight controls," she quickly reminded him.

"Hand me that wrench, please?" Claude pointed to a tiny
wrench by Marguerite's hand.

She gave him the miniature tool and asked, "So, what do you
suggest?"

"I suggest you let the military handle his extraction." He
popped a wing into place and screwed it in.

"They aren't going to do that. Jacques is already on some sort
of probation and apparently getting caught by pirates is not a
favorable move. The first thing I did was ask them to go save him.
They said no, getting servicemen away from pirates is not their
priority. They seem to think that if he wants to be a pirate, then
he can, and if he doesn't, then good luck," she said with disgust.

"Well, then I suggest you go carefully and quietly. Learn the
lay of the land. Find out where he is, and be sure to make friends
wherever you go because I know I can't talk you into not going."

"As opposed to what?" She watched him place a little motor
inside the bird and pop its other wing into place, then close it up
carefully with miniscule screws.

"As opposed to usual Marguerite style—guns blazing and no plan at all," he smiled at her and playfully punched her in the shoulder. "You smell a lot better, by the way."

"Thank you," she said as she watched the little bird come to life in Claude's able hands. It jumped upright and hopped around the table a few times before flapping its wings and coming to rest in front of Claude.

"Not many like Hector these days. Everyone watches for the pigeons and their huge scrolls. If you are in trouble, best to use a smaller, less noticeable messenger." Claude pulled a tiny gilded box out of a drawer in his work table and opened it up. Inside was a scrap of pencil, a stack of tiny papers, and a carrier tube.

"Now, who do you wish to write?"

Chapter Twenty-Three

Marguerite did her best to write her request in legible, yet tiny script on two pieces of the miniature paper. She let Claude affix the tube to the bird, and then he programmed it to fly directly to her father. "Are you sure he will help you with this? Your father isn't that interested in your globetrotting schemes," Claude pointed out.

"My father and I have made great progress over the past year. I know he isn't thrilled with my life choices, but he also agreed to support me when he can."

Claude handed her the little bird. "Would you like to do the honors?"Marguerite took it gingerly in her hands and kissed it for luck before she tossed it into the air and it flew away. "What can we do for your wife?" she asked.

"Louisa is doing all right. She just needs to stay quiet and rest. Maybe you could help me make supper?" Claude suggested.

They spent the rest of the day helping Claude with his settlement, talking about the old days and catching up on the new. Outil helped repair his autocart, and Marguerite successfully avoided Louisa until dinnertime. Louisa grunted as she passed Marguerite on her way back to her room from the washhouse, which was better than the tongue-lashing she'd received earlier that morning.

Marguerite climbed into the loft that night, feeling better than she had in days. Good food and warm blankets made a huge difference. She resolved to do all she could for Claude and his little family while she was there in person. She prayed her father would humor her request as quickly as possible.

In the morning, Outil woke Marguerite early, and they set to work in the kitchen. Marguerite hadn't grown up cooking or cleaning, but she wasn't completely oblivious. She'd picked up enough working her few days in the kitchens of the Henrietta that she could make a decent meat pie. Plus, Outil had been programmed to serve in many different capacities.

Once they got going, they realized that the kitchen, although organized, was in need of a deep cleaning. Outil scrubbed and Marguerite cooked, which allowed Claude more time to work in his shop. Eventually, he came in for breakfast. "This place looks amazing. You two have been working hard. And what is that I smell?" Claude looked pleased, and this made Marguerite glow with pride.

"I made a meat pie and two loaves of bread, and I've got a pot of stew going for tonight," she said. "Outil has been cleaning like her life depended on it."

"Well I can't thank you enough," he said as he sat down at the table and Marguerite joined him.

"We've tried to be quiet for Louisa. Was she well this morning?" Outil asked as she served breakfast. "Yes, she was well. I told her not to leave the room today. She can enjoy some quiet time in there while you two are here to help." Claude took a bite. "This is delicious. Really. Excellent work, Marguerite. I'm seriously blown away. Who knew the Princess of La Rochelle would ever learn how to cook?" Marguerite slugged him in the arm and took a bite from her own plate, savoring her success.

"Why don't you have a bot, Claude? I thought you'd have an army of Outils running this place by now," Marguerite asked.

"Well, it's been a tricky situation with the Indian wars and government work. I have to report occasionally to the field office to do repairs, but since Louisa has been in bed, they have graciously agreed to bring most work to me."

Marguerite lowered her voice as far as she dared. "Louisa said that you are in debt to the Iroquois. How is that possible? What do you owe them?"

Claude was in the middle of chewing a much too large bite, but her questions made him set his fork down and rub his forehead. "It's not so much that we are in debt, as we are in an alliance. They came 'round during the skirmishes last year and Otetiani and I struck up a friendship. His braves protected our land and home during the worst of the battles and helped me bring in the harvest; I supplied them with all the mechanical supplies and repairs they needed."

"The steam cycles?" Marguerite raised her eyebrows in question.

"Yes, I thought those up last winter when I was dealing with a pile of autocart parts. They needed to get through the forest trails more quickly, and I figured two wheels could be balanced like a horse if you were going quickly enough."

"They are really brilliant, Claude. You know that, right?" Marguerite ate a few more bites then added. "You really should be patenting these ideas and selling them. You could be a very wealthy man in no time, my friend."

"I know, Marguerite, but I haven't quite decided if I want to be a very wealthy man. The first thing the Royal Corps of Engineers will do is ship me back to Paris, and I just don't want that. Neither does Louisa. We love it here. We love our land. It's our own land and our own home that we built. Otetiani is a good friend, and I trust his people with my life. "

"Why can't you just go out on your own? Have your own shop away from the Royal Corps?"

"Because we need the money. We only produce enough food here to feed ourselves. I don't have time to farm the entire property and keep up with the demands of the King and the Iroquois. You've seen my shop. It's ridiculous how hard it is to get parts out here. But maybe now that there is a peace treaty, supply ships will be more inclined to venture away from Montreal." He shook his head and continued eating. Marguerite let the matter drop and finished her meal, watching Outil finish the cleaning. Even if her father didn't come through, they would, at least, leave this place cleaner than they'd found it and full of fresh food.

"Thank you for the meal and the help. I'm going to take a bit into Louisa and see if she's up to eating." Claude stood from the table and patted Marguerite on the shoulder.

Outil handed him a plate and waited for him to leave before she sat next to Marguerite and whispered, "There is a lot you could do to help them, m'lady."

"I know, Outil. And I'm going to help them. I just need to get to Jacques first. Why don't you go look for Hector?"

"Yes, ma'am." Outil rose from the chair and opened the door, just as they heard voices in the back bedroom.

"Princess of La Rochelle? Really Claude? I've cooked pies and bread for you for the past year, and you never dote on me that way."

"Louisa it's not like that at all. You are being ridiculous. She's trying her best to help. Taste it, it's nowhere near as good as yours, but I can't be rude. She spent all morning cleaning and cooking. You have no idea what a feat it is to get her out of bed before noon on any given day."

Marguerite stood from the table and straightened her blue cotton skirt. "I think I'll join you." Outside another fine spring morning was under way. She and Outil walked to the barn and stopped to pet the horse.

"I suppose I will just have to accept the fact that she hates me," Marguerite eventually said.

"It could be a side effect of her miserable state," Outil offered.

"I never, ever want to have children, Outil. I can't imagine being that huge and miserable."

As she pronounced this, Claude came running out of the house. "Marguerite, I need you two to sit with Louisa. I think she's going into labor. I need to run to the fort and get the midwife."

"But I don't know anything about labor! What on earth do we do?" Marguerite wailed.

"Just sit with her and do whatever she says you should do. I shouldn't be more than an hour." He pulled open the gate and threw a lead around the horse's neck. "I'm so sorry. There is a bit of a mess in there, too. Just keep her comfortable and I'll be back as soon as possible." Claude jogged away from the pen, the horse in tow, and Outil shut the gate, trapping the goat.

"A mess? Why aren't you driving the autocart? Do you even know how to ride a horse?"

"Cart isn't trustworthy enough. I ride just fine." He pulled a bridle off the wall and put it on the gentle mare, then swung up on her bareback like he'd been doing it his whole life. "I'll be back. Just make sure she's comfortable." He kicked the horse, and it bolted off down the road.

Marguerite looked at Outil, "Please tell me you have some sort of training for childbirth?"

"I do not, m'lady. However, I do know that we should boil water."

"What for?" Marguerite was aghast at the thought of baby soup.

"I have no idea."

The two trotted off to help the woman who hated them and found her lying in a very wet bed looking very miserable.

"Oh, my!" Marguerite exclaimed, hand to heart.

"I will get clean blankets," Outil answered and left the room. "What on earth is all this ... damp?" Marguerite asked as she took a careful step forward.

"My water broke, you ninny." Louisa was in no mood for patience.

"But, it's not time yet, right? What do you want me to do?"

Louisa groaned. "Get your hands scrubbed and fold up a quilt for me on the floor."

"Yes, clean hands. Of course." Marguerite ran to the kitchen and rolled up her sleeves, then scrubbed at her hands furiously in the bucket of left over water.

Outil came down the ladder from the loft with a clean quilt. "She wants it folded on the floor for some reason?" Marguerite told her.

"Yes, m'lady," Outil said.

Just for good measure, Marguerite filled a pot with water and set it to boil on the fire next to the stew, then she joined Outil in the bedroom. Louisa was kneeling on the quilt by the side of her bed. Outil was gathering up the soiled linens and asking in her calm automaton voice, "Do you require anything to drink?"

"No," Louisa groaned. "My back hurts horribly. It feels like I'm on fire. Can you just push on it, please?"

Marguerite looked at Outil who shrugged her silvery shoulders in confusion. "Of course," Marguerite said. And she got down on the floor behind the laboring woman and put two hands on her shoulder blades.

"No, lower, at my waist," Louisa commanded. Marguerite moved her hands lower and pushed gently. "Push hard. Please," she groaned again. "Oh, Lord have mercy on us all. Lord save us. My mother died giving birth to my baby sister. I don't want to leave Claude alone. I can't leave this baby alone. Save me, Lord."

Marguerite's chest tightened, and she felt tears involuntarily well up in her eyes at overhearing this private prayer.

"I'm so sorry," she offered.

"Save it for someone else and just push!" Louisa snapped back.

Claude arrived with the midwife one hour later. A frantic Outil met them at the gate carrying cleaning supplies from the wash house. "There is a baby, Master Claude! You have a baby!" The trio entered the house and was greeted by the screams of a newborn infant. Claude looked worried, but the midwife, an old Iroquois woman, assured him. "This is good! Strong lungs means a strong baby." Marguerite heard them enter and stuck her head out of the bedroom door. She was grinning from ear to ear and had a mess of blood and who knows what else smeared all over her dress.

"It's a baby!" she beamed.

"I should hope so." Claude raced past her. "How is Louisa?"

"She's much, much better." Marguerite jumped out of the way and watched as Claude knelt by his wife's bedside. He kissed her hand, then the baby's head. The old midwife pushed her way past Marguerite and joined the little family at the bedside.

"This is a very healthy baby," she pronounced smiling.

"It's a girl." Louisa smiled and cuddled the baby to her chest.

"Well, it is a hungry girl. Let's take care of this cord and get her eating," the midwife said with authority, shoving Claude out of the way.

Marguerite took that as her cue to leave. She looked one last time at the happy group and the tiny little miracle in Louisa's arms. She knew that she would never forget this day. Something inside of her had come loose, something she didn't know existed. Claude smiling at Louisa, the tiny wailing infant in her arms, was the perfect picture of happiness, and for the first time, she ached for that kind of happiness. She scrubbed herself as best she could in the washbasin and joined Outil outside.

"You did a fine job, m'lady," Outil said.

"Thank you. You weren't so bad yourself," Marguerite replied. They watched the birds fly in great throngs around the tops of the budding trees. The fresh spring air danced around them carrying the smell of fresh, green life, and Marguerite thought about how strange life could be.

"I want to make sure Jacques has a ride home if he wants it. There is a good chance that he may not want it after the way I behaved, but I need to know that as well. Do you think I will ever learn to slow down and be wise, Outil?" Marguerite kicked at a stone in the ground.

"There is a chance that you might," Outil said. "However, I suspect you will be in the grave by then."

"Outil! Are you teasing me?" Marguerite laughed at the bot, incredulous at the unexpected humor.

"Possibly," Outil turned and patted her mistress on the shoulder. It was a very human gesture for a bot, and seemed to fit the magic of the afternoon perfectly.

An engine roared in the distance. Marguerite stood from the spot where she'd leaned on the fence and walked to the lane, trying to see who might be approaching. As soon as she saw the single front wheel and the long black hair flowing behind a goggled face, she took a step back and wondered what she should do with herself.

"Who is coming?" Outil asked as she joined her.

"It's Otetiani," she answered. They both stepped back as not one, but four men on three steam cycles rolled into the yard. All of them were striking to behold. They were the very embodiment of power and pride in their leather clothing, which in the daylight, Marguerite could now see was decorated with beads of all colors. They propped up their cycles, removed their goggles and retrieved parcels from the backs of their rides.

"Lady Marguerite," Otetiani walked up to her and gave a short bow. "It is good to see you with both feet on the ground, although I do not wish to know whose blood is on your dress. Have you killed a bear this day?"

Marguerite blushed as she looked at her mess of an outfit. Was this very serious man actually teasing her? She decided to pretend like she was wearing her best ball gown and held her head high as she nodded back at him. "I happen to have delivered my first baby today, thank you very much, Monsieur Otetiani."

"I did not realize you were a midwife as well as a pirate and a Lady of France." His face did not break a smile, but he was definitely teasing her.

"I most certainly am *not* a midwife, nor a pirate, but I would like to know how I can help you. Monsieur Claude is busy attending to his wife at the moment."

The other men gathered around with their paper-wrapped parcels, a few of them grinning at her, another looking confused at this high speaking woman covered in blood questioning their leader. "Forgive me, Lady Vadnay, these are my brothers. We have only come bearing gifts for the baby." He motioned to the men and their packages. "That is quite lovely of you. Let me send Outil to see if they can receive you yet." The whole group followed the bot to the front of the house, but Otetiani reached out and put a hand on Marguerite's shoulder.

"Lady Marguerite, forgive my forwardness. I find you to be an interesting person, and knowing that you are here with only a pack of food and a pistol, I brought this for you." He handed her a paper-wrapped parcel.

"Oh, my, thank you." She took the bundle and unwrapped it carefully. Inside was a simple dress, made of soft brown leather with delicate white beads sewn on the neckline. "This is so lovely, thank you, Otetiani."

She smiled at him, and he nodded back, stone-faced as ever. Looking up at his lovely chiseled face, Marguerite saw the bright blue sky behind him and a wisp of white clouds float by. Behind the cloud, a splotch of brown suddenly appeared. Marguerite all but forgot her companion and her manners as she jumped for joy and called, "Outil! They are here! Daddy got my letter. They are here!"

The Henrietta drifted closer into view and began to give up altitude. She dropped anchor and Lucy, Louis, and Captain Butterfield waved from the deck.

Chapter Twenty-Four

"I will agree to take you on this trip, but only if you swear on your mother's grave that you will behave yourself." Captain Butterfield sat across from Marguerite on a stool in the barn. "I only came this far because I've heard a bit about this Claude of yours. Word travels fast in New France. I wanted to see his handiwork for myself. Not much to look at, eh?"

Marguerite looked around the barn that served as a smithie shop and sighed. "He really does deserve more. That's why I asked my father to send you with the money. You have it, right?"

"I do, and plenty more to pay for your passage to North Carolina. I hope you appreciate this father of yours. Not many wild young aristocrats have daddies who support their rescue missions."

"Father is fond of Captain Laviolette, and he understands how the military works—always leaving men behind," Marguerite stood and walked over to a broken clock on the wall, and flicked carelessly at its exposed cogs. Captain Butterfield stood.

"We need to get going. Are you ready or—" The Captain looked Marguerite over from head to foot. She was still wearing the blue cotton dress smeared with the evidence of the afternoon.

"I'm just going to change. I haven't wanted to go in the house and disturb them," Marguerite pulled at the dress.

"Your father sent a trunk of clothes. You can change on the Henrietta if you'd like."

"Oh, I think I will just jump in the washroom and slip into this." She lifted up her brown paper package and made to leave the barn.

"You know, Lady Vadnay, I didn't think much of you after your shenanigans out there—fool-brained rich girl—but this is the right thing to do. You keep your nose clean this time, and my opinion will be repaired."

"I'm so glad, Captain. That is very nice to hear," Marguerite smiled as she skipped quickly on her way to the washroom. A few moments later she was ready to go—buckskin dress and boots on, hair braided and pack set to go. She noticed the handsome Iroquois men appreciating her new outfit. She smiled and turned round for them. It was soft and warm and beautiful, in a simple way. The only thing it was missing was pockets.

Claude came out of the house to see them off, with Outil close behind. He stopped short when he saw Marguerite's new outfit. "Well, this is unexpected," he remarked.

"It was a gift from Otetiani. He noticed I didn't have any clothes—unlike other men around here." She laughed and shouldered her bag.

"Listen, I'm so sorry for the mess you walked into here. You must come back when things are settled. Louisa is doing very well, thanks to you and Outil, and the baby is going to be just fine. We just can't thank you enough."

Captain Butterfield approached them as they spoke. "Here's the paperwork you asked for, Lady Vadnay."

"Give it to Claude. It's for him anyway," she gave him a hug and looked for Outil. The automaton was talking to Otetiani and looking at his steamcycle closely. Claude took the papers and stuck them in his pocket, before he took Marguerite by the arm and started to walk her to the Henrietta's lift.

"I just want you to know that we named the baby Francine Marguerite," he said quietly and gave her hand a little squeeze.

Marguerite looked at him sideways. "Oh, Claude. Please, you don't have to do that. Louisa doesn't need to have any reminders of me hanging around. You should let her call the baby whatever she wants."

"But it was her choice. She agrees with me. She's grateful for your help and feels terrible about the way she's acted." He was earnest.

She hugged him again. "Just make sure you two are happy."

"Be careful. And take this with you." He reached in his pocket and pulled out a small gun.

"What is this?" Marguerite took it and admired the fine workmanship her friend always brought to his projects. Little brass gears turned as she moved the weapon back and forth in her hands. A weight inside shifted with the movements, and fine filigree decorated every inch of free space.

"It's a gun, but it doesn't fire traditional projectiles. The sliding weight inside creates friction as you move, which turns the gears and loads the energy tanks. The natural movement of your body will keep it loaded, and you can fire a stunning shot of power to anyone within close range. Simply shake it vigorously for a second shot in thirty seconds. Not very handy at long range, but more than adequate in a hand-to-hand altercation. Just don't point it at anyone you like. There is enough potential energy in a full reserve to knock a person out for several hours if you hit them in the right spot."

"Oh, Claude! Thank you." Marguerite tucked it in her pack and climbed into the lift with Butterfield and Outil.

"Stay safe," Claude called again.

"You too!" Marguerite watched as Claude opened the papers her father had prepared. She let a smile spread across her face as the realization dawned on his.

He suddenly looked up and yelled to her. "Marguerite! You are ridiculous, you know that, right?"

"My behavior is absolutely justified. Go do something amazing, will you?" she called back.

Outil leaned over and asked, "What did it say, m'lady?"

"It was a statement of finance. Father has agreed to be Claude's benefactor, and he transferred the rest of the money I had from the cricket treasure to Claude's name. He should be able to make himself a real steam forge and some bot helpers now."

"That was very good of you, Lady Vadnay," Outil replied with surprise.

Otetiani stood at Claude's side and lifted one arm in a farewell gesture as his companions climbed on their steamcycles and prepared to leave.

"You never introduced me to that one. Does he like to fly? We should bring him with us." Captain Butterfield elbowed Marguerite in the ribs and pointed to Otetiani.

"He is quite magnificent, but no, I doubt it would be a good idea to bring him with us, even if he would come." She couldn't imagine being able to think straight with the possibility of running into Otetiani around every corner on the ship. She needed to focus on Jacques. On deck, Lucy and Louis were waiting to greet them with smiles and pats on the back. Captain Butterfield called to the crew to pull anchor and head out.

"Take her as high as she can go, steamers. We're heading over the border. Going into Brit country, then pirate land. You can thank Lady Marguerite for the wages. Let's keep the sail up and the motors running. Up and out!"

The crew cheered, and Lucy pulled on Marguerite's arm. "I can't *believe* you survived! You are a wicked crazy thing. Come on, you get the benefactor's quarters this time around. I'll show you where they are."

The ship sailed into the aether as Marguerite descended the stairs with Lucy to a much larger cabin with a much nicer bed than she'd had the last time on the Henrietta. A giant trunk was waiting at the foot of the bed as well. Marguerite opened it up and found a letter from her father on top of several dresses of different styles. On top of all of this sat three of her special order flight suits. Marguerite's heart filled with gratitude.

My Dearest Marguerite,

Thank you for bringing young Claude's predicament to my attention. He is a talented man, and I am most interested in seeing his abilities come to their full fruition. I fully expect you to return to me whole and happy with an expanded reservoir of wisdom from which to draw upon for future endeavors. My heart goes with you, as does a significant amount of my liquid assets. I pray you will not squander either. I pray for Captain Laviolette as well. It is a godless people he has fallen into. Do not assume to undertake this errand without assistance. Captain Butterfield has offered to guide you and protect you as best she can once you reach Cape Feare. Please be cautious and remember that you carry my heart in your chest.

All of my love,
Lord Vadnay

Marguerite smiled at the sweet words coupled with the formality of the signature. They truly had come a long way since the days of bickering over suitors and boarding school. "What does he say?" Lucy bounced on the balls of her feet as she stood next to Outil, both waiting for Marguerite to finish.

"He says we must come home alive," Marguerite smiled as she folded the paper up and tucked it into her pack with her goggles. She added the small gun to the collection and then turned to her companions. "Now! We need to make a plan!" She clapped her hands and looked from one to the other.

"I thought you had a plan," Lucy said.

"Lady Vadnay's only plan is to fly south and get Captain Laviolette," Outil offered.

"Right, but we need to work out some details, like how we find him once we are actually there," Marguerite said as she looked out her little porthole.

"That would be a good idea," Outil said.

"I'd suggest we meet with Captain Butterfield then," Lucy said as she joined Marguerite at the window.

"Magnificent, isn't it?" The wild green and blue landscape below them was crowned with white clouds and glowing with bright spring sunlight.

"Yes, it most certainly is. There is nothing quite as wonderful as flying. Let's get above deck and find the captain." The three made their way back to the deck and found Louis scampering around with the other deck boys and a bot, trying to keep the ship's course on track.

"Hello, Louis," Marguerite called. "Where is Captain Butterfield?"

"Hello, m'lady! She's down on the bridge now. Calling up orders on the pipes," he smiled broadly as he answered. "Might I say, m'lady, that I watched you bounce off the envelope of that ship and get caught by the pirates, and I'm mighty glad you survived and that you weren't set on fire."

"You may say that, and I will join you in the sentiment. I was very grateful not to be set on fire as well." Marguerite felt the chill in the air growing as the ship rose into the aether, and she took in Louis's lack of a proper deck jacket. She would have to rectify that as soon as possible. The boy was already too thin. He needed a layer of fat and a layer of wool on his bones to do his job properly.

"Louis, is there anything you need? We are heading to the bridge," she asked.

"No, Lady Vadnay, but it is ever so kind of you to ask," he replied with a moony kind of look in his eyes.

Oh dear, Marguerite thought, *time to leave*. "Very well, we will see you in the mess."

The bridge was one level below deck and at the bow of the ship. Windows lined the walls, providing a clear view of their course. Instrument panels were crammed into every space available. Most looked to be made of spare parts and added on after original construction as an afterthought. Captain Butterfield sat in an overstuffed blue parlor chair in the center of the whole mess and was calling out orders to the bots and women manning the controls. A black pipe extended down from the ceiling above them. The Captain leaned over and called into it off and on. Marguerite guessed this was the pipe system Louis spoke of.

As Marguerite approached her chair, Captain Butterfield swung around. "Welcome to the magic room, Lady Vadnay. A bit cobbled together, but she does a lot of good things. How can I help you today?" Marguerite noted the change in the way the Captain addressed her now that her father was paying for the voyage. It was a welcome change, but also slightly annoying. She proceeded anyway.

"I was just wondering if we should come up with some sort of plan for extricating Captain Laviolette."

"Ahh, yes. Well, first we have to survive the border crossing and the Brits. Then we have to get through the storms, and then

I agreed to help you *find* Captain Laviolette. However, I'm not sure if we will be extricating him."

"What do you mean?" Marguerite was growing tired of people telling her what she couldn't do.

"Well, there are two options when you are captured by Captain Douleur. You either sign on as crew, or you are tortured for information and then dropped on a deserted island. It's been at least a week since your Jacques was flown away with, so by now he's both broken and dying in Nova Scotia, or he's hoisting the mainsail and stoking the boilers for Douleur. Let's just hope he didn't get dumped in Britland. There's no way our Frenchie vessel will be welcomed there, even if we are just picking up a fallen friend."

"Well, how will we know?" Marguerite rang her hands with worry.

"We won't till we get to Cape Feare. It's the only safe harbor for us, and unless Douleur stopped off in New Amsterdam, we'll find her there." Captain Butterfield turned and cried at one of her bots, "Get more steam out of that back boiler. We've got to get higher than this if we want to dock at the tip of the Bombay Tower and avoid the land rockets."

"Land rockets?" Marguerite wrung her hands with more earnest.

"The Brits hate us, deary. Or have you been living under a gilded rock for the past fifteen years?" Captain Butterfield snorted.

"Bombay? We're not going all the way to India, are we?" Lucy asked.

"No, deary. Wrong hemisphere. The Bombay Tower is in Bombay, New York. It's the border guard station. All ships flying into Britland have to stop and check in there. It's about as advanced as the Brits have gotten with their technology. Stands up into the clouds with lookouts and refueling stations for aerships. Also provides a nice little base for shooting Chinese fire rockets at unwelcome visitors."

"How are we going to get past there? We are obviously a French ship, and no, I haven't been under a gilded rock." Marguerite walked to the closest control panel and scanned the buttons, trying to make sense of them.

"You think I'm making this trip just for you? Oh no, dear. I have a cargo bay full of French silks bound for the Republic of Charleston. The Governor there has six daughters, and they do love their ball gowns."

"I believe I have a solution to our navigation issue," Outil said.

"I was able to give Captain Laviolette a tracking beetle before we were parted on the Renegade. It is a long range sensor I've been working on for a while now. I was planning on giving it to you, Lady Vadnay, when I realized how easily we were parted at sea. But, as things looked to be a bit harrowing for Captain Laviolette, and you were not yet reunited with me, he agreed to test the bug. The signal is very faint, which helps me to calculate distance. I'm fairly certain it's coming from North Carolina."

"That's brilliant, Outil!" Marguerite cried and squeezed the bot's arm.

"Thank you, m'lady. We will certainly find Captain Laviolette there. If not the Captain, then at least the trousers he had the beetle sewn into."

"Oh dear," Marguerite said, her enthusiasm draining.

"I agree. Oh dear," Captain Butterfield echoed.

Chapter Twenty-Five

The Tower of Bombay was not quite what Marguerite expected. It was, indeed, a tower of angular metal configuration. It looked to have been quite splendid at some point, but over the years the copper fittings had turned green, and most repairs seemed to have been made with inferior metals and wood. It stood, at least, two thousand feet from the spring green earth below it. There was a lightning rod at the top, suspended by three trusses over a massive funnel for catching rainwater. Pipes and wiring ran from the uppermost level, down as far as Marguerite could see. Smaller water tanks perched precariously here and there on the way down as well, and various flags of different countries flew from each tank. The whole thing was crisscrossed by a network of catwalks and stairs. Two lifts ran right up the middle on chains attached to pulleys just under the rain funnel. They paused at what appeared to be small compartments for people to man out of the elements. Each one she could make out was also equipped with a slot for a gun, or as the captain had said, a rocket. The largest was at the top. It had a water tank and a British flag flying in the high aether wind.

They pulled the Henrietta up to the topmost filling tank and prepared to dock. Having only traveled a few miles, they had no need to refuel, but they still needed to supply the border guard with papers.

A plank was extended from the nearest refuge and a stocky, dark-haired man in a British military outfit walked to meet them, his face stern. Two younger men followed, also in uniform, and also in what appeared to be bad spirits.

"Time to work some more magic," Captain Butterfield said as she hoisted herself out of her chair and pulled open a cabinet under one of the control panels. "Ah! Here we are. Papers for the pretty silks. You lot stay here. I'll return when the inspector is satisfied."

Marguerite watched her leave and turned to Outil. "I'd very much like to see those silks myself. I wonder if they actually are the very latest from France."

"The cargo hold is just two flights down from here. We could be down and back in no time," Lucy offered. "I've seen them myself. Quite exquisite."

"I'm not sure this is a good idea. I believe we should wait here as the captain asked and then survey the fabrics when the inspectors are gone, m'lady." Outil stepped up to meet the girls as they tried to leave.

"Outil, it will only take a moment. I'm sure they will be busy with paperwork up above for ages." Marguerite pushed her way past her bot and continued to the stairs just outside the bridge. As they headed down at a leisurely pace, chatting about what had transpired between their last meetings, they reached the cargo hold at the same time as they heard voices coming down the stairs behind them.

"Oh, dear. Do you think that might be them?" Marguerite asked.

"Could be. We better get out of here. Captain won't like running into us. Maybe we can make it back up one level before they are on top of us." Lucy started back up the stairs. They heard the men descending, and they ascended as quickly as possible. Then another sound echoed through the confined space.

"Captain, is Lady Vadnay down here? I have great news for her!" Louis's clear, young voice cut through the air and rang all the way to the bottom of the stairwell.

A strange voice boomed out, "Lady Vadnay? You reported that you had no idea of her whereabouts, Captain Butterfield. What is this boy doing looking for an internationally wanted criminal in your stairwell? Hmm?"

Marguerite turned to Lucy and mouthed the words *internationally wanted?* Lucy shrugged and motioned for them to move quickly to the next door up, which was only a few steps away. Marguerite didn't hesitate. She skipped as quietly as she could up the stairs and pushed on the lever for the door in front of her. "That boy was bonked on the head in the midst of our last battle. He had a bit of a crush on the Lady and seems to be stuck thinking she's still on board. Of course, I'd report her to you. I may be a privateer, but I'm no smuggler."

Marguerite heard this exchange as Lucy slipped past, and she carefully re-latched the door. As the men approached, they heard their continued conversation.

"I find this very hard to believe, Captain. After we are finished with your cargo hold, we will require a full search of your ship. Bristol, report back to the tower and order more men up here, right away."

"I don't think that will be necessary. I'm on a tight time table. The governor of Charleston is expecting me by tonight at the latest with this cargo," Captain Butterfield explained.

"And I can't be held responsible for one of your reckless, young terrorists entering our country or aerspace. I'm sure the governor would understand."

"I will ask for a full written explanation then, from your hand, detailing why we were detained for no good reason at your tower, General, and I'm sure his daughter, Avery, will want to know why her silks were late. You are attending her ball next month, I assume."

"What is she talking about?" Marguerite hissed to Lucy.

"The governor's daughters are the hottest ticket to the top of Britland these days. Every military man on the continent is in line for a dance with them, hoping for a strategic marriage." Marguerite knew all too well what that meant. She felt sorry for the girls. It wasn't many months ago when she was in the same position, forced to endure grumpy military men and flippant aristocrats looking for a wealthy bride.

The British official seemed flustered now. They stopped walking just outside the door where Marguerite hid. She tensed as he stammered. "No, I, well, that is to say, I haven't received my invitation just yet."

Butterfield jumped on his hesitation with no mercy. "Oh, I am so sorry. Invitations went out months ago. Yours must have been lost in the post. Those blasted French pigeons are so unreliable. I may have an extra in my cabin, however, if you'd care to go. Not that you have time—important man like yourself."

"Russell, count the bolts of fabric below. I will escort the Captain to her quarters and make sure it is secure on that level of the ship." The footsteps quickly faded in different directions, and Marguerite smiled as they sprinted down the corridor, then up to the deck.

"Ah, I needed some fresh air after that. Butterfield is going to kill Louis though," Lucy said.

"Why would she do that? He didn't know any better. He's just a kid. I didn't even know I was being hunted internationally. Ridiculous." Marguerite tossed her braid and took a deep breath of the fresh air.

"Well, then you two are the last to find out. Everyone knows about the rich girl who tried to single-handedly take down Douleur's ship, against orders and with no regard to the well-being of her shipmates."

Marguerite gave Lucy a critical stare. "That wasn't at all what happened."

"I'm just reporting the telegraph that went out to all military personnel. Seems they want to make an example of you."

Marguerite walked to the edge of the ship and looked over, straight down the tower of Bombay. It was somehow dizzying to see the apparatus reaching up from the ground to meet them.

"We'd better head back down before they catch us up here," Lucy tried to fill in the silence.

"Yes. I suppose so." Marguerite leaned back from the edge and turned to head for the stairs. "We can wait in the mess until all of this passes." Just as they approached the hatch they had exited, two hats bobbed up from below.

"Oh, no," Lucy said. But she was too late to warn her friend. The Britlander and Butterfield had already seen them. *Maybe he doesn't know what I look like*, Marguerite thought, as she smiled prettily at the ornery little man who now grasped a gilded letter in one hand.

"You!" he cried. "You are under arrest!" He sprinted out of the stairwell and straight at Marguerite, but she was too quick. She dodged him and ran for the other end of the deck.

"Apparently he does know what I look like," she said as she tried to figure out her next move. If she went back down, he would only follow her. If she stayed up here too long, there would be a swarm of soldiers on the deck in no time. She only had one option.

She ducked around the masts and riggings until she came to the gangway. There was no way to hide on the ship, in a snap decision she decided she might be able to lure the Brits back to the Tower of Bombay and ditch them there. She bolted across the gangway toward the small cabin perched on the top of the tower.

"No!" Lucy cried from behind her. Marguerite looked back for a moment and saw the officer in hot pursuit. He raced past the last pile of barrels before the gangway, and a small foot stuck out at just the right time, sending him sprawling to his belly. Marguerite saw this from the tower where she raced up the stairway that wound around the little shelter. She was heading for the small refueling barrel perched at the top of the tower just below the rain funnel. Soon both guards were helping their general up off the gangway then racing to pursue her. Marguerite reached the end of the stairs and climbed out onto the cold, wet tank. The top was a small flat circle. Beyond that was nothing but a straight drop to the soil below.

Somehow she'd never been afraid of heights except for the day Jacques forced her to climb the rope ladder between ships. This was turning into much the same kind of situation. She knew she was safe as long as she was steady. She knew she was just as high as she always flew on a ship. Sometimes they even flew much higher. The difference was that there was no ship beneath her now, no rails, no cozy little cabin to hide in. She was completely exposed on top of a two thousand foot tower with angry men pursuing her. Her knees suddenly felt weak, and she began to think this spur-of-the-moment idea may not have been the best course of action.

Marguerite forced herself to focus on her goal. She needed to get back to the ship, and then they could fly away and leave the British tower guard behind. The deck of the *Henrietta* started to fill with curious onlookers. One of which was Outil. Perfect. She called out to the bot. "Outil! The rope!" Her arm wasn't one hundred percent better, but she knew she could hold her own this time. "Fire her up!"

Her nerves were another matter entirely. She saw Captain

Butterfield hollering commands into the closest pipe as Outil quickly untied a rope on the main envelope of the *Henrietta* directly across from her precarious spot on the tallest tower in the world. Then she accidentally looked down.

She couldn't look down. She wouldn't look down.

She looked down again.

She knew it was illogical, but as she felt the tower sway and creek with the wind, her thoughts suddenly turned to the fact that it wasn't exactly a sturdy structure. She took a step to steady herself, and her foot slipped on the cold, wet surface. She righted herself quickly, but her heart was now pounding its way out of her chest. This plan was positively suicidal. She froze in place, and time seemed to stand still with her.

There was no chute. There was no Jacques. There was no escape. She could hear the three soldiers thundering up the stairs behind her, hollering what she could only guess were obscenities in English. She heard her name from below and dared to open her eyes to see Outil standing ready with a length of rope. The *Henrietta's* engines were roaring to life, and the ship was pulling out. Outil threw the rope, and Marguerite knew she had to move her body.

Just move, she told herself. And she did. Both arms reached out and grabbed the rope as it swung past her head, but she wasn't fast enough. Outil jumped forward and retrieved the returning line and threw it again as fast as lightening. This time, Marguerite was ready. She focused on the life line and grabbed with both hands as tightly as she could. She ignored the pain in her shoulder, closed her eyes, and jumped off the Tower of

Bombay. The men behind her swore and yelled, but their voices faded away as she flew through the aether.

I really must stop doing this.

She opened her eyes just in time to see Outil standing right in front of her, ready to catch her. But she was moving too fast. She hit the bot at full speed, and they both sprawled on the deck as the little ship burst into full speed ahead—which wasn't nearly as fast as Marguerite would have liked. She vowed then to figure out a way to get her hands on The Dragon's technology. There had to be a way to get these ships to sail faster.

"You are bad luck and not worth your weight in pine needles. No wonder they locked you in the brig. I'll do you one better. Josephine, lock her in her room. The bot too. I'll let you out when we are in North Carolina—if I have forgiven you." Just then the sky erupted in colors and flashes of light all around them.

"Blasted Chinese rockets!" Captain Butterfield swore. "Get out the water cannons. We are going to be lucky to make it past Virginia now. Soak the envelope! Fire back!" The battle was fast but glorious. Water and fire were everywhere. The rockets exploding on and around the deck were deafening and colorful, but Marguerite knew that one strike to the shabby brown envelope holding them aloft with explosive gasses would knock the entire ship out of the sky like a dead bird.

She ignored the captain's order to go to her room, dodged the big girl, Josephine, and with Outil's help grabbed a water cannon. She pointed it at the envelope, watching for incoming rockets. She successfully joined a few others in soaking the vile weapons before they did any damage to the ship, but as they finally flew out of range of the Tower of Bombay and the battle ended, she also soaked the captain. Butterfield marched up to her and took the hose. "Your quarters, *now!*"

Somehow Marguerite knew this was an order she couldn't ignore. She marched below deck sullen and wet. Outil followed, a persistent squeak coming from each step of her now soggy gears.

Chapter Twenty-Six

At least this time, Marguerite had a porthole to watch out of. As they sailed south along the coast of the British Colonies, she saw much of the same landscape of her own New France. Thick forests and winding rivers covered and cut the land below her. She faced port side, so there were no mountains, but every now and then she got a glimpse of the ocean.

The horizon soon began to change from bright blue to fiery orange, and then a soft pink fading to deep purple. A vast net of stars covered her and a deep black settled below. Pinpoints of light speckled the land in random places. Glowing clusters marked the more populated towns, like Virginny and Baltimore.

She changed into a flight suit and dried her hair as best she could with a spare blanket, then threw herself on the bed. No one had bothered to deliver any food yet, which irked Marguerite a bit. The battle was over; surely everyone had eaten by now. But the feelings passed quickly as waves of guilt washed over her as she thought about her foolish wrong turns.

"Outil, I swear to listen to you the next time you give me advice." She pronounced with as much resolve as she could muster.

The bot simply nodded her head. "Yes, m'lady."

"You don't think I will. I can tell. You think I'll just go on doing whatever fool thing comes into my head," Marguerite sat up and faced the bot that was standing in the corner, waiting to power down for the night.

"No, m'lady. I know you are penitent for your mistakes, and you wish to be a better person. I do not think I can guarantee that my advice will always be the correct path to choose."

"Well, so far you've been right as rain." Marguerite flopped back on her bed. "And I am a fool."

"I disagree. And I have good news, m'lady. Upon my last check, the beetle frequency is much closer. I believe we have almost arrived at Cape Feare."

A knock at the door startled both of them. "Yes," Marguerite called.

A key was fitted into the lock, and the mechanism clicked, allowing it to swing wide. Louis stood there, looking sheepish and smelling horrible. He was carrying a tray of what looked to be a cold stew and bread.

"Dinner, Lady Vadnay," he said quietly as he entered her room and placed the tray on the small table.

"Louis, what on earth happened to you today?" Marguerite sat up and smelled at the food, trying to rid her nostrils of his stink. "You smell like you lost a fight with Fifi."

"Yes, miss. You aren't far from the truth. Captain put me on special duties this afternoon. I was packaging up Marguerite Bombs."

"Packaging what?" She set down the fork she'd just picked up and looked at the poor boy.

"Well, Captain liked your little trick you played on Captain Laviolette so much, she ordered me to make up some more packages just like them—only with some gunpowder to boot. We've been saving Fifi's wastes for the past week. It's not a pretty job." He sighed and looked, even more, embarrassed.

"Ha! That's excellent news. Why don't you go get cleaned up and head to bed," Marguerite offered.

"Can't. That's the other news. We're docking in Cape Feare in the next ten minutes. Captain will be down to see you before that. She said to eat up and get ready."

"Well, thank you, Louis." Marguerite cringed at his filthy clothes and terrible smell, but patted him on the back, and returned his happy grin.

"My pleasure, m'lady."

He left as quickly as he'd come, but she didn't lock the door this time. The food was better than going without, and Marguerite took quick bites as she went through her pack and trunk, trying to decide what to take with her. She had her goggles ready and her gun in her waistband when Captain Butterfield showed up.

"Oh, no," she said when she saw Marguerite's outfit. "You will put on your best gown and put away all that gear, and you will do *exactly* as I say for the rest of this night or I swear to you, I will leave you and, any other fool who helps you, in this godforsaken city of pirates and walking parts. Are we clear?" She stood with her hands on her pudgy hips, her face tight as a knot and her eyebrows raised, waiting for a reply.

Marguerite felt it only fitting she say, "Yes, Ma'am."

"Now, put on your prettiest ball gown. Outil, put this around her wrists. You are booty tonight, and that is that. Booty does not speak. You will follow me to the tavern where my messengers have informed me Douleur and her crew are celebrating their victory over the French. They've been at it for the past three days, ever since they arrived. My lovely little helper also let me know that Douleur has a thing for silks, and I just happen to have a cargo hold full of them. You are the model, the bot pulls a sample load, we trade for your boyfriend and we get out of here. Is that clear? No shenanigans, no crazy rescue attempts. No trying to get even. You will also not let anyone know your name. Tonight you are Eunice."

"Eunice?" Marguerite pretended to gag. "What is it with you and terrible names? First the Henrietta, now Eunice?"

Butterfield had moved to the trunk and opened the lid to look at the wares inside, but now turned on Marguerite, her face just as stern, but also cracked with a bit of emotion. "I'll have you know, this ship is named after my tiny daughter. She was the most beautiful, perfect thing you ever laid eyes on. I lost her and her father to the Barbary pox on a run to the Canary Islands. So I'll thank you to keep your opinions to yourself, *Eunice*."

"I'm very sorry, Captain." Marguerite was sorry. She hadn't ever considered that the rough, ill-tempered woman could have had a family, much less children. She also couldn't imagine what it would be like to suddenly lose all of that. She thought of Lucy as well, having lost all of her family to disease, and was simultaneously grateful for her health and sorry for her big mouth. She wanted to stop putting her foot in her mouth but wasn't quite sure how. She wasn't sure how to keep from getting herself into situations that required her body to fly through the air either. She would have to work on both of those.

"It's neither here nor there. Make my night easy, and I'll forgive you. Marguerite looked at Outil again. The bot nodded slightly, and Marguerite sighed, remembering her promise. Captain reached into the trunk and pulled out a blue silk gown of the latest style, and a slightly less elegant green frock. "This one will do for you," she held up the blue. "And this one I will take for your friend, Lucy."

"Very well," Marguerite nodded, taking the gown and laying it on the bed. "Just let me finish my food. I need all my strength to keep my mouth shut." Twenty minutes later they were docked and showing papers to the local authority—if you could call him that. He wore a Britland military hat, but his cloak was shabby and clearly not originally his own, as it bore the emblem of a French aerman. The rest of him was dressed in gunnysack, and it didn't appear that he was fond of shaving. He had several companions at the dock house that were drinking heavily and weren't worried at all about a ship coming in after dark.

They received no warnings or questions about criminals or illegal activity. There wasn't even a search of their goods when Butterfield mentioned that the silks were for Captain Douleur's private collection. "This is a strictly don't ask, don't tell community," Butterfield was able to whisper to them once the pirates had left them alone. They marched right off the lift and out into the city. Outil pulled a cart, and Lucy and Marguerite walked behind, a slender chain connecting their bound wrists to the end of the cart. Butterfield took the lead and marched them down muddy streets and dark buildings to a street that shown with yellow lights, both flame and artificial.

As they turned the corner and the lights came into full view, Marguerite couldn't help but gasp. The lights didn't just come from windows. They were strung across the street. A bonfire burned in the center outside of a tavern. Men and women danced and laughed, stumbling drunk and merry with life. Everything was covered in a film of dust, it seemed. They marched past makeshift autocarts and peddler carts loaded with fine wines. Some of the labels Marguerite recognized from her homeland. Their little parade was only gawked at by bots, of which there seemed to be an unusual amount out in the streets without a human at their side.

Eventually, they came to the doors of a tall wooden building crammed between two other shorter buildings. It was night, and Marguerite couldn't make out many details, but it was most assuredly the loudest establishment on the block. The doors were thrown wide, and the light poured out into the street adding to the effect. Music came from within, as well as laughter and the occasional body, stumbling or being tossed out the door.

Butterfield led them to the door and instructed Outil to stay with the cart. It only held a few bolts of cloth, but Marguerite knew their worth was high above that of any peddler's rum. Bots and humans mingled inside. Game tables were set up on the perimeter, and the center was open to dancing. On a chair in the middle of all of this noise, stood a man in a strange suit of bright colors throwing balls up in the air and catching them in difficult positions. The crowd cheered and whooped every time he caught another, and each time he threw the next higher. A bot was sitting at a clavichord in the corner, pounding a quick melody on the keys and leaving Marguerite to wonder that they hadn't already broken from the heavy hand.

A tall, brown-skinned man with tight cotton pants an inch too short for him and a leather holster filled with bullets slung over his chest stood at the door. Two guns rested on his hips. One hand idly fondled a gun while he reached the other out and stopped Butterfield. "There's no soliciting tonight, slaver. Wait till morning," he growled.

"I'm not waiting another minute. These lovely ladies and the silks are here for Douleur. If the day breaks on this shipment before she sees it, it will be my head and your neck." Marguerite did not like the term *slaver* and instantly tensed. She tried to slip her hand to her gun in her pocket for comfort, but remembering her hands were bound, she let them fall lamely in front of her. The man grunted again and nodded across the room to an antiquated copper bot, which also nodded and walked to a corner in the back of the roaring tavern. The first man kept his arm out and didn't move until the bot returned. A very tall, very striking woman followed him. She was wearing all black, and although she held a strong drink in her hand, she was nowhere near being out of her wits.

"Butterfield," She said the name like it was something foul she accidentally ate for dinner. Captain Butterfield bowed low and yanked on the chain indicating the girls should do the same. They both dipped their heads, and all three rose to see the look of annoyance on the woman's face. The two captains together made a strange pair. Butterfield wore a frumpy brown cotton shirt and jacket with the worn pants of a deck hand. Her hair was as wild and unruly as ever, sticking out from all sides of her tricorn hat. Her face was brown from years on the open deck of a ship, and her eyes were a dull brown behind droopy lids. Douleur, on the other hand, was tall and thin, but her slender arms were lined with the definition of muscles used to hard work. Her black dress was of the finest silks and design, and she stood with a regal air. Her brown waving hair had the slightest hint of grey streaks but was combed up in a fashionable style. Her face was a porcelain picture of loveliness, but her eyes were penetrating and sharp, giving away her true nature of cruelty and contempt.

"Captain Douleur. So very nice to see you again," Butterfield seemed, for the first time, to be a bit out of her element, nervous even.

"I can't say that the feeling is mutual. What have you brought me that couldn't wait until tomorrow?" She looked at the girls with disinterest. Marguerite tried to be patient and watch the night unfold, but it was not easy.

"Silks from Paris, Captain. There are more outside on the cart."

"And two servants to boot." Douleur lifted her glass at Marguerite and Lucy.

"That remains to be seen, Captain." Butterfield forced a tight smile. It was a bold statement considering the situation and Butterfield's obvious insecurity around the famous pirate queen.

"Have your bot bring the silks to my back room. The girls can come with me. Boots, take the chain." Captain Douleur nodded to the copper bot to take the chain.

Up close, Marguerite could see that the bot wasn't antiquated as much as neglected. He stood six feet tall with wide square shoulders and thick limbs, quite the opposite of the slender, streamlined Outil. He'd probably had a fine polish at one point, but no one had cleaned his gears past oiling in a while. He was covered in patches of green patina, and the lower half of both legs and feet were solid green making it appear as if he was stomping around in tall green boots. It was easy to see where he got his name.

Marguerite bumped into Butterfield, intentionally trying to get her attention so she could ask what she should expect now, but the square woman just walked out of the tavern without acknowledging the girls. Marguerite was feeling better about the fact that she'd shoved her goggles and gun in the pockets of her skirt, but less happy about the fact that she didn't think she could get her hands out of the chain without help.

The bot named Boots pulled them through the crowded room following Captain Douleur. As they passed beside the man on the chair throwing balls, he reached out a foot and poked Lucy in the back of the head, never missing a beat. The crowd roared with laughter. Lucy tucked her head in annoyance and gave a quick look of annoyance to Marguerite that said—this better work.

They weaved past the crowd, eventually coming to a private

room in the back. The bot led them in and closed the door, blocking out most of the din. Marguerite was impressed with what she saw. The furniture was of excellent taste, finely crafted, and looked extremely comfortable. Any of the pieces before her would not have seemed out of place in her own home in France.

There was a card table in one corner, several armchairs with downy seats, and two settees flanking a fireplace big enough to roast a whole pig in. A door on the other side of the room opened revealing yet another bot and Captain Butterfield, followed by Outil, whose arms were filled with bolts of silk. Captain Douleur lay languidly on a settee and motioned for Outil to come near. "Lay the bolts here." She indicated the other settee. "Yes, I'll take these. Do you have any others?" She looked closely at Marguerite and Lucy, lingering far too long on Marguerite's face.

Marguerite's throat tightened and she fought down a wave of anxiety as she wondered if this fearsome pirate captain known for torture and cruelty had seen her the day she'd accidentally attacked Douleur's ship. Maybe she'd been given notice to watch out for Marguerite, the *international criminal,* just like the officials at the Tower of Bombay. Either way, she didn't like the woman's stare, and she looked away as long as she could bear it. When Douleur did not relent, Marguerite sighed out loud and met her scrutiny straight on. *She obviously sees something in me. No use in acting like a helpless simpering debutant,* she thought. Douleur quickly turned to Outil who was laying out three more bolts of bright colored silks and satin on the small sofa. "I do not care for the peuce," Douleur said. "But I'll take the rest. What is your price?"

"One thousand francs." Marguerite, Lucy, and Outil all turned to look at Butterfield in unison.

"That seems quite high," Douleur said. "Unless you were meaning to throw in the girls and the bot as well. I like the looks of this bot."

Butterfield didn't even hesitate a heartbeat before she replied. "Done."

Douleur waved a hand at a woman standing in the corner Marguerite hadn't noticed before. She was wearing men's clothing, plus two pistols, and a sour expression. She walked to a small chest and opened it, pulling out gold coins.

Marguerite forgot herself and charged at the pudgy little woman, yanking on the chain, which in turn yanked Lucy off balance. "You said you'd trade the silks for Jacques. What kind of game are you playing? I am *not* for sale!"

Captain Douleur sat up with a look of amusement on her face, "Jacques Laviolette? Have you come to save your lovely Captain? Boots, fetch Captain Jacques, please." She sat back on her sofa smiling and took a sip of her drink.

"Unchain my hands at once," Marguerite demanded. "We will sell you the silks for Jacques Laviolette's freedom, and that is all."

"This one is fiery, Butterfield. Where did you pick her up?" Douleur continued to look amused as Marguerite struggled to wiggle her hands out of their chains.

"I picked them both up in Montreal. They are more trouble than they're worth. The bot is quite amazing, though. Almost human. I should raise the price."

"How about I let you keep your life?" Douleur looked at Butterfield in a way that made Marguerite's heart ice over. This woman was cruel. She could easily see Douleur doing any of the things she was rumored to have done. It was Lucy's turn to be upset now, "Captain Butterfield, I have served you faithfully for years, why are you doing this?" Big tears spilled down her warm brown cheeks.

"My girls, if you've served with Butterbuns here for years, then the first thing you should have noticed is that she's always only in it for herself. I'm fairly certain these silks were destined for the governor of Charleston's brats. Am I right?" Douleur's expression had softened again, but the edge was still there.

"Oh, no, Ma'am," Butterfield stammered. "I picked them up off a frigate stranded outside New Amsterdam."

"I don't care where you got them—" Douleur started but was interrupted by the door opening.

"What is it now?" a familiar deep male voice filled the room. Marguerite knew it at once. She turned to see Jacques walk into the room, a free man, no chains, and no whips. He was whole and unharmed and looked surprisingly good, considering he was being held captive by the most feared pirate in the world. His pants were the same, and his shirt sleeves were rolled up. Gear grease smeared his arms and hands, and a bit was on his face, but other than that, he seemed well rested, if not in ornery spirits.

"Jacques!" Marguerite tried to move to him, but the chain jerked her back. Outil took two steps forward, but Jacques held out a hand to stop her and stepped toward Marguerite.

"Eunice here thinks you remember her," Captain Butterfield

said. Jacques looked at Butterfield carefully, his eyes soft, but his face unyielding.

"I have a lot more to do before the *Dragon* is ready for flight, Douleur. I don't have time to answer to every girl who thinks she knows me. We'd be here all night if that were the case."

"Oh, I know your reputation precedes you, but there's no need to be unkind." Douleur grinned wickedly. She was enjoying this scene a bit too much. Marguerite was confused; Lucy looked terrified, and Jacques stood there useless in the room full of pirates. Marguerite's only hope was Outil. She looked to her bot with pleading eyes. Outil looked at the bot holding the chain.

"I do know that bot, however," Jacques said as he pointed to Outil. "She would be quite useful to me. She knows her way around an engine, if I remember correctly. And we can always use more serving wenches." Jacques nodded toward the two girls—Marguerite fuming and Lucy weeping.

"Well, you got your wish. I just bought them from Butterbrains over here. Boots, give her the gold and show her out. I suggest you leave port tonight, Captain." Douleur stood up and walked to Marguerite. "I want this one delivered to the ship. Send the silks to my dressmaker and Captain Laviolette, get back to work. Take the bot and the girl with you."

"What about me?" Lucy whimpered. "They need help at the bar. Can you balance a tray?" Douleur was looking much too closely at Marguerite again.

"I'm not going anywhere without Lucy. Wherever I go, she goes. We are a package deal." Marguerite stared back at the pirate queen.

"You go where I say you go, or your little friend loses her lovely curls and her ears. Understand? You'll both be branded in the morning."

Marguerite wasn't quite sure what to say to that. She knew it wasn't a bluff. She knew she shouldn't push this situation, but she couldn't let Lucy go, not to this crowd. Not when it was Marguerite's fault that Lucy was here in the first place.

"Captain Douleur, if I may," Outil's soft lilting robot voice cut the tension. "Mademoiselle Lucy is my mechanic. She is excellent with bots, and I fear her talents would be wasted as a bar wench."

"You don't say?" Douleur looked from Outil to Lucy then back to Marguerite. She turned in a quick movement, sat on the settee and sipped at her drink again. "I want both girls in my cabin. Give them uniforms and lock them down for the night. We sail at sunrise, Laviolette."

"Do you want to hobble on the wind? Or would you like operational engines?" Jacques barked back without apology.

"It's your neck, aerman. Get the work done or die." She waved a hand of dismissal. All around her, people sprang to action clearing the room. Marguerite watched as the large woman with the guns handed Butterfield the cash and motioned her to the back door. Marguerite couldn't hold her tongue much longer. She knew she'd promised herself and Outil that she would be less impulsive, but watching Butterfield pocket the gold and walk toward the back door made a fire burn up her insides. Then the dowdy older woman turned around and smiled at them.

"Good luck girls. I probably won't be seeing you again."

Marguerite snapped. "You double-crossing, back-biting, piece of worthless dung! I'll see that you are hanged as a slaver and a traitor to the crown! You'll never get another legal job again! My father will see to that! You'll be hunted like a dog!"

"Get them all out, Boots, will you. And gag that one." Captain Douleur waved impatiently at Marguerite. The green clomping bot walked to a table and took a few strips of cloth from the drawer then walked up to Marguerite who was still ranting as Butterfield walked out the door and let it close behind her.

"This won't hurt if you will just let me put it on you quickly," the bot said.

"Of course, I won't let you put anything on me, or in me, or the likewise. I won't be bought and sold and manhandled—" Marguerite was cut off as the bot grabbed her by the back of the neck and pushed one piece of fabric in her mouth then expertly tied the other around her face holding the first in place. Then the bot picked up a pistol, motioned them all out to into the night, and closed the heavy wooden door behind them. Marguerite hung her head in defeat.

Lucy whispered through tears, "What are we going to do?"

But Marguerite's mind was already formulating a plan. She watched Jacques lead their way through the dark back alley. Surely he had a plan, and they could get out of here together. But even if he didn't, at least, she'd found him. He was here. He was alive. Her heart ached at the sight of him, and it broke with the thought that he was still angry with her. He could be angry with her forever after everything she'd done. He may never speak to her again. Maybe he had decided he liked being a pirate. Maybe he had more options. Maybe he didn't want to marry her anymore, and he was out to conquer the world with this cruel new boss. Maybe Marguerite was worse than Douleur, always dragging innocent people into her messes and getting them killed.

Marguerite knew she was working herself up into a useless frenzy. She didn't know at all how he felt, and she was no good in a frenzy. She tried to calm herself as they approached the entrance to the gangway full of pirates and bots coming and going from the *Dragon*. But as Jacques stood to see them on, he fell back into step beside her.

She could smell him; he was that close, but he continued to treat her like a stranger. It was almost overwhelming. She thought she might actually faint with the stress of the entire situation, something she hadn't done in years. But when no one was looking, his soft, warm hand reached over, found her bound ones, and squeezed. It was a small, quick movement. No one saw them, but it was real. Marguerite felt it.

He still loved her, but would things ever be the same?

Chapter Twenty-Seven

E ven at night, the *Dragon* was magnificent. It was right alongside the *Renegade* when it came to fine ships. The craftsmanship was of the finest quality. Every bit of metal gleamed from being freshly polished. The whole ship buzzed with the dull hum of engine song. Normally Marguerite would feel a thrill at being so close to such a magnificent vessel, but tonight her anger and frustration overrode her curiosity.

She had to focus on pushing her emotions aside and set her brain to work. She watched the deck hands and counted them— only three tonight, and they all seemed a bit tipsy. There were four bots, however, that were rather too on task. There were three anchors holding the ship to the lower dock of a small aership tower. She supposed the towers with giant ramps made it easier to load and unload quickly, as opposed to civilized ships that weren't rushing to rid themselves of illegal cargo.

Jacques continued to lead the way onto the ship and then down the first set of stairs. Below deck, everything was lit by silver light. It was cool and cast a gloom on everything, making their situation seem even more dire. Marguerite kept trying to get Jacques's attention again, but he paid her no heed. He just kept walking until he came to a door before the bow of the ship. They had to be close to the bridge. This must be Captain Douleur's cabin.

Jacques opened the door and held up an arm indicating the girls should enter. They had no choice with Boots, the hulking, yet very quiet copper bot right behind them. Jacques signaled for Outil to stay by his side. "I can handle them from here, Boots. Thank you," Jacques said.

"Sir, I should chain them to the rings as the captain ordered," Boots reminded Marguerite of her father's own Faulks back home. What she wouldn't give to see that bumbling hunk of metal again.

"I've got it. I know how she likes them. Remember, I spent a few days there myself." Boots nodded and walked back up the hall the way they'd come. Jacques didn't waste a moment. He whisked all four into the room and shut the door, locking it behind him.

Inside the room was all black and red velvet. The walls were hung with thick curtains, and the furnishings were all padded with the finest of cloth. The bed was round in shape and filled all the free floor space. Along one side were several port holes. Along the other side, metal rings hung from the ceiling and others lay attached to the floor. On the wall were sharp instruments that appeared to be from a doctor's kit, along with what was obviously a branding iron with a large swirling "D" as the insignia.

"She tortures people in her bedroom?" Lucy gasped.

"Yes, she does," Jacques answered. "Outil, can you cut these chains?" He pulled up Marguerite's hand and examined her wrists.

"Jacques! You are alive!" Marguerite was blubbering like a fool now. She couldn't get her words out fast enough, but she knew she had to say them, before she was tortured, before they were all dead, before he left this room and she might not ever see him again. She didn't even care if Lucy heard.

"I love you, and I'm so very sorry. You have to know how sorry I am that I got you captured and tortured. You weren't tortured were you? Oh, she hasn't branded you, has she? Deep down I think I only wanted to be with you. I know you probably don't want me anymore, but I don't think I could live another day if I didn't have your forgiveness. Oh, please, forgive me, Jacques. Please?" This was the very bottom of the barrel. Her face was wet with tears, and her nose ran into her mouth. She could neither pat it dry nor hide her shame and sorrow. But if this is what it took, she would humiliate herself every day to show how grateful she was that he didn't die because of her stupidity. She'd do anything to convince him that she loved him.

"Marguerite," he said as he pulled a handkerchief from his pocket and wiped her face himself, cupping it with his free hand. "I am just fine, very surprised to see you here in the middle of pirate country, but then again, I should have expected you wouldn't leave me behind. Of course I forgive you, and of course, I still love you, and of course, I want to marry you still. I am the one who should have apologized. You had every right to be on the *Renegade*. I should have told you about my mission and had you help me instead of pushing you away. And yet, your crazy stunts have actually made my job so much easier."

Outil stepped in with her multi-tool hand and easily cut the chain holding Marguerite's hands together then moved onto cut Lucy's. Marguerite threw herself on Jacques. "What on earth are you talking about?" She stood on tippy toes and held him as tightly as she could with both arms around his neck.

"I couldn't tell you in Montreal; it was classified. I still shouldn't tell you; except that now you are here, I need your help. With your brains and my brawn, we can be free of this place in less than an hour."

"Tell me what? What are you talking about?" Marguerite leaned back and looked at his face. He wiped the rest of her tears away and handed her the handkerchief.

"I'll tell you while we search. We need to find the plans for the ship. I know they are kept in here somewhere. I saw her looking at them one day when she thought I wasn't watching." Jacques moved to the wardrobe in one corner and started digging through the dresses and fine black aersuits hanging in perfect order. He turned to Lucy, Marguerite, and Outil. "Hurry! Start looking in those drawers. It must be in here somewhere."

Marguerite was still stunned, but she did as she was told and opened the top drawer of a bureau. It was filled with fine undergarments of every variety. Marguerite blushed as she pushed aside the private items of the most feared woman on earth and asked again, "What did you want to tell me?"

"My mission was not to accompany the fleet back home. They knew Douleur would come flying as soon as she heard about the size of the shipments bound for New France. The King made sure that the information was leaked. My assignment was to somehow infiltrate her ship and find out as much as I could about the technology she is using and where it came from."

Marguerite stopped her search and stared at him as he frantically checked for secret compartments in the wardrobe. "You mean, you meant to get yourself captured all along?"

"Well, not exactly captured, but yes. That's how it worked out. And after a couple of days on the rings, she accepted me into her crew and even into the engine room. One of the liquidizing boilers sprung a leak, and the whole thing almost blew sky high on the way home."

"So, you knew all along that you were going to leave me for pirates, and you didn't tell me?" Marguerite was stunned. It had been a bad day for surprises. "You wanted to get caught by pirates."

Jacques had moved onto a trunk under a porthole while Lucy and Outil looked through a side table and smaller chest by the bed. "I didn't want to get caught by pirates, and I didn't want to leave you." Jacque looked sideways at her standing there staring at him. He took two quick steps and pulled her into his arms. "You didn't want to get married, and a single officer can't turn down a commission, especially when he blew his first and last ship to smithereens. I had no choice. But we are here now, and we have a chance to get out of this." He held her close and kissed her cheek. "Please, help me find the plans. I almost have the boiler repaired, and with Outil's help we can understand how it works and fly the whole ship away!"

"But what about the crew? How are we supposed to overpower them?" Lucy asked.

"I've had a chance to speak to some of them. They are all here against their will. Most of them wouldn't mind a change of leadership. We just have to get back to the engine rooms and get this bird in the aether."

Marguerite suddenly felt very weary as well as foolish. She turned back to the dresser and thought about what he'd said, as she continued to dig through the unmentionables and trinkets. It was true, if he'd been married, or even engaged, he could have turned down the commission. It just never occurred to Marguerite that he *would* turn down a commission. She certainly wouldn't have. Especially not a marvelous undercover job like this. Or maybe she would have?

She dug through the drawer as she dug through her feelings. There were buttons of strange makes lining the bottom of each drawer. Some held clothing, some strange devices like those on the wall. The bottom drawer was filled with papers. Marguerite pulled them out one by one, focused on discovering schematics for a ship. She would have time later to process the truth of the past month's events once she survived this night. She had to survive this night and then she would make up her heart and mind about her next step in life. As she knelt on the floor and tried to quickly sort through the mess, she had to keep throwing her skirts out of the way. Finally, out of frustration she stood up and walked to the wardrobe. "I've already looked there, my love," Jacques said.

"I'm not looking for your paper; I'm getting into something

more functional. If we are going to steal a pirate ship, I need to dress the part." She pulled down a flight suit and started to peel off her dress.

Jacques cried "Oh!" in alarm and turned away. *Good,* she thought, *maybe he's not a rake after all.*

She pulled on the warm, yet light, fabric and fastened the buttons; then she filled her new pockets—Hooray! It had pockets!—with the strange pistol Claude had given her. She pulled her goggles on over her up do and set back to work on her drawer. She set aside each useless paper and finally turned to Lucy, "Can you come help me with this? There are just too many for me to go through alone."

"I should put on a flight suit as well," Lucy said as she tried to kneel on the floor in the billowing green frock.

"Help yourself." Marguerite nodded to the wardrobe still standing full of clothes.

Lucy stood again. "Don't look, Captain."

Jacques turned away and groaned as he pored over the contents of the trunk. "These are all employment agreements. Who knew pirates were so thorough in their paperwork? It's maddening. However, they do make quite a bit more money than I ever would in the Royal Aerforce.

As Lucy joined Marguerite again on the floor, Marguerite pulled out a bundle of letters tied with a red ribbon. She began to untie it until the script in the corner of one page caught her eye. It was familiar. It certainly wasn't a set of plans for a ship. But she knew these were important papers, so she slipped them in her free pocket and kept digging as she tried to place how she knew that script. They soon were at the bottom of the stack and had found nothing but more contracts and a few personal telegraphs.

Marguerite stood and put her hands on her hips as she turned about the cabin studying the contents and layout. *If I were a vile pirate in possession of priceless engineering documents, where would I hide them?* She thought. *Probably next to my other most prized possessions.*

It was clear that Captain Douleur enjoyed her silk undergarments, but Marguerite had been through that drawer. She continued to scan the room and think. Her gaze fell on the rings attached to the floor and the shining silver tools hanging from the wall. Anyone who enjoyed torturing people in their room, and owned tools like this, having kept them in such polished and sharpened order, obviously prized them.

Marguerite took a few steps closer and shuddered as she reached out to touch the edge of a massive knife. It was as sharp as a razor. A hook hung next to it, long and slender, also polished to a high shine and sharp at the tip. She supposed this wasn't for any kind of yarn work. A small saw hung next to that, then a piece of thick wire with wooden knobs at either end. Marguerite didn't have the stomach or imagination to wonder what that could be used for, but she did notice a slit in the wood just behind the tools. She took hold of the hook holding the knife to the wall and pulled carefully. Sure enough, the whole section of the wall slid out revealing a secret compartment. "I've got it!" she cried. "She had them behind her tools."

"Brilliant, my girl," Jacques cried as he crossed the room and took the plans.

"Now what?" Marguerite asked.

"Now to the engine room," Jacques said. Then he regarded Marguerite for a moment, his hand on the door handle, ready to leave. "Marguerite, in that outfit, you look just like her." The door swung open, startling them all. Jacques jumped back and reached for a weapon that he didn't have. Captain Douleur stood in the doorway with a pistol in each hand, Boots at her back.

"She looks like whom?" She asked. "I hope you were going to say me. Because that would be very fitting," she said as she lifted her pistol and pulled back the hammer, pointing it at Marguerite.

"Why is that?" Marguerite barked back.

"Because you are my daughter."

Chapter Twenty-Eight

All eyes were on Marguerite as the room waited for her to reply to the statement. Marguerite could only muster one word, "Liar."

"I assure you, it's true. All you have to do is look at your face to see the resemblance. I could spend the next ten minutes telling you my tale of woe, how your father was a tyrant and chased me out when he got tired of me, but wouldn't let me take my baby daughter along. But that is old news, and we have much bigger problems. What is a mother to do with four very naughty children? Hmm?"

She motioned with the gun for all of them to move back, as she stepped in the room and Boots closed the door behind them. "I knew *you* were not to be trusted from the start," she pointed at Jacques with the barrel of the pistol. "Honest eyes, tell no lies. I was certain when I saw the way you looked at my girl here, then proceeded to lie about knowing her. You even called her a wench. Tsk tsk. It only turns tacky when you lay it on too thick."

Lucy took a step closer to Marguerite, and Douleur drew her other gun with her free hand and pointed it at her. "You are pretty, but I can already tell you are useless—only good for menial labor, at most. Possibly fetch a price in the Jamaican slave market, but your skin is much too dark to get any real money out of you there." Marguerite reached down for Lucy's hand and squeezed it.

"The bot is extraordinary, and I can deal with her programming. I especially like her voice. Very nice, feminine touch. You must let me know where you picked her up. I'd take a ship full of bots like her, much better than this old bag of bolts." She indicated Boots with the nod of her head.

"So that leaves you, Marguerite." Captain Douleur smiled a strange smile. It seemed to be full of nostalgia and sadness, but there was still cruelty underneath. "You grew up very, very fast. I'm under no delusion that we can sail off together, the happy mother and daughter pirate team, but there must be another way to deal with you besides killing you. No?"

Marguerite was as fast as lightning. She pulled the little gun from her pocket and fired straight at Captain Douleur without a moment's hesitation. The captain fired as well, but her two guns were half a second behind Marguerite's. As the blast of electricity from her tiny pistol struck Douleur between the eyes, the balls from the pirate's pistols found purchase in Lucy's arm and Outil's head.

The bot fell helplessly to the floor, and the girl stumbled to her knees as the pirate captain crashed in a heap. "No!" Marguerite didn't know who to turn to first. Lucy was bleeding, the red liquid dripping on the ground caught Marguerite's attention first. She jumped to the drawer still open in the bureau, grabbed a silk camisole, and pushed it onto her friend's wound.

"I'm alright. She just grazed me a bit," Lucy said between tears. "Check Outil!"

As Marguerite turned to the ruins of her dearest friend, Jacques was already in action. He had Captain Douleur's hulking automaton, Boots, by the arms and was trying to wrestle him down. A useless move for a human to make against a bot of that size, but he tried nonetheless.

The lead ball had hit Outil in the left eye, tearing off half of her lovely face and rendering her circuitry completely dead. As Marguerite stared at the amazing network of gears and cogs that made up her friend's inner workings, she began to sob fully. She was so overcome she didn't register the robot voice behind her.

"Master Jacques. There is no need to subdue me. I am not a threat to you." Jacques let go cautiously and looked at Boots who stood still over his mistress laid flat on her back on the floor. A black mark was seared across her forehead. The bot lifted up one foot and kicked her hard in the ribs. Captain Douleur groaned but did not wake up. "How do you like this useless bucket of bolts now?" he asked in his monotone voice.

"Jacques!" Marguerite wept. "She killed Outil." She lay her head down on the bot's hard metal chest and let her whole heart spill out in tears and sobs.

"Marguerite, it's not too late. We can get her to Claude. We can do this; we can save all of us. What on earth did you shoot Douleur with?"

Marguerite gasped through her tears, "I don't know, just something Claude gave me." She handed the weapon over to Jacques. "He told me not to point it at anyone I liked. I couldn't think of anyone in the world I liked less than her right now, so I just shot her."

"You did well, my love. This is going to be alright. We are going to make it. Just stay with Outil. Boots, can you help me?"

"Of course, Master Jacques. But only on one condition." Jacques looked surprised at the bot. "What is that?"

"You call me by my real name, Bradley."

"Excellent. Bradley it is. Let's tie this pirate lady up and get her ship back in the air."

Chapter Twenty-Nine

Because the *Dragon* had such a terrible reputation, they had no problems flying north along the coast. Any ships they passed steered far away from them, and none questioned their path. A few Chinese rockets went up from New Amsterdam as they flew past, but nothing that was a serious threat. Marguerite guessed the new governor wasn't as friendly to pirates as he'd been made to sound.

Jacques and Bradley successfully repaired the engines and had them flying with a loyal skeleton crew of now ex-pirates who were more than happy to see Douleur bound and gagged in the brig. They steered the *Dragon* away from land until they reached New France. Then he ordered the French flag flown high, and they sailed up the Saint Lawrence River to Montreal where they took a sharp turn to starboard and sailed on to the northern forest.

Marguerite spent the entire day and a half voyage in a cabin far away from the Douleur's awful captain's quarters. Outil lay on the bed and Marguerite lay next to her, her head on Outil's lifeless chest. Only as they began to drop out of the sky in sight of their destination, did she rise and look out the porthole. The thick pines of the north were there to greet her once again. She continued to gaze through the trees until she could make out the shapes of Claude's empty barn and humble cottage. She pulled her goggles down and adjusted for distance. Claude stood in front of his house, wearing his own goggles and looking back up at her. He waved up at the ship in welcome. She assumed someone had hailed him from the deck or sent a wireless telegraph or pigeon. She wondered what had become of Hector, the little Spanish swallow.

Marguerite helped Jacques push open the gate; then they carried Outil's body out together. Marguerite burst into a new fit of tears when she saw Claude approaching.

"Can you save her?" she wept.

"Of course I can." He motioned for Jacques to carry her to

the makeshift smithy forge in his barn. Marguerite felt a warm arm around her shoulders. She turned to see Louisa smiling with concern at her.

"If anyone can fix something he already dreamed up and built, it's Claude," she said in low voice.

Marguerite sniffed a bit as she watched the two men with the lifeless metal form. "You're right."

"I have someone I want you to meet if you can spare a minute." Marguerite nodded, grateful for the kindness, as Louisa led her to the house. There in a cradle in the back bedroom lay the most lovely baby girl, all peaches and cream skin, with a perfect little nose and dark lashes brushing pink cheeks. She was sleeping soundly, dressed in a white eyelet gown. A blanket of soft wool was tucked around her in the handmade bed.

"She's just lovely," Marguerite whispered. It felt wrong to talk louder than that, almost like she was in church.

"She is strong and healthy; we couldn't ask for more," Louisa said as she smiled down at her baby.

"Outil would have been completely fascinated by her."

"Will be," Louisa corrected.

"Will be," Marguerite echoed, barely audible.

A knock at the door made both women jump. Marguerite moved first. "I'll get it. You stay with your baby," Louisa nodded, and Marguerite left to see who was there. A very tall, highly decorated aerman stood in the door flanked by four officers of equal pomp and circumstance.

"Lady Marguerite Vadnay?" the man boomed, a harsh contrast to the sweet sleeping baby.

Marguerite answered as she stepped outside and closed the door, "Yes, that is me."

"I am Admiral Auboyneau and I hereby accuse you of high treason, obstruction of His Majesty's orders, theft of an escape boat ... " He continued to list several other crimes Marguerite was fairly certain she had committed. She sighed and held out her arms waiting for someone to chain them again. *This is becoming too much of a habit,* she thought. But they were not bound. Instead, the admiral kept talking.

"We have also been informed that you have helped to complete a mission of great importance to His Majesty and have not only discovered the technology behind the pirate ship the *Dragon* but have brought the ship to our aether along with its infamous pirate captain. Because of these special circumstances, I, Admiral Auboyneau, by the power vested in me, do hereby drop all charges against Lady Vadnay, under the condition that she never again volunteers for duty in His Majesty's Royal Aerforce or any other branch of the French military, and that she hereby be released from her services with a dishonorable discharge."

The Admiral then leaned in and whispered in her ear, "We had to issue some sort of punishment or they'd have our heads. We felt this fit the crime." He stood back and returned to his full height. "This concludes your service to King and Country. We thank you for your efforts, your success, and your willingness. Godspeed."

With that, the admiral bowed low and then stood in a more relaxed fashion. "Now, where is this Douleur? I can't wait to get my hands on her."

"She is locked in the brig of the *Dragon*. I think you'll find ample evidence in the captain's quarters to hang her." Marguerite couldn't quite believe she would ever speak of hanging someone in her life, much less her own mother. Then again, she hadn't had time to really think about the fact that suddenly she had a mother again—and a pirate mother to boot. She wondered if she should get to know her a bit better, find out why she left. Was it really because she just wanted to see the world? Or had something more sinister happened? And why hadn't she let Marguerite know she was alive all these years?

It was a lot to take in. She was definitely going to need a soft bed, warm tea and a few nights of good sleep before she would be able to sort this mess out.

"Marguerite!" Another voice called to her from where the military ship had dropped lift. "Dearest!"

She looked past the admiral and his men who were now heading for the *Dragon* and saw her father scurrying toward her on the dirt road. It was almost a comical sight. His cane flopped out of rhythm as his short legs hopped along at a much faster pace than he was used to. His perfectly pressed dress trousers were covered in dust, and his monocle bounced right out of his eye and flopped on his chest. Marguerite made her own quick move toward her father, and they met in an embrace.

"My dear girl, they told me all that has happened. I couldn't be more proud of you. I mean, that is to say, you could have gone about all of this in a less haphazard fashion, but I'm so grateful that you're home."

"Thank you, Father. I am very glad to be home as well." And

the tears sprang to her eyes again. She stopped trying to fight them. She cried whenever she felt like it now. She'd cried for Outil all the way home. When she wasn't crying for Outil, she cried for Jacques's safe return. Last of all, she cried for herself. She reached into the pocket of her flight suit and pulled out the bundle of letters tied in red ribbon and handed them to Lord Vadnay.

"Did they tell you about—her?" she said.

He took them from her and turned them over in his hands, peering at them as if they were some sort of strange new contraption. "Where did you get this?" he whispered.

"I found them in Captain Douleur's cabin," Marguerite pointed up to the *Dragon*. "I thought I recognized the script when I first found them, but there was no time to read them. It was only later when I realized that I recognized it because it was your handwriting."

"Marguerite, are you saying what I think you are saying?"

She nodded her head. "I believe my mother is alive."

Her Father took his monocle out again and wiped it off with a handkerchief. "My dear girl. We must talk through this. Maybe not tonight, as you look completely worn to the bone, and I know you are worried about Outil, but soon. We will speak of all of it soon." She nodded again and wiped her face on the handkerchief he now offered to her.

"Did you know? Did you have any idea?" She searched his face for any hint of a lie.

"No. I had no idea where she was, honestly. I paid various men to track her for several years, but after losing her in the pirate-infested Indies, I figured she was gone for good." He placed the letters in his vest pocket and took her hands.

"Let's go up to my ship. You can rest there."

"That sounds very appealing," she said. And father and daughter caught the next lift back into the sky.

Chapter Thirty

Marguerite hadn't slept in the past few days. She wondered if she would ever sleep again. Lucy joined her in the night and the two played cards and talked until Lucy finally returned to her own cabin before dozing off. Marguerite lay in bed staring at the ceiling, replaying everything she'd been through in the past few weeks.

She thought about all of her stupid decisions, some of her more daring successes, and she tried not to think about Captain Douleur. She decided she would refuse to associate her with the word *mother*. The woman was a beast. When she allowed herself to dwell on their encounter, she shuddered at the comparison her father made in the library not so long again in Montreal. Was she really just like her mother? Was there some sort of magical tie that bonded a child to its parentage even when they are not raised by their hands? Could all of these desires to be daring and to travel be in her blood?

A tapping at her door early in the morning brought her away from this morbid train of unanswerable questions. Marguerite was so fatigued and so used to having Outil answer her door and filter the visitors for her that she hadn't thought before calling out, "Come in!"

The latch turned and Jacques stood in the doorway, the morning sun shining in through her porthole onto his greasy clothes and jubilant expression. "I have wonderful news. Claude worked through the night with the parts we found on the *Dragon*, and Outil should be functioning again this afternoon."

Marguerite sat up, gathering the covers about her chest in an attempt at modesty. "That is marvelous!"

This happy news was just what she needed to pull her mind away from all of her troubling ancestral thoughts. She smiled at Jacques who suddenly registered the situation and Marguerite's clothing—or lack thereof.

"Oh, dear. So sorry. I'll be back later," he whispered and started to close the door.

"No," Marguerite reached out for him. "Please come here, for just a moment. Hand me my shawl." Jacques looked at the floor and smiled. Then he looked up and down the hallway and slipped inside, closing the door quietly behind him. He picked up the soft pink wrap and was at her side in an instant. He took her hand and held it to his lips then ran his fingers over her cheek, cradling her face.

Marguerite wrapped the shawl around her shoulders and whispered, "And what of you? Is His Majesty satisfied with your service?"

He kissed her hand again. "Why yes, he is. He has offered me a promotion and command of the *Renegade* once again. An actual command this time, not a cover for another operation."

"And do you think you might take it?"

"That depends," he smiled at her.

"On what?" she wasn't going to give him any leeway.

"On whether or not I am compelled to take it by my low status as a single man in this new world." He smiled at her as he kissed her hand again and held it at his lips.

"I believe you are safe to pass up this particular commission without any fear of the law hunting you down," she said with a smile. Then her face suddenly turned dark.

"What is it," he asked.

"Only, I just can't believe you'd still want a harebrained woman like me as your wife."

"I don't want a harebrained woman as my wife. I want Lady Marguerite Vadnay as my wife, and she's anything but harebrained."

"Do you really mean that?" she asked, hating how pathetic she sounded. But she needed to know. She had to be certain.

"Yes. I mean that."

"Then the answer is yes." Jacques leaned in slowly and Marguerite closed her eyes, savoring the moment before their lips met, when a fierce banging came at the door.

"Why does everyone seem to think I need to be up early this morning? Stay here." Marguerite walked to the door and opened it a crack. A deckhand stood in the hall, his face flushed and his breath coming in large gulps. "What's the matter?" Marguerite's chest tightened.

"It's her, miss." He gulped a few more breaths then finished. "She's escaped."

"Who?"

"Douleur! They were escorting her back to Montreal to stand trial, but she got away. I thought you'd want to know."

"Oh, cogs and sockets. Thank you."

"Yes, miss."

She closed the door behind her and turned to Jacques. "Maybe you should consider that commission after all."

THE END

The Truth Behind the Gears

The late 1600's are infamously remembered as The Golden Age of Piracy. The seas of the world were an open playground for every sea-bordered country and scoundrels of every sort. There were new laws governing the waters that didn't govern the land, and there were also unspoken rules, codes of conduct, and traditions springing up across the globe. Many of these customs and the reality of a life at sea have been forgotten, especially in popular culture portrayal.

Cinema and works of fiction often show the navies, while not always commanded with integrity by those in charge, were the best organizations with which to see the world and learn the sailing trade. In truth, the organized navies, England's in particular, were far from the clean, well dressed, well fed, and highly organized institutions as they are often portrayed. Unless you were from a noble family and could secure a position as a commander in the higher ranks of a ship, you were most likely drafted, or impressed, to serve and forced into a life that bordered on slavery. Sailors were expected to work long hours, rowing, bailing water, manning guns in time of battle, and all on promised pay that was far below what they could expect to earn on a merchant vessel. Once a ship was finished with its commission, the men were free to return home, but many never made it that far. Commanders often sacrificed sailors before cargo and held back the best rations for themselves, leaving the men to go without clean water or food and forcing them to forage and raid local ports when landing.

These harsh conditions led to the not surprising problem of desertion and piracy. Many sailors would jump ship for a pirate vessel if given the chance. Unlike the navies of several countries, pirate ships were held only to their own codes and were often run more like a democracy. The captain of the pirate ship was usually chosen by the men for his (or on rare occasions, her,) ability to read, write, and keep records. The pirates kept track of everything they stole and kept careful books on who was to receive what part of the booty. Men could expect to be paid immediately, and handsomely, after a successful raid when living the pirate lifestyle, as opposed to the legitimate service as a navy sailor where low wages were rarely paid and often held back to keep the men in service.

When major decisions were being made, the entire crew of a pirate ship, from the youngest deck boy to the captain, often voted. Mutiny was rare and only happened when a captain tried to go against the wishes of the crew. Many crews also developed their own codes of conduct in regard to the types of ships they would plunder and how they would treat captives, especially women. Some were ruthless and uncaring, but others were honorable, allowing women and children peace and safe passage to land. Conduct varied greatly between ships, but the basic foundation was the same; voting, even wealth distribution, and no need to answer to anyone as long as they were on the sea.

Several pirate crews worked so efficiently together that the governments of the world took notice. While it angered some, many governments approached successful pirate captains and offered them pardons if they would work as privateers, which was essentially a pirate with the protection of a government. Privateers had to give a portion of their spoils to their patron country, but in return they were protected from being tried for piracy in any country. If they were attacked by an unfriendly country, they could report it as an act of war, which also provided them with a buffer.

It's no surprise that so many men opted for the life of piracy in the late 1600's and early 1700's. Considering other options, it wasn't a bad lifestyle for a penniless young man trying to avoid impressment to the navy. A few women also took to this lifestyle with much success. Cheng I Sao was one of the most feared women on the seas, commanding a fleet of nearly 50,000 pirates in her prime. Mary Read and Anne Bonny found each other during a high-seas battle where Mary was disguised as a man and doing quite well for herself. They both started plundering openly as women alongside "Calico" Jack Rackam and were soon feared for their ferocity and ability to fight and drink as well as any man. And the leader of them all, Grace O'Mally ruled a fleet of twenty ships in the 1500's, a time when women were rarely educated and were restrained to their homes. She gave the British navy a run for their money on the coasts of western Ireland her whole life.

While the truth is far from glamorous, it is, nevertheless, fascinating. Captain Douleur is based largely on these famous pirate women. They were ruthless scoundrels, sometimes worse than their male counterparts, using their womanly assets to avoid punishment and to lead unsuspecting sailors and merchants to their deaths, but they were also far ahead of their time in the struggle for equality and women's rights. They proved that women could keep up with men, even in the criminal arts.

Lady Marguerite is based on my ancestor, Marguerite Sauviot, who actually did sail the Atlantic to Canada as a young girl on her own in search of a new life during a perilous time.

Because of their infamy and careful record keeping, there are several documents on pirates and privateers of all types that have survived the centuries through court records. If you are interested in learning more about pirates, I suggest you visit your local library and check out the books listed below. If you are interested in your own ancestors, pirates or not, I highly recommend the free website: http://www.familysearch.org

Who knows? Maybe there's some pirate blood pumping your heart toward adventure after all.

- *The Pirate Hunter: The True Story of Captain Kidd*, Richard Zacks (Hachette 2003)
- *Under the Black Flag: The Romance and Reality of Life Among the Pirates*, David Cordingly (Random House Trade Paperbacks 2006)
- *Pirates of the Carolinas*, Terrance Zepke (Pineapple Press 2005)
- *Blackbeard: The Life and Legacy of History's Most Famous Pirate*, Charles River Editors

ACKNOWLEDGEMENTS

My husband is a saint. He is always going to be the first person I thank, always. Without his shining halo, I'd never be able to write a word. I'd be slaving away in a messy kitchen somewhere with cockroaches licking my toes. Thank you for *everything*, honey. Next comes a list of people who helped me in life and with this book, in no particular order.

Amy Jameson—agent extraordinaire, Chris Coray & Emma Nelson—amazing CPs and lovers of all dark things, Erin Isgett & Sarah Baird, Eric Ehlers—Ninja Monkey, Judith & George Holt—who let me invade their office and saved my sanity, Carole Rummage, The Straitjacket Writers, The Kidlit Drink Night Podcast crew, my SCBWI Carolinas family, Southeast Regional Library and librarians everywhere, Month9Books, the makers of Paul Newman's sour licorice sticks, the woman who invented chocolate—because we all know it was a woman, and all the little birds outside my window, especially the cardinal with no feathers on his head. Rock on, baldy.

LEIGH STATHAM

Leigh Statham was raised in the wilds of rural Idaho, but found her heart in New York City. She worked as a waitress, maid, artist, math teacher, nurse, web designer, art director, thirty-foot inflatable pig and mule wrangler before she settled down in the semi-quiet role of wife, mother and writer. She resides in North Carolina with her husband, four children, five chickens and two suspected serial killer cats. If the air is cool and the sun is just coming up over the horizon, you can find her running the streets of her small town, plotting her next novel with the sort of intensity that will one day get her hit by a car.

OTHER MONTH9BOOKS TITLES YOU MIGHT LIKE

THE PERILOUS JOURNEY OF THE NOT-SO-INNOCUOUS GIRL

BONESEEKER

Find more books like this at http://www.Month9Books.com

Connect with Month9Books online:

Facebook: www.Facebook.com/Month9Books
Twitter: https://twitter.com/Month9Books
You Tube: www.youtube.com/user/Month9Books
Blog: www.month9booksblog.com

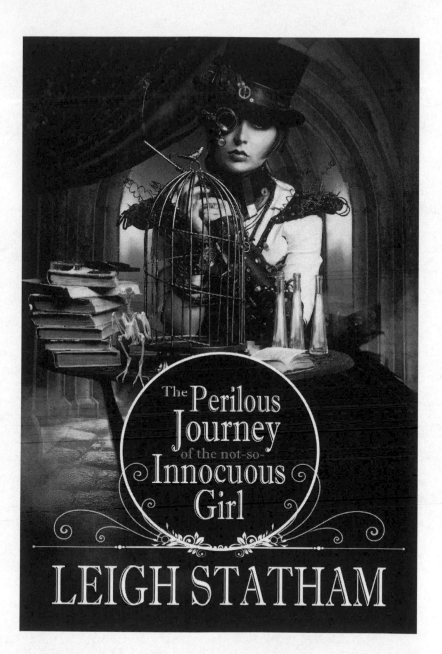

The Perilous
Journey
of the not-so-
Innocuous
Girl

LEIGH STATHAM

SHE WILL DISCOVER A TRUTH
THAT SHOULD HAVE REMAINED HIDDEN

BONESEEKER

BRYNN CHAPMAN